# AMONG THE PINES

## STORIES

## MATT ANDERSON

# Contents

No single step on an expedition is without experience, be it joyful or bitter. We are all summations of experiences, all part of each other's expeditions. Although the stories contained herein have been produced over a period of years, this book could not have been made without those to whom I owe a monstrous debt of gratitude.

To my grandparents: Bill and Lucille Nyberg, and Arvin and Bonnie Anderson.

And to my proofreaders, without whose assistance this book would likely exist in a much less satisfactory condition: Karissa Anderson, Evan Anderson, and Shi Grey Sky Franklin.

# Picture of an Elm Tree

We wear our memories in our skin.

They read like musical notation, like sheet music, the lines and marks on the old man's skin. Stretched and knotted, pockmarked and scabbed over; they infer a song about a man that has been through seventy years or better and is not inclined to talk about a single day. No formality, just dour honesty permeating him from his bones to the sweat that collected in his whitening hair. The axe in his hand is a contradiction, bright new cedar haft stuck into a familiar and well-used iron head. The blade is inches shorter than when his father used it, years of grinding it down to make sure it stayed as sharp as ever.

The elm was waiting for him in its own special place at the top of the hill. Sixty feet, one hundred twenty years, if the old man's grandfather had been truthful all those years ago. Old rock elm, split apart by lightning in its youth and so it grew to resemble an American elm more closely in its form, but still resolutely a sour old rock elm, its own histories imprinted in its hard bark. The wind was caught in its broad, serrated leaves, hissing at the old man's approach. Its boughs nodded in what one might perceive as respect, but the old man wasn't naïve.

1

His wife had hated the tree. She didn't like the way it had grown strange, so tall and so bitter. The hill which faced the farmhouse was on the eastern half of the acreage, and every sunrise that held the promise of beauty and grandeur was consumed by the hoary silhouette of the elm. If trees could gloat, she would say on more than one occasion, then that tree was having a damn dinner party at their expense.

The old man had always promised her he'd cut the tree down, but it was a promise that kept getting knocked back in lieu of other projects, of jobs he'd had to take to make ends meet, of necessities that warranted more attention.

He'd kept that promise in his pocket even after all his kids grew up and left the nest, fostering families of their own. Even after the leukemia went to war with his wife and she'd held the fight for six years until it finally, mercifully, ended her.

You and me, the elm tree would sometimes say, a gleeful whisper on the wind – you and me, old man, and when you're gone it'll just be me, forever and ever. I was here before your grandfather was yet a seed hunting for a womb, and I'll remain here when your children's children are rotting in the earth...you know I will.

The old man paused at the top of the hill, turning back and staring down at the farmhouse. It looked nice in the noonday haze. His wife wanted so much of it fixed up and looking nice for neighbors or visitors they never have over. Still, the old man felt he did a good job of it anyway. He sighed as he took off his plaid work shirt, returning his attention to his quarry. Going to be a long, hard day, one in a great string of long hard days.

A small bole stared like a dark expectant eye down at him. He knelt and put a hand on its bark, felt its coarseness against his skin, the dips and ridges and pockmarks, felt its story. There was nothing reverential about this act; the old man was feeling the spot where his axe had gouged out better than a foot yesterday, straight into its heartwood. The splintered chips were gone as well, blow away in the night breeze.

He heard the tree whisper: You're tired, and old. I will go on. How about you?

When there's a problem, you fix it, and you do it before the problem gets even worse. That's what he was told when he was a boy helping out his father fix up and varnish a post for the mailbox, shy of a century ago. They didn't have any varnish and his father didn't like going into town, but they had spare motor oil and that worked a treat. When you got your own land, you got responsibility; when there's a problem, you fix that problem. That's all there is to it. The old man hefted his axe and began another long day.

No one in his family or anyone he knew would call it meditation, that point where repetitive action yielded a heightened mental state. The old man would just call it what it is: "thinking." As he worked, his body shielded from the sun by the arched limbs of the elm, he contemplated all the other things that had to be done once this task was finally taken care of, chores around the house and out by his brother's cabin, the bills that still had to be paid, and wasn't that a bitch? His wife dies, his kids all flown the coop, and his heart so old it was a wonder it hadn't kicked a decade ago, yet still he had to continue paying off the back thirty.

It wasn't so bad, he mused. He was glad to have had the time he had. He'd lived a good life with his wife and had good kids, and that was a damn sight more than some had. He didn't like thinking he was lucky, such a thing was apt to ruin something that was there, but all in all, he had a good time.

There were bad times, sure enough, but there were good times, too. He supposed that was the most important thing.

Time slipped by as thought countered thought – it was only the awareness that the sunlight wasn't where it was supposed to be that brought the old man out of it. All the trees about the farmhouse, the aspen and birch and graceful pines, hummed with the oncoming evening, the sky so soon all the colors of a peach. Insects were making a meal of him and he swung at the little monsters, fat and witless with his flesh and blood. There weren't enough dragonflies.

Once he was done, his body red and stinging and every muscle weeping for relief, the old man breathed in the threshold of the night, looking down at the neat pile of shavings and hunks of wood pooling at his shoes. This time, the axe had bitten deeper into the elm than before, deeper than yesterday or the times before. The bones in his hands were ringing all the way up to his shoulders.

Could let you rot, the old man thought at the tree, hoping that it could hear him. Let this wound fester in your body, and then you'll know what it's like to get old, get sick and weak and finally die before your time. Before you did any of the thousand things you wanted to. Yeah, could do just that.

He took hold of his axe and grabbed his work shirt, gave it a hard flap against the wind to shoo off the grit, wood shavings, and bugs, then he turned and headed back home. Blood was pounding in his ears, heart a wild rusted piston, bones creaking like the timbers of a Hollywood pirate ship.

It wasn't the voice of the tree that made the old man stop, stop and turn around to look up at the hill. It was just a breeze, a suggestion of something out of place, aberrant. The tree was standing there, tall and

4

strange and black against the sky. What it had lost it had somehow silently grown back. Not a single scar denting the memoried bark of its trunk, not a sentence missing from its stories.

A big smoky grey moth flapped by the old man's ear; a funerary dagger moth, they were called – he remembered it from some nature documentary on PBS. It circled his startled face before lighting on the tree, just on the lower rim of the gazing bole. It crawled an inch, another – it twitched once, legs and wings curled into its body like plastic in a fire. The small pale body fell into the grass, already lost to view.

Its leaves whispered: you're a child. A child and a fool, swinging sticks. Now go home and sleep, child. I'll be right here tomorrow.

The old man sighed, exhaustion digging in deeper, setting root. He stooped on his way back to the house, counting up all the things that had to be done in the morning, all the chores that have to be taken care of. The elm tree was at the top of the list.

# Spring is Emptier

"You're going to be safe here," he says, and he truly believes it. Right here in the shadows of his double-wide, the menace in his eyes is little more than receding stars in a dawn sky. His thin brown beard, wet and matted like grass in the summer rain, tilts up into a smile. A languishing spring whispers through the open window, curling the black-green drapes. Behind the half-inch-thick plexiglass, she stares at him with her own black-and-yellows, the single light bulb throwing light on her scales and now he can see the tigroid design on them, marbled black and pale yellow over mottled green, like so many pike and musky that had been caught in the lake. But she is special. So very, very special.

Without knowing that he was doing it, without being aware of much else outside of his own half-recalled memory, he reaches down between the slats of her cage and grabs her breast. Fingers running over the cold protrusions of nipple and areola and he wonders about the women in his life who have left their scars inside of him, trying to remember the faces he'd promised himself to forget. Forgettable whores, he decided back then and still believes now, believes as much as *her* being sent from God above to keep him company.

His first wife, may she rot in peace (because she never gave him any), had been a cheerleader in the same high school he went to, had cheered his name over and over on the football field and cheered for him more than once in the back of his '88 Camaro. But a bad tumble in his first year of college broke his clavicle and ruined his chances of potential scholarships. Soon enough, his formal education started circling the drain and Maisy abandoned ship while she had the chance. No note, no phone call, just a big FUCK YOU inscribed in the dust on his Camaro.

The painkillers were fine for a little while, they took away the feelings of uselessness and the bad thoughts he'd have for a little while, but they kept bubbling up, dark shadows breaching his consciousness. He went to church every Sunday, and what solace the drugs couldn't give him he found in the shadow of the cross, the smell of rosewater and mildew and burning candles.

Loss became his lot, like old Job himself. He'd given up on college, and the damage to his neck made finding an occupation that paid decently and wasn't too physically strenuous a rarity. He had to foreclose on the house because he couldn't make either of the payments for his mortgage and his old college tuition; had to buy this ramshackle throwback from the eighties from his cousin Stu, who'd left it entirely as it was, with the rain-damaged ceiling and warped lacquer flooring, strips of vinyl painted into a profane exaggeration of mahogany curled up like arthritic fingers. He had to get a job at the paper mill in the next town over, inhaling the cancerous fumes day in and day out and going home with that shit coating his lungs like he'd never get rid of it.

On a whim, he took to fishing, inspired by tales of ancient fishermen who became legends among their time and entombed in posterity; Noah, Thor, King Midas, and the rest. And now he could add his own name to that list. What came up for him in the dark east edge of Eagle Lake had dashed all his fears, and now he wouldn't be alone again.

She slaps the side of her tank with her sinewy tail. Mud-murky lake water spits up through the slats while browned pine needles and leaves stick to the plexiglass, and the stupor in which he'd put himself shatters. He jerks his hand away from her breast, its chill lingering on his palm. He sighs and shakes his head and notices the erection in his khaki shorts, straining to rise beyond the swell of his gut.

He looks at her for a few seconds longer—he'd intended to only glance at her, but you don't give something like her the slightest of attention; he stares long and hard, at the undulations of the water and the rippling of her body and the kind of large bright eyes belonging to a woman that was neither child nor adult, but some heterogeneous, alien mix. He sits down in his chair and thinks about his forbidden fruit until he ejaculates into a diamond-pattern bed sheet and he slips into sleep.

Free to dream about anything he wished, but mostly he dreams about mottled black-and-green scales, tiger stripes, pleading wet eyes as deep as the deepest parts of the lake.


That day hadn't been very much. The sky hemorrhaged another dusk over the lake, vast depths of orange and red painting the clouds the color of plum skin. Clouds of midges raced overhead; dragonflies darted like living jewels among them; an otter swam up through the reeds on the east side of the lake and seemed to watch him for a while before growing bored and diving back down. He'd been feeling strange, prone to peculiar thoughts. After several hours drifting in his old paddleboat, he decided to put away the cooler of minnows and the plastic container of leeches (both bought at Roy's Hardware for fifteen bucks total; sixteen-fifty with the snuff) and use his old wedding ring. It felt fitting and somehow satisfying, to put the expensive piece of metal to some functional use beyond its symbolism. He set the tip of the rod over the port side instead of swinging it, fearing the ring would fly off the hook.

If there had been any pull on the line, it came from nibbles that never made it up to his hands. Finally, with two hours in and the sun drowning itself across the lake, he felt the pole jerk in his hands. The sun and the slow rhythm of the waves was nice, and at some point he'd closed his eyes and dreamt of fucking. Suddenly aroused from his melancholy, he opened his eyes and saw the tip of his fishing pole pull down into a U shape. He gave some slack, counted to four, then jerked upward, grabbing for the net at the bottom of the prow and nearly tipping the whole damn thing over.

He fought for maybe twenty minutes, maybe half an hour – too long for him to think he'd hooked anything he'd expect to see in these waters – before he'd reeled it in enough that he could see the flash of predator green. No way the net could help. Its bulk and strength suggested that it had to be at least four feet, maybe five, and no walleye or catfish gets that big, not in this lake. Had to be a muskie, he thought, and a wintry gust of fear swept over him. He knew stories about men who tried to singlehandedly take these monsters on, only to be pulled down and drowned, or bitten so bad they'd had to go to the hospital. He reached into the water and, like Thor himself, he heaved the serpent out of the depths.

"Holy mother of God," he'd said aloud, too stunned to say anything else. Her black-yellow eyes stared up at him, hoping-pleading eyes just like the Henna'd and rouged women he'd picked up along the train tracks outside of the city, or on the corner of Hapsburg and Ninth, where they waited in a loose line of mascara and vinyl, sequins glinting like scales, lips puckered to suggest and tease.

Her skin was a paler shade of camouflage green, and partly translucent; sunlight seemed to show him the pale curve of her ribcage beneath the dermis, the dark trails of veins and arteries. She was woman from her reed-like yellow-green hair down to her thin waist. There the woman ended, and her scales blazed in the fading sun like zircon and malachite. Where one would expect her feet to be was a muscular torso tapering down into a tail, the spines like the tines on a pitchfork, the wide caudal fin the same color as old parchment paper.

He chained her right off the property, keeping her in the water so she wouldn't suffocate. He drove a shaft of rebar into the ground, bent it at a sharp angle so the rope wouldn't slip off. The rope was heavy-width twine, the kind his father used to use for hauling steer, and he looped it around her wrists in a thick knot. He didn't dare make a sailor's knot, superstition telling him that she might know some preternatural way out of it.

Her long, dexterous fingers terminated in translucent claws that pulsed with blood vessels beneath. Her teeth belonged to something he'd fantasized lived in deeper waters far away from here, rows of little pins like glass.

The skin on his hands was gouged and torn, bandages crisscrossed over his palms and knuckles. Something had gotten into the wounds, turning the surrounding flesh red and itchy. When she bit, he hardly felt her teeth until they were rapping on the nerve endings seconds later. She was quick but he was strong, and the air made her weak enough he could haul her to shore.

The fish caught by King Midas of Crete gave him the ability to turn things into gold by his touch; Vainamoinen fashioned a harp out of the jaws of the giant pike; the man of some ancient fairy tale, presumably from France or Germany, was given three wishes by his own catch. Treasures of the deep.

She was an answer to his unspoken dream. Even if she didn't know it, even if she didn't want it, she'd made him the happiest man on earth.


He didn't intend to kill Rosalyn. It just happened. Like so many things out of his control, it just happened. They'd both been drinking that long cold night dead smack in the middle of November (as a waitress, Roz had a nice discount on drinks at the Walleye bar, and they both made good use of it when they wanted), and she'd undone the latches on her mouth and let fly at him about spending his money so freely when what he was getting in his paycheck couldn't cover a bee's ass. He let her go on, even though she'd bought enough for both of them herself. He would let her have it once they got in bed, and then they'd get on with the next day. They were just playing the same old song and dance.

That whole week had seen ice-rain slushing the roads, freezing into sawtoothed encrustations when the sun went down. It pooled around the steps leading up to the trailer home and all around it, forming a hard crystalline carapace over the snow. Roz hadn't let up for what felt like the past hour, and he gave her a playful shove to get her to quiet down and maybe try to coax out her friskiness. He shouldn't have been so surprised when she slid over the ice on her heeled boots and cracked her head on a big moss-covered hunk of shale. He was still drunk, and tired, and in his state he'd forgotten about the rock. When he woke up, he spent the next five minutes trying to get her to wake up until he finally saw that the red spreading away from her wasn't part of her jacket.

A man alone always tries to do his best, in all things. He tries to think straight and remain calm, and to hold to logic and reason above uncertainty. But a man alone is flawed. Fear overtook him that night, gave him temporary clairvoyance. He saw himself, the cameras trained on him while red-and-blue police lights were uplighting his face, two county cops in their pressed browns frog-marching him to their sedan, escorting him to the courthouse down in Hinckley, and from there to the looney bin an hour's drive away in Rush City...

The remainder of his lifetime taking pills from a little paper cup (the kind you used to get your ketchup in at McDonald's, he remembered), nurses and orderlies examining him, doctors telling him what was wrong, not having a single word that left his mouth be noticed by anyone. That was a future he wanted no part of, so it was out of horror of this grim future, more than anything else, when he took the axe out of the back of the trailer and hacked until she wasn't a single Roz anymore.

Some parts of her he buried in the yard (the ground hadn't frozen to the point where it seemed denser than tin), and some he threw out into the lake. The lake had frozen over already, and even a warm day wouldn't undo what had been done. By that time, the pieces will have drifted away, whatever was still left after the fish and snapping turtles had had their fill.

The lack of Roz, indeed, the lack of what made life worth living for any man of his age and means, was a powerful hunger that ate away at him, chewing away like an ulcer. The need for company, for affection from the softer species, was a constant need that buzzed inside of him. It drove him to seek out and haunt those places he'd always heard about, from passing comments at work or a sly tale at the bar, but had himself never been.

There had been four women after Roz—five, if you included Maisy, if you wanted to be chronological—and most of them had been good to him. Some were not; some had to be reminded and corrected. Some just ran away. Some followed Roz into the lake. None of them had what he wanted, none had the special effervescence that he was searching for.

None of them had ever given him that warmth and state of mind that drove away his unrest. None of them had what *she* had.

He began to doubt anyone else ever would, until that day. "I love you," he whispers in his sleep. Whether he is in the same room with her tank while she watches in her perpetual fascination, or he is sitting on the toilet lost in another of his reveries, or he is outside raking the yard, or fixing up the damn bitch pipes secreted in the RV, he would occasionally pause and whisper those three words.

He supposes he had never really experienced anything close to what people called "love," but what he knows he feels for the woman in the tank, he realized, is the deepest, truest, most undiluted feeling he's ever had. He would gladly suffer any hell if it meant being with her, just as he knows she would do for him.

"I love you," he says again, quietly, spring caressing his lips and face with warm delicate fingertips, a moth dancing around the light bulb in a supplicant's pirouette, the faint splashing of his jewel in her tank.

On the final day of spring, in the grey pre-dawn light when everything is shrouded in gloom and wariness, he watches her moving laconically back and forth in her tank. Perplexed, he understands that she is trying to shift all of the dirt and sticks over to one side of her container. It seems a perfect time to show her proof of his affection.

This time, when he binds her wrists with the thick bailing rope, she doesn't struggle. She whimpers in that muted way of hers while he carries her down to the edge of the lake, but he can see the adoration in her eyes and he knows she isn't afraid. "Gotta get this done, honey," he tells her, gently, and he pretends that she understands him. "We can't have you looking like the ugliest thing since my brother split his pants the last time he tried out for the lumberjackin' contest. That was up in Cedar Rapids, I think." He sets her onto the ground long enough to tie up the loose end of the rope to the stake, then he picks her up, delicately, as though she were something made of ancient porcelain or carnival glass, and deposits her into the lake.

With a ragged cloth, he cleans the grime and algae from her body, scraping and pressing against her flesh until she is gleaming in the clear water. He sees the throbbing red veins inside her caudal and dorsal fins where the sunlight pours over her, ignoring the unseemly spines. His eyes rest on her peculiar sex, and he sighs. When the top of her head rises above the surface, lake water falls across her cheeks like tears.

He swears when his fingers get caught in the knotted cords of her peridot hair, managing to tug them out only after a brief struggle. She ducks down under the water, but her eyes remain on him, always on him. His heart reverberates like a gong when he looks at her.

"Did I never tell you that my dad used to take me fishing here?" he asks, and he can't remember if he'd already told her this story or not, but he decides that since he started, he might as well finish it. "It's not a big thing. Lots of fathers took their kids fishing in this lake. Not many people had boats, so you had to get your time in before the damn lily pads took over this side of the lake. You can see the power lines up there by the freeway, all the bobbers and lures snagged by kids or drunks or drunk kids grabbing for too much distance. You can probably see the big Red Devil on the far side—that one belonged to my dad. Hell, he just up and beat my ass with a stick when that happened!"

He lets out a boisterous chuckle that makes his stomach undulate beneath his polo shirt. A passing otter pauses to take notice, then continues about its business.

He strokes her face with his calloused hand, brushing away the water that isn't her tears. She shivers, and his heart flutters when she bends her head down into the palm of his hand.

"I love you," he says, and then "I'll be right back."

He brings the tank out of the camper, pulling it as gently as he could without tossing around too much filthy water. Once at the doorway, he upends its contents over the steps, watches it cascade and wash into the soil. He wonders if there is some other way to drain the water out, but it would probably cost him a few thousand dollars to install.

Using his rag, he scoops out the dead leaves and pine needles and other things he doesn't know how had managed to get in there. A film of brown-green scum clings to the bottom, demarcating where the water level had been; he sneers when he grabs at it, smearing it across the glass. The smell infiltrates his nose and pulls at his stomach, organic and pathogenic. The smell reminds him of ammonia, even though that isn't at all what it is. It all smells like Eagle Lake; fish, mud, clams, and frogs. It abdicates the scent of coming summer, enveloping and devouring it and turning it into yesterday.

It takes him the better end of twenty minutes, but at the end he sets the tank down, gives an appreciative nod to his own handiwork. It is free from all contaminants now, purified, almost holy in its transparency, and again worthy to contain his beloved. He drags it over to the where it stood before and grabs the big bucket from off its hook. Another chore he wishes he could streamline.

As he marches back to the lake, the sky has bled itself out as the sun is cresting the horizon. Sheets of golden light lay over the back yard, shadows from the row of ash and elm trees forming obscure shapes on the ground. The clouds seem to dissipate against the might of the sun.

"Almost finished, honey," he says to her, nearing her stake. He watches for an acknowledging ripple tossed by her tail, but there is nothing. The surface of the water remains unbroken and smooth as obsidian. He frowns and swallows a lump of fear. She just hadn't heard him, was all. Trying to control the knotting sensation in his stomach, he steps to the edge of the lake and peers down—

"Shit!" he shouts, shouts so loud his voice carries far across the lake. She's gone; she's left him, just like the other ones. The whore had up and left him, swam off to someone else. His face contorts, and before the half-remembered voice of his father can tell him to get a grip and stop acting like some old squaw, the despair has hunched his shoulders and dragged his body low. He swings the bucket, wanting to feel something give beneath his power.

"You bitch!" he screams. "You goddamned bitch-whore-slut!"

The lake calls back to him with his own voice.


She had timed it perfectly, or at least as well as she could. To a woman born below the waves, there was no poison nor venom nor unguent more toxic than the air. When the man leaned over to inspect her she concealed her form, covering herself in threads of glamour so that all the man would see was water, ruined cattails, and the torn ends of the rope. She watched him turn on his feet in a mad dance of rage, swinging the bucket at his imagination. She waited at the shore, not even daring to massage the burning feeling in her wrists. Her lungs were no better—she was certain that something was lodged inside of her chest or the thin group of gills beneath her breasts; each breath was a step toward deeper pain.

She doubted she had much longer, but she was nothing if not patient.

After a time, the man returned to the edge of the lake, his face red as the sunrise and spittle falling from his lips in quartzite strands. Maybe he didn't believe his eyes, or he was suspicious that his eyes were lying to him. Her vision was greying at the edges, as though clouds of ash or silt were pulling in from all sides. There was a terrible burning itch in her gills.

He turned away from her and she struck. She grabbed at his ankles and used her diminishing strength to pull his legs out from under him. He cried out, silenced when his face struck the ground and rebounded. It was a satisfying sound, almost pleasurable when it traveled through the water, but his legs kicked out when he landed, the soles of his heavy hiking boots slamming into her face and tearing loose the flesh on her cheek. Stunned, with rancid pain spreading across her face, she retreated back a pace and paused.

She could feel the alchemy of emotions and sensation washing off of her captor, shuddering: his mouth flooded with the taste of pennies, salt and metal, and he was certain the coarse, solid things that fell out of his mouth were not pebbles. He swallowed one and cried out against the ground. His nose was broken, stars were falling through the blur in his eyes, and he couldn't feel half of his face. For a moment, the thought of betrayal didn't enter his mind. When it did, he buried his fingernails into his palms and beat at the earth to get away from the water.

The pain, or anger, or just the final shred of the desire to survive filled her with enough strength to reach out and pull the man who had baited her, caged her, and tormented her, down into the water with her. He thrashed just as she had, but he was dazed and bleeding. She coiled in the water and swam a few yards from the banks, dragging him by the ankles. He was easier to manage here, where she had more power.

She might be too far gone, she felt, but she at the very least knew she had more control. He was kicking out at her, pummeling blindly with his feet, and occasionally his boots would strike their target. She let go of him when the rocky mollusk-imbued lakebed gave way, dipped down into a steep drop that fell twenty-some feet and she swam down. Here, her little bed of weeds and mafic igneous rock quivered for her, and the bones of small mammals and fish and the barren shells of clams were woven into articulate statuettes, placed delicately along the lakebed. She looked at it, hope and sadness clouding her eyes as she fought for breath. Then, flicking her powerful tail, she darted upward toward the splashing.

She pulled him under again, this time clasping her clawed hands around his neck. White and pink bubbles burst out of his mouth while he continued to thrash, throwing foam and grit. She flinched when he hit her, but she didn't let go. Above all, she wouldn't let go.

Soon, the bubbles stopped. He blinked once at her, surprise and despair in his eyes while he descended into her home, the sunlight fading from his face.

Her gills fluttered, trying to expel the sediment and algae that had already done their damage. She scratched at her throat, scales like flecks of peridotite glittering as stars revolving around her head. Blood clotted her eyes, making the awful sunlight brighter than it was; she dove down, down where her bed was waiting for her and her small garden of art told her it was safe. She pushed the corpse of the man away and lay down, curling and coiling, and in this quiet and familiar darkness, she closed her eyes and waited.

Her body became reeds and cattails, mucusy silt and freshwater pearls. Later, after the sun burned away the last wisps of fog that hovered over the lake and the fish, otters, and snapping turtles came around the strange field of bone statuettes, all they saw was the body of the man. Soon enough, there wasn't much left of him at all.

# Shrine of Sunless Days

There's something you need to know. Consider it an apology, if you want, or merely an explanation, though neither one is quite apropos. Neither one really hits the nail on the head accurately enough. In the end, I don't think it matters anyway.

In our memories, events and moments add up and consolidate into a whole, the joy or pain or promise or regret they contain. It builds up, like nacre on a shell, forming our defenses against what we cannot expect. When we are plunged outside of the comfortable zone of the mundane, we're subject to events and stimuli we cannot control, that we don't expect and, occasionally, don't want to have happen. The shell that protects us from those moments takes much longer to form, but is infinitely denser than anything else. The shell becomes a filter, however, for language and perception. It changes the way you think and behave, changes what you say to the people you meet, however infrequently that might be, and what you think of them. What you think they think of you. It changes the world.

My shell shattered in the summer of 1997. Sometimes, I trip on the pieces.

We were eager to bury our trepidations about beginning our senior year of high school under a veneer of righteous adventure, about getting the hell out of this dinky flea-bitten town and doing something big, being something big for the rest of our lives. Bury the children we used to be under the floorboards and be some kind of a success. Do *something*. We filled our world in ways our parents had in their own generation, with friends and beer and nighthawking around the county or in the cities, searching like rats for the next morsel that would keep us alive, or at least offer us an ample enough reason to live. The scariest things on the news were Bush junior and Marilyn Manson.

Although my memory isn't quite as it was back then, only charcoal rubbings of sculpted bas reliefs, I can remember that it was a cloudless Friday noon; the sky like the smooth surface of some pretty fabric, satin or silk dyed with cobalt or woad; a firm wind was roughing up the pines and the underbrush outside of town, filling the air with those smells intrinsic to a Minnesota summer; squirrels called out to each other in their shoe-squeak voices as they darted between the trees and through beds of old loam.

There were four of us then—four youths embittered by the education system and the hegemonic cliques they favored. We were tossed adrift from those we had considered friends when we were younger, discarded in favor of better people, so we'd gravitated toward each other. Not for support, not merely for motivation, but for mutual survival.

That day, Damien's parents had taken him to go scouting for colleges, so it was just the three of us. We found the day walking along the railroad tracks that ran through town like a suture, heading south toward the cities and the old station in Hermantown. We knew we wouldn't walk that far, as much as we dared ourselves to do it. Toby had taken a distant lead, grabbing agates from the sides of the rails, brushing his long sweat-shiny black hair out of his eyes every time he bent down and came back up with a specimen. A silent starved-crow of a boy that always looked bedraggled, like he'd just flown in out of a bad rain. Charlie and I were passing around a can of PBR as we balanced over the rails. PBR was easy to get because all of our parents drank the stuff.

Suddenly, Toby sprang up and ran over to us, big half-moon grin on his face. "Here, take a look at this," he said. He handed me a little rock, about as big as a marble but flattened into the shape of a big fingernail, the color of a burnt cookie.

"So?" I asked him.

"Hold it up to the sun."

I did, pinching the stone between thumb and forefinger and proffered it up to the empty sky. Sunlight filtered through the stone, which was not transparent, more translucent, murky yellow-brown. There was something embedded inside of it just off-center, a nebulous whorl of something cloudy. For a second, it made me think of a maggot, curled up and suffocated in its sulfide prison.

"Wow," I said. "It looks like a chunk of carmel."

"*Cara*-mel," Charlie corrected.

"Fuck you." I made as if to whip the stone at her. Both Toby and Charlie flinched away, and I felt a pang of injustice. I'd been to two or three counselors for anger and self-control by then, reinforcing my parent's belief that I was more a financial drain than the dream child they wanted. There had been incidents in and out of school, though a more accurate term ought to be *accidents*. I was a little better around my senior year, but reputation is parthenogenic.

So, their actions weren't unwarranted, but it still annoyed me. I tossed the rock back to Toby. He fumbled it and swore, rooted in the gravel while Charlie and I kept walking. She passed me the beer and I nursed at it. It was way too hot out, the beer was sour and warm, but it was something. Charlie looked over her shoulder at Toby, adjusting her sunglasses when she and I exchanged a look that we'd seen others give us. *What a freak*, we said between each other, but here there was a degree of familiarity, of affection.

When he came back to us, Toby was taking out a joint, greased the end with his lips. "Can I see your lighter, Charlie?"

"Where the fuck did you get that?" I asked him, suspicious and a bit miffed. I don't like weed, not during the day, not during a day like this, when shit was boring but just bearable. I suspected it was that disgusting shit from Canada, already not wanting anything to do with it.

"My cousin sent a package from his station in Kuwait, with a few of these taped to the lid. Far as I'm concerned, it's an early birthday present."

Charlie took a puff but I declined. I had a hundred reasons why I didn't think smoking a joint from the cousin of a friend who was stationed in the Middle East was a good idea, but I kept them bottled up. Another thing to file away. It's easy to bottle things in my family. I drained the rest of the beer and set it down on the track. I brought my boot down hard, feeling every inch of the thin aluminum crumple beneath me into an obliging oblong disc. Charlie and Toby started discussing politics while I grabbed the disc and chucked it into the trees.

The second when your feet step onto the tracks, you can't help but be filled with the sense that you're going *somewhere*. Direction and location were irrelevant, erroneous. You felt like a bird heading south for the winter, or a blood cell traveling through an artery, which I suppose are euphemisms as apt as they are redundant. This was why we enjoyed doing it, and why we did it so often; the feel of aged steel bleeding heat up through your shoes, wooden beams like an extended ribcage or the disks of a spinal cord, casting shadows where insects or frogs skulked to get out of the sun, walls of trees on either side like tired voyeurs. Nobody stopped us, nobody told us it was illegal. Even when you passed through the woodland corridor and the rails were cutting through an open plain, it still felt like you were restricted to one space; you never went backward, you just turned around and kept going *forward*.

We spent that first day of summer hobnobbing on the railroad, play-acting characters from TV shows or Jack Kerouac novels and being what we considered to be intellectual. We drank what our parents hadn't nailed down and smoked cigarettes that stank too much of menthol or cloves and exchanged scraps of local and foreign news, regurgitated rumors from the television or the old folks that hang around the gas station and shoot the shit without buying anything. We were allowed to forget about the mothers who said things we didn't want to hear, or the fathers who forgot to pull the punch at the last moment, or the indifference of teachers, pretending that this guise of a world we were crafting for ourselves was enough to justify whatever tiny rebellions we were making.

Sometimes, when I'm lying awake at night and trying to find sleep in the blue-green ceiling, I'll inevitably float back to some ponderous memory and try to figure out if it was real or not, or if I was remembering everything in a way that hadn't really happened. Some cerebral noise pocket or firewall, my own brain trying to tell me to stop this crazy bullshit, remembering the past that didn't need to be remembered. Better to just forget things and move on, learn how to heal. But I won't forget, and I won't move on—either because I won't or I just fucking can't.

Charlie was the first to see the animal. I sometimes remember that it was me, or that it was Toby, or that it was Damien, who wasn't even there that day, but I *know* that it was Charlie who found it first. The scraggly little mess of grey fur, shattered guts, and rent bone lay between the tracks, unidentifiable and writhing with black flies and ants.

We could have kept walking, gone right past it. Turned around and headed back into town. Instead, Charlie circled it and said "What the hell is this?"

I swore, or maybe Toby swore with my voice. We crowded around the mess, silent and oblivious mourners.

I scoffed and said "Some Native you are," but Charlie didn't react. I wanted her to look at me, throw me a withering look with those Cola-dark eyes that said she knew I wasn't being racist, just a bitch; I wanted to distract her so we didn't have to look at that thing.

"Looks like a grey squirrel," Toby said. "Red squirrels like to chase them around and kill them when they get too close to red squirrel territory. They're the bigots of the rodent world."

"No, it's not a squirrel," Charlie said, and she knelt down closer to it. I wanted to haul her up and push her away from it. Even from where I was standing, I could smell it, trapped cadaverous gasses heated and expelled, threaded with something that left a horribly briny taste in my mouth. "Look at the fur. It's too long and wiry."

I snapped. I started walking away, kicking up gravel. "So it's a damn cat, so what? Poor bastard probably couldn't jump out of the way of the train in time."

Toby glanced back at me, giving me a look that said he didn't know what I was doing, but I ought to just stop and calm down. He turned back to the little body and I heard Charlie say something about a fifth leg, a lack of any head, or at least an intact head. They pondered over the funereal geometries of the dead animal, trying to discern its identity. They couldn't *smell* it. They couldn't *feel* it.

It was an animal overtaken by forces it couldn't hope to stop. That's what I hated about it.

"Oh, screw this," I shouted and stomped away. They couldn't see just how *wrong* the corpse was, how blatantly incorrect by any set standard. I felt their gazes behind me, expressions exchanged. After they were finished with their fruitless research, they made it back to me, silent, a gloom hovering around us. It made me a little less angry.

Every path leads to somewhere. Even when there's never a beginning point, there's always still the next destination.

We all knew about the house nestled inside the crook of red oak and grasping tamarack, about three miles out of town on the north side of the tracks. It was the kind of western style house you see scattered across rural Minnesota like seeds, little houses sometimes supported by little farms, with little differentiation in characteristics by the families who had built them. The Søldenberg house was a victim of time and weather; the paint which had once made the whole exterior look like a robin's egg had been almost entirely ripped away, little patches beneath the eaves and around the foundation had faded to the color of beer suds; all the windows were broken eyes staring into and from nothing; the timbers were worm-eaten and dangerous, structurally unsound; a water pump older than the town, the same color as old blood. It had been built in the late 1800's by a small family that might have been German or Swedish—here the history becomes murky and entirely dependent on whom you ask.

If it was a truly haunted house, it was haunted by some incorporeal element rather than any human spirit. You had a sense that time was moving forward too quickly when you walked through the sea of Indian paintbrushes that covered the front yard, or that it was moving awkwardly when you looked through the jagged translucent teeth of broken windows into dilapidated rooms.

To us, it was just another graveyard to hang around in.

Toby and Charlie were lagging behind, discussing rocks or something and trading the blunt, so I was in the lead, not very far from the Sødenberg house. So I saw the woman first. She had materialized from between the trees like a wood nymph too curious and too brave. Her skin was the color of beach sand. She looked a little bit older than me, though it might have been the way she carried herself. She walked up the ditch and onto the tracks, the wind combing through her long black hair. The night could get lost in hair like that.

She didn't appear to see me, just turned on the tracks and started walking down the same direction as me. Her green dress hugged her body without appearing too tight. I watched her for a second or two before I called out to her. I can't remember what I said, that first thing. I might have said "hey, there," or just "hello." She stopped and looked at me, curiosity floating in the emerald pools of her eyes. She didn't say a word, didn't make any gesture in acknowledgement. I thought I could see a grin tilting the corner of her mouth but I couldn't be sure.

She mumbled something, the wind in my ear taking the word away. When I walked up to her, her dress seemed to shimmer and become blue, then green again, as if the fabric consisted of the same microstructures found on the wings of butterflies. Or fairies.

"What're you doing here?" I asked.

"What're you doing here?" she replied, mirroring the inflection.

I scowled at her. "You don't have to be a smartass. Who are you?"

Her thin copper-colored lips grinned. "I fly with birds, I swim with otters. I like to sing and dance with sons and daughters."

I wasn't too far away when her grin became something else. Something about her just…changed. The features of her face sharpened, hardened, cracked like splintered wood. I heard a sound like thunder rumbling from her throat, and when she opened her mouth I heard the earth shattering behind her teeth.

Her throat bulged and pushed out, something was rising up through her esophagus. When the little animal pushed it's mashed head out past her lips, one golden eye hanging from a crinkled retina, it mewled, wailed. I wanted to scream, I *must* have screamed, because the next thing I knew, Charlie was grasping my shoulders and telling me to calm down.

Or—

Or it was night, perfect summer night beneath a blazing hot full moon. I walked down the quarter-mile stretch of unpaved road in front of my single-story house, nestled in the crook of a field. My parents were going at each other again, and I didn't want any part of it, wondering if they even heard the front door when I slammed it shut. I was sick of their vain plays for dominance, sick of being part and parcel and casualty of their damn wars.

A couple miles down the shaggy dirt road was a river, too small to have a name, though I knew it managed to snake around the houses and

30

roads to reach Perch Lake. A bridge forded it, crumbling concrete bracers beneath, making it look like the remnants of a fortress.

The river was the only thing that brought me serenity, the only thing that made all my disgust and contempt evaporate. It made sounds smaller than a whisper beneath my feet, while the wind hushed the trees. I sat down on the edge by the rocks, pushing my knees up to my chin and held them there. There used to be a guard rail, but it had been removed a decade ago. I don't know why.

But the night didn't make me feel any less abandoned. It was a sensation I knew I didn't deserve, because I'd just abandoned my brother Lucas to their abuse, but by then I didn't care. There were times I'd planned to escape, just get in mom's station wagon and head south to the Twin Cities, or west, out of the state entirely. But it was my brother that kept me anchored here.

The trees rustled as bats swooped and chirped in the air. I heard a big splash in the river; there used to be fish here, a long time ago, but now only turtles swam here anymore. It was probably a deer sliding into the stream to get away from the heat. I looked down into the black waters, black glass capturing the moonlight. To be dead…I wondered what it felt like, if it felt like anything. I wondered if there was beauty there.

"Hello," she said, her voice like the wind and the stream. I turned around, seeing no one there—a footstep disturbed the gravel, and I turned the other way, seeing her standing there, smiling. Weird, I thought, realizing that although I heard her voice coming from the right, she appeared from the left.

She gave me a perplexed look, and I managed to unglue my tongue from my mouth long enough to say "Hi." She floated toward me, her summer dress diaphanous and gleaming in the moonlight like evaporated topaz.

"You new here or something?" I asked, fearing that she would ask me what I was doing here, alone, at night. I didn't want to be the topic of conversation. "I don't think I've ever seen you before. You from the Cities?"

"No. I've lived here for a long time."

I narrowed my eyes at her—all that crap about small town folk knowing everything about each other is largely exaggerated, but most of it is spot on. "Yeah, right. For how long?"

Her smile was like the moon revealed by parting clouds. "Long enough to recognize when someone is feeling lost in the world, and their own thoughts aren't much help."

She knelt down on her knees beside me, looking down at the river. The moon was trapped in her eyes. I felt blood fill my cheeks. "Whatever," I said. "It's not like it's your business."

"No, probably not."

The quiet filtered into the anticipating dark, intercut by the crickets and night birds. After a while, she said "Have you ever wished on the morning star?"

"What?" I glared at her. Not because the question was out of left field, but because I was just thinking about the last time that I'd wished on that morning star, on that star or planet or nebula or whatever that point of orange-red light really was. "No, I don't, not anymore. Why?"

She looked down into the darkness below the bridge, and then up into the sky. "Let's say a person's thought moves at the speed of light, and let's further say that a person can project their thoughts outward. Light moves at 186,000 miles per second; if that star up there really had any power to grant wishes, it would take about ten years for it to happen."

"Huh. Do you think it does?"

She looked at me, and I fell into the dark pools of her eyes. "Does it have that kind of power, you mean? Probably not, but I'd rather not step on anyone's toes if it does."

The smile on her face was bright, pilfering starlight and hiding it in the thin spaces between her teeth. For a moment, I felt everything just wash away, the anger and the neglect blew away like so much cornsilk. I smiled back at her.

I heard the truck coming around behind the trees, and I knew he had his high beams on, saw them slicing through the pine needles and bracken behind the brook. It was natural, he had no reason not to have them on, in the dark nondescript backroads, but when the light lanced my eyes as the person drove past, I called out some obscenity and showed them both middle fingers. Juvenile bravado—if the truck had stopped and went into reverse, I probably would have leapt over the side of the bridge.

There was something else I noticed then, but I can't remember if it was real or if I made it up on some night years afterward. It's another thought riddled with the bacterium of nightmare and imagination, what I want to believe and what I can't handle. When the truck came around, the young woman beside me wasn't there anymore. She was just gone. As the driver went and the night filled in the gap that the light had touched, she was there again.

"Jackass," I heard her say, the upward tilt of her voice telling me that she was still smiling.

"Really," I said.

The grass at my knees moved, and I saw what was twitching and scraping its forelegs at me. I cried out and jumped away from the young woman and the large black thing that had crept up the support wall. I recognized it for what it was, one of Minnesota's most intimidating predators; a wolf spider. I'd been bitten by one before, once on the back of my calf, and the pain will always make me associate the number eight with anguish. This one was as long as a pen, black and blue—I instinctively slapped at my back, brushed off my arms and legs of anything that might or might not have been there.

I watched as she extended her hand down to the rock, the spider skipping onto her palm without any apprehension. I watched as she made the spider dance in the moonlight.


Can either of these scenarios be real? Are they just dreams, or can I allow myself some comfort in the idea that they're just corrupted or deformed memories? One, a threat, the other, an act of diplomacy. The days, weeks, months I've spent talking about this with the handful of people I can open up to about it—my brother, my boyfriend, my therapist, a few unfortunates that are jinxed enough to find me when I'm off my tits with brandy—just keep going on, like a hallway in a carnival funhouse with no ends. I keep running from A to B with the blind hope that there might be a door or a window, but I never get that flighty dreamer feeling that I've found the exit.

Was she even real, that woman I met in the summer of 1997, or was she something that I wanted to believe in, to give myself something to cling to when I had nothing else? Sometimes I'll think these thoughts, and sometimes I'll believe them, and when I do I end up calling Charlie. We both pretend that I've forgotten it's been twenty years since that night, and she married a climatologist from Arizona, and where she lives now it only rains when it's not blistering hot, and she has higher responsibilities than tending to the mind of a bargain-bin schizzo who can't tell if she's dreaming or not.

It might go something like this:

The dial tone goes for three rings, and then it clicks. "Hello?"

"Charlie, it's me," I'll say. "It's Ashley."

"Oh," she might say, or it might be something like "Shit, Ash," or she might let out a heavy sigh. I'll wait for her to say "Did something happen, Ash? What's wrong?"

"No, nothing happened," I'll say, even though I'm thinking about that day and I want to say *Yes, something did happen and I can't get it out of my mind and I just want to talk to someone who might understand because you were there.* But then I'll remember that Charlie wasn't there, not on that particular day. "I just wanted to talk to someone."

"What's wrong with…" she'll ask, always referring to that last person that I was dating. "Wait, something did happen, didn't it?"

"Charlie, please," I say, and I use that begging word that I've never used, even when I was a kid. "I just want to talk to a friend from the old days."

"Cut the shit, girl," she says, or something to the same effect; something that cuts me off and shoves my thoughts out where they belong. "Damn it, I know why you're calling. You need to stop doing this to yourself, Ash. It's not healthy."

"But I need to talk to *you*! You're the only one that remembers what was going on back then."

Sometimes she swears here, and other times she just sighs, and the sound is so sad and tired that I want to hang up, but I don't. I want to hear her voice because she's proof that at least part of my memory really happened. "I thought you were getting help. Aren't they doing anything for you there?"

"The help isn't helping," I'll say, and as childish as it sounds it comes across as vaguely poetic in my ears.

"Okay...We can get together and talk sometime. When are you available?"

"You don't have to, Charlie—."

"Bullshit! This is exactly what you want, and I fall for it every fucking time," and I wait for her to calm down while inside my stomach, joy and guilt are wrestling for control. She tells me when she can meet and I tell her my schedule and we argue about a meeting place. Sometimes, we actually do meet up. Then we indulge in meaningless topics until one of us grows bored or busy and we have to let go. I'll go and pour some brandy into my favorite glass and down it as quickly as I can—it's bad for my meds but it's good for my mind.

I might be lying to myself, but I know that Charlie is just as guilty. She was with me on that final night of July, and so was Toby and Damien. Our friend Jodie was having a party and we were all grateful for it—Jodie Torgeson lived way out in the woods like me, but there was a big meadow behind her place, a hilly rise surrounded by a ring of trees. She wasn't as popular as some in high school, but she knew her backyard was a coveted party spot, and she lorded it over everyone like a Parisian baroness.

Cars and trucks were parked far behind us by the garage, and after a brief hike the night was set aflame with a bonfire. Kids were seated on felled logs, looking like clumps of fungi. The stars were out, all crystalline and making a glistening diadem for the moon. Led Zeppelin and ACDC, Metallica and Alice in Chains. It was another backwoods bacchanalia, with cheap beer flowing in time with the music, old loves and bitterness crossing with everyone. Some attendants had older cousins or siblings who were off from work or college, if they had the money to go to college, who were handing out weed. I remember seeing a bong that was shaped like the rubbery monster in *Night of the Demon*, the one from 1957. A train howled in the distance.

Charlie and I were dancing together by the fire. It was a cold night and she'd given me her leather fringe jacket. I can't remember if I was high or merely drunk, or perhaps cruising on the mingled chemicals of both narcotic and barbiturate and burning oakwood, when I saw the woman standing by the ring of trees. Her green-blue dress seemed to be woven from jeweled thread, moving like ice. She was looking at me, watching me, little silver smile playing behind her lips. I stopped dancing when I saw her, and, perhaps seeing that I had finally noticed her, she turned and stepped quickly through the trees.

The branches moved, the leaves moved, so it had to be real. She had to be real. I ran away from the fire and headed for the trees. To the east beyond the conifers, past a low descent through the woods, was a small lake populated by minnows, bluegills, and a community of beavers. A tiny peninsula stretched out into the center of the lake, but the ground between me and it was steep and marshy, and my mind was somewhere between here and Saturn. I stumbled once or twice, and on one occasion I fell face-first into a murky pool.

Windfalls tore at my cheeks and neck when I got up; I wouldn't notice until I woke up the next day and saw the damage I'd put myself through. Didn't matter to me then, and it hardly matters now, when I lie awake beneath sweat-cold sheets and relive all of it.

The woman in the dragonfly dress was waiting for me, standing on the edge of the peninsula, where the trees grew in agonized tangles, branches twisted into hideous knots. She was leaning her body against one gnarled alder, its roots piercing through the bank and down into the water. It looked like a mangrove here. I was crashing through the brush, losing my footing once and sliding down the edge into the water. I panicked, convinced then that there were things other than beavers and small fish in this dark water. Things that only find the moonlight bearable.

I heard someone call out my name, someone somewhere far behind me. I ignored it—they probably wanted to stop me from talking to her, from finally knowing who she was. I clambered back up the bank, water soaking into my shoes. It was deadfish cold, like the stars.

It was pulsing in my head, throbbing with urgency and *need*, to need to know who she was. That single thought diminished everything else. Like a wave when it touches down and wipes away any impression or structure in the sand, shuffling some of the fine grains into a uniform smoothness, dragging some back into the water.

Finally, I reached the tip of the peninsula, stumbling to the strange alder where she was standing. She shifted her weight and stepped away from me.

"Wait up! Who the hell are you?" I slurred. There was no answer, unless you count the mosquitoes and my own voice echoed back. She didn't acknowledge me, pretended that I wasn't even there, even though she was so close I could reach out and grab her shoulder, spin her around, and make her tell me everything. I wanted to stare into her face as she tells me who she is, her name, why she's everywhere in my head. Ghost or delusion, I could make her tell me.

She turned away, but her eyes remained on me as she stepped around the alder, her dress gleaming like eyes in the dark. I heard the sound the fabric made as it caressed the tree roots and shrubbery, a gentle hiss, like a November whisper. I, and anyone with a modicum of sense and an adherence to reason and logic, would expect a body who walks behind an unmoving object, and remain in motion, ought to appear on the other side, but she did not. She was there, and then she wasn't.

Then, there came a splash off to my left, nothing more than a muskrat-silent rippling in the water, and there she was again. She floated on her back, eyes closed to the moon while her arms were outstretched, her dress billowing around her like fallen leaves. She was floating in starlight.

The anger was just gone. I thought she was drowning, drowned, dead, dying, someone that needed saving, and I stepped in. The water was warmer than I thought it was, though it made the cuts on my face sting. There were shouts behind me, my name screamed out into the air. I wondered who screamed and who could have heard anything all the way out here, where screams can be reduced to tiny mutterings.

She was right there, right within my reach, fingers' length away from my saving her. I could have saved her, whoever she was. Instead, arms grabbed onto my shoulder and around my arm and started pulling me back toward land. "No!" I screamed.

"Ash, what's wrong with you!? Get back here!"

"Get the hell off me! She's drowning!"

"What!?"

I howled, shrieked—I tried to tell them that she was drowning. Couldn't they fucking see her!? Couldn't they see that she was dying, maybe already dead? I recognized Damien and Charlie, their touch and voices as they kept me from saving her. They were killing her, and they were making me into a witness. An accessory.

"There's no one there, Ash!" Charlie shouted in my ear, which by now was muffled by lake water. Everything was blurring together, fusing into a dark oil portrait left out in the rain, stained and running. "Goddammit, stop moving!"

"No! We have to help her!" I cried. Damien and Charlie fell into an argument, words mixing into a dull babble in my ears. There were pieces of the exchange that I could hear— "What if there is someone there, Charlie?"…"Take a look! She's the only one that's here!"…"Listen, I'll go take a look"…"No, you have to help me with this bitch!"—

With a lurching heave, Charlie pulled me back onto the muddy shore, sodden and cold. I gave her a fight until she clocked me on the jaw. There was hardly any pain, thanks to the alcohol, but the jolt made me seem like I'd woken up. Like the constellations were kicked back in place, even though I knew they hadn't moved.

Damien was out in the water, the mirror-sheen encircling and rising steadily above his waist. His sharp freckled face was splattered with mud, water streaking his rusty-brown hair back across his scalp, and the look he gave us as he turned around was one of the first things I never forgot and what the dreams couldn't mercifully warp. That suspicious and annoyed expression changed his features into something feline and sour. Even when the woman in the dress colored like dragonflies and scarabs reached out of the water and pulled him down below, leaving a wake of fading concentric ripples and an archipelago of bubbles, his face didn't change, like he didn't see it coming. Just another whisper in the dark.

Charlie called out for him, and after some time, I did, too. Even though I had seen it happen, I still called out his name if there was the barest chance that he was still there. Some others from the party came over and helped us search until the police came around—the party had thinned considerably by then. They questioned Charlie and I thoroughly, barely leaving out the third degree. Weeks were spent with people combing the woods and dredging the lake, but no body was found.

The only trace of human interaction they found there were Damien's footsteps in the water, and a scrap of ragged fabric. They figured Damien must have been messing around with one of the girls at the party, because the green-blue fabric seemed to come from a woman's dress.

There's a period between the time someone dies and their name becomes a ghost legend, some kind of intermediary for the incorporeal. For Damien, it was approximately six years—five years after the funeral and six after that night. When I'm buying gas for my old Nexus, weathered white like bird shit, or some cat food for my overweight Himalayan, or anything that might help dull the nightmares so that they seem like only illusory terrors, I'll overhear some teenagers talking about the ghost boy who died in the lake behind the Torgeson house and how badass it would be to go over there, maybe have a party, have a bonfire, bring the beer and pot. I want to tell them to forget it, to stop and think about what they might do or what might happen. I want to tell them to stay close to their friends for the rest of their little lives and don't talk to people who walk through the trees as if they were smoke, or who make spiders dance, or who float on the water like leaves as if they might be dead. But I don't say a word. I pay with my VISA and get the hell out of there, back to my house and the familiar depths inside.

I've become a shrine to her. A shrine where there is no light or succor, just the dull flicker of dusty candles illuminating photos that have lost their image, memories faded of all but their substance. If there ever was any.

# Lakeview Properties

"Paul, the lights have gone out."

Paul Conifer peeled his eyes away from the World News long enough to give his wife an incredulous look. "What're you talking about, woman? The lights are just fine."

He was going to say more when he noticed his wife, actually saw her standing there by the dark green curtains, looking out into the fading rosy dusk. The concern in Eleanor's brown eyes said it all. She wasn't talking about the house lights.

He jumped off the sofa, just about threw his hip out like he did a couple winters back, when his good-for-nothing grandson said he'd help plow the drive and never did. Eleanor stepped aside so he could look out the window, past the yard and toward the blue-grey waters of the lake. A ring of some sixty-odd stakes surrounded its shores; each one was topped with a bulky single-thousand-watt work light, aimed toward the water.

Not a single one was lit.

"Oh, *hell*." He immediately went to the phone on the nightstand and began dialing.

"What's Eric think he's doing over there?" Eleanor said, one hand holding onto the curtain, the other beginning to shake against her floral blouse. "You don't think he went into town, do you? At this time of night?"

Paul nearly swore – his fingers fumbled against the numbered buttons, and he had to depress the receiver more than once to restart it. "No. Even if he did, he would've told the Jacobson's he was heading out. God, I hope the bastard hasn't gone on a bender."

The dial tone buzzed in Paul's ears for a long time, too long to dispel the worry that was knotting in his stomach. Already the hairs on his arms were saluting his fear. "C'mon," he muttered, "C'mon, c'mon, Eric…"

Another buzz, and finally there was a click on the other end. "Yeah?"

The single word was blurred, disjointed. "Eric, what the hell are you doing? The lights are out, for God's sake!"

There was a cough, hard and damp. "That you, Paul? Nice to hear from you again. Been so long since we talked. Yeah, the God's-sake God-damned lights're out."

Paul waited, listening for the man to go on, and when he didn't, he lost it. He shouted, "Well, what happened!? You got a short over there or something? The wind take down a power line?"

A cough, and Eric spat something out. "No, no, no, Paul…no, nothing's wrong with the lines. It's all just right as rain. I just can't do it anymore, Paul."

*Oh, Christ in a henhouse.* He looked over at his wife, and he must have looked how he felt because her eyes went wide and she turned her attention back to the lake.

"Look, Eric…I know it's been tough, but—"

"You know me, Paul. You know me better than most of the other geezers around the county, and it hurts me to say this but you don't know shit, Paul. It took up all the money Joanne and me scraped together to make sure she had the best hospital care, an' when that ran out, it ate up my pension. An' none of it did an ounce of good. An *ounce* of goddamn good."

Paul winced at the hurt in the old man's voice, self-contained sobs lacing his sentences. Eric Stone was one of the oldest shoreline residents, one of the few to know the history of the lake. He'd been a few grades ahead of Paul and Eleanor when they were all attending McGregor High School, near a thousand years ago, and now that he was well into his seventies he'd been unofficially designated the Head Honcho in charge of the lights. The Big Watt Kahuna. The Warden.

And the warden had finally reached his breaking point. Paul cleared his throat, hoping to assert some control. "Eric...Joanne passed a year ago. We need you here, right now. The sun's going down, buddy, you need to put the lights back on."

A sniffle, a clink of glass on a hard plastic table. "Well, Buddy's dead, too. Didn't know that, I bet. He'd been going blind steady since last March, Paulie. And the goddamn tumors on his body, you'd think his skin was like the highways once the construction crews get on 'em. Like they was ticks that latched on after he'd been out in the woods. I just couldn't stand him suffering like that, Paulie, so I had to put 'im out."

The pause on the line was awful, a nail scraping silently against bone. On TV, the world news had wrapped up and the local news was starting. Storm damage down in the cities and over in Asenath, freeway repairs and burglaries. Things that happened in other places. Not here.

"*Paul.*" He looked over at his wife, saw her still staring out into the lake, her bottom lip vanished between her teeth.

"Eric, you're going to listen up, damn it! Everybody on the shore's counting on you to get those lights going!" and, not sure what else to say, he added "You've got a duty to this community!"

"Buddy was the last straw, Paulie. The last straw for me. When Joanne died, my world went with her, but I still had Buddy around. To remind me about things, right? We got him for Christmas – Joanne was so happy that year. That damn basset hound could've outlived all of us if it hadn't been for the cancer. Bet it was the same cancer she had. That kind of misery doesn't stop, Paul, it just keeps growing. Got nothing left anymore."

"Don't you think like that, Eric. Don't you fucking think like that! Look, I need you to get over to your shed and get to the generator, alright? Get to the genny and start 'er up. You do that, and…and me and Ellie will come over with some beers and hash things out. That sound good to you?"

"Sorry, Paulie."

And then the line went dead.

And even over the news, they both heard a small, sharp *pop* from the small grey house on the other side of the lake.


It had started, as far as Paul Conifer knew (and what he knew was gleaned from the scraps of info that was spat at him whenever his father had one lager too many and wasn't fit to walk out the door) back in 1898, when the three families that lived here at the time held a conference of sorts. In the early dawn hours, they'd gathered in the parlor room of Meredith Rook's big two-story on the west side of the lake, enjoying the buns and bread and hot coffee at Miss Rook's disposal. Eventually, the idle prattle ceased, and Miss Rook heaved her not-quite-two-hundred-pound frame into the middle of the room and told them all a story.

It was a very brief tale, though one they could all nod and find relation with. A Norwegian girl who married an Irishman named Rook and settled in Minnesota by a very pretty lake, hoping to have a very pretty farm and raise a very pretty family. About an Irishman named Rook who tried saving his daughter from the thing that pulled her into the waters while she was playing on the soft dark sands, and was himself taken.

Each family went around the room, telling different iterations of the same story. Livestock or pets or family members who wandered too close to the water at night and never came back. Some found only in pieces, but most of the assembly were sensible enough to merely know that fact, and not say it aloud.

"Now, what can we do?" Miss Rook declared, fists on hips and stamping her shoe on the floor, looking like a latter-day Madame Thérése Defarge.

"They can't stand fire," one man said.

"Bah. Devils from below spend eternity bathing in fire – it's the light they can't abide." This from Jessup Martin, father of the young man that was found on the northern banks the month before. Only his upper torso was identifiable.

"That's true," Franklin Green said. He was the youngest at the conference, and he might have made a living off his daddy's insurance practice, but all were victims here, all had a grievance and a voice. "One of 'em got into my barn last night, and when I shined my buggy's light on the damned thing, it scuttled away."

Soon, they quickly engineered a plan. They'd constructed the thick poles and set them into the shoreline, which in those days were topped with oil lamps. They all decided to set aside some of their wages into a pool to purchase the lamps and the oil. To the salesmen who were happy enough to turn a profit, nobody would explain why they were needed. Dozens of drums were purchased, the steel easily resold back to the government when war broke out.

Over time, the lamps were replaced with strong bulbs, each in turn replaced as technology advanced. Two of the families moved on, but the assembly grew to seven houses. Those new families who settled here either fled to safer places and never came back, or they learned to live with it.

Like the hard winters or the tough soil, you learned to live with it.


"He was soused, wasn't he?" Eleanor asked from the passenger seat. Paul leaned hard on the accelerator, as hard as he dared on the gritty dirt road. The old Chevy vibrated and slid along the gravel, and his heart jolted each time he struggled to regain control. Eleanor was holding the rifle against her plaid jacket, and he didn't want to jerk the wheel too hard.

"To the barn and back. He's stuck on what happened with Joanne some time back. And you remember Buddy?"

"What happened to Buddy?"

"Eric told me he was dying slow, full blind and everything. He put him down last week."

Ellie shook her head and clutched the gun. "Poor man." She turned her eyes to the window and Paul heard the sharp intake of her breath. He looked out the window, too, saw the surface of the lake was roiling, foaming, red-gold sunlight captured in tattered scales along its surface. He braved the turn and hit the pedal harder.

By now, other residents had begun to notice what was happening and were rushing out of their doors. Joe Montague was rubbing at his chin while behind him, his wife Terrie was ushering their daughters into the house. Judith Coxcomb, the lake's resident sculptor and, as the rumor mill went, a professed lesbian, was already pacing along her porch with her expensive crossbow. Others had the presence of mind to have a firearm in hand. Tom Singer was hailing them from the front yard, beer paunch hanging dangerously over the elastic of his brown shorts. Paul could just barely hear him shout "What's going on?"

"Get back in the house, Tom!" Eleanor shouted, a lot louder than Paul would have thought she'd be able to at sixty-five. Tom blanched, distracted by the lake. In the rear-view mirror, Paul thought he saw Tom dart back for his small barn, where, as the rumor mill went, he kept a small, one-man bunker, complete with marijuana garden.

They pulled up into Eric's drive and already had boots on the dirt before the cloud of sand that had been kicked up by the drive flew up and met them. While Paul was fumbling with the doorknob, Ellie kept the rifle aimed toward the lake. Heavy things were moving under the water.

He threw the door open, jumping when it banged against the wall, left a dusty imprint in the plaster from the doorknob. The smell of mildew and forgotten dog food slapped him hard, but he rushed through the foyer with Ellie on his heels.

Seeing the names of friends you grew up with in the obituaries, that hurts. Seeing them slowly tearing themselves apart by old regrets, that hurts, too. Seeing what that regret leads to, seeing your friend lying in his favorite patchwork sofa, rifle still clinging to his limp hands, the back wall painted in red and pink and abstract angles of fragments of bone and maggoty brain matter. That shit can drive you up the wall and back down at high velocity. Paul wiped his mouth with the back of his hand.

Behind him, Ellie whispered, "Oh, god, Paul."

"I didn't think he'd…" but the sentence faltered before he could finish it. Had he expected it to happen? He might have. Give a man enough sadness, enough beer, enough time, and what else was there?

Another splash, much louder.

"The genny," Paul muttered. Did Eric have the shed locked up? It wasn't winter, there wasn't any need for it, and every family around here knew not to futz around with the very thing that kept them safe. But who knew what else Eric had been doing before this? He might have boarded up the door out of pure spite, or booby-trapped it. Ellie ran outside, but Paul stayed in the room, breathing in the smell of blood and mildew and dog food that will never be eaten. He broke his gaze away from the flower that Eric's scalp had become, following the blood pattern of his checkered shirt to the carabiner attached to a loop in his jeans, holding a number of old keys.

Sweat lining his hands, he pushed himself forward until he was standing over the body. He reached down, grabbed at the keys – how could a body smell like this on the inside, all fuming and rotting? Was that just the brain? His eyes disobeyed his own command and looked into the darkly gleaming hole, saw that the veins were still weakly pumping blood inside.

Paul ripped at the carabiner and managed to pull it loose before he stumbled away from the sofa and spilled his breakfast, lunch, and dinner onto the grey shag carpet. He expelled until his stomach cramped and he was dry heaving, making the pain all that much worse. A thousand miles away, beyond the pounding of his heart in his ears, he heard something growing louder.

His wife burst through the doorway. "Paul! *Paul!* He's locked up the shed!"

Still hurting, he lifted the carabiner and tossed it to Ellie. Spry enough for a woman half her age, she caught it before it hit the floor and dashed back out of sight. Paul stumbled to the front door, coughing bile into his mouth and wiping at the corner of his lips. Behind blurry eyes, things were falling apart. Above, the sky had been usurped by a sheet of purple-pink clouds, darkening by the minute. The lake seemed like it was vibrating now, sloshing around as a child might shake a bowl of chicken soup. If he squinted through his rheumy eyes, he thought he could see the bright flash of scales, mossy green or charcoal black, a large hand or paw webbed like a frog...

He jogged over to the shed, the door already hanging wide open like a broken jaw. The 30-30 was propped up against the wall. Inside, Ellie was making it sound like pulling the chain on the motor was a Grecian labor.

The claws were scrabbling at the rocky jetty not far away from the jeep. Across the lake, other figures were frothing and milling onto the sand. Paul grabbed the rifle, checked to see the clip was in, the safety off, his hands were steady enough. He thought about getting in the jeep and making a break for it, leave Ellie and the whole community behind, get to safety, start over where there wasn't no lake full of monsters. The shame of it hit him then, burning his ears and cheeks. How could he even consider it? He liked to think he knew the difference between bravery and cowardice, but to have, for one instant, forgotten where the line was, infuriated and embarrassed him. To put his mind out of it, he pressed the butt of the rifle against his shoulder and watched the lake through the steel sights.

"Come on, bitch!" Ellie shouted. He heard another sharp yank on the chain and the motor growled to rickety life. The mass of volts traveled through all one thousand eighty-nine feet of copper wiring circumnavigating the lake, taking more than a couple anguished seconds before the circuit was completed. At once, the post lights flickered, died, and shakily ebbed to life as the sloshing blue-brown waters were gutted by incomprehensible lumens. From above, one might be astounded as seemingly a new sun formed down below.

The writhing waters slowly subsided and subsumed, ripples growing, gathering, echoes of echoes. But not before Paul saw a head break through the surface not far away, a coarse beaked head like a snapping turtle attached to a muscular neck, an orange eye brilliant with clever malice. Even as the eye slid back into the depths, Paul felt it still frozen on him, seeing him clear through the water, the Cambrian slate, the sentinel lights, and would keep following him once he got back into the safety of his bed.

He didn't know when Ellie stood beside him, how long she was there or when she had put her hand on his shoulder, but the look she gave him helped to calm him down. He would have jumped into the driver's seat but his hands were shaking so bad and his legs were paining him, so Ellie escorted him to the passenger seat and drove them both home.

Eric would have to be seen to, calls made and neighbors informed. He didn't relish at the prospect. Later, though, later. They could think about other things after a long night's rest.

# Three of Wands, Reversed (1996)

The boy pulled himself deeper into his jacket, ruffling into the black faux fur as he looked at his watch. For what felt like the hundredth time of the evening, he pulled back his sleeve and counted how long since his sister told him she'd pick him up at the Trolley Station Store in town. How long it's been since that promise became a sting. It was turning his stomach into foliated knots, the waiting, the hoping.

Where was she? He turned away from the bubbling containers of minnows and leeches and checked the aisles. There was a time when he couldn't look over the tops of the partitions, but now at seventeen he was tall and gangly enough. There were a few men in the store, buying up cases of beer and chips and last-second fireworks as the evening of the Fourth loomed.

He caught one or two of them throwing glances his way, curious jocularity and amused disgust in their sharp eyes. Some were strangers passing through their shitheap little town, nestled as it was like a small blackhead as 210 ran through it, but some were townies, people who knew him and would talk. They'd mention to their friends and coworkers and family members about the boy dressed up like a girl, lipstick and all, standing alone by the minnows and the leeches, impatiently checking his watch like a hooker trying to catch a john.

He caught Tom Green's eye over by the register, all animal viciousness pouring from him when he said "Jesus, tranny. You gonna buy something or you just going to stand there looking to get fucked?"

Barbed laughter fluttered through the station like bat wings. He knew Tom Green up through eighth grade, before his father had to pull him out of school so he could help run things at his home-owned sawmill business. After that, the asshole quotient multiplied by a factor of ten.

As if he's ever felt the suffocating grip of this place, constricting like a bony cage so intensely you felt it would be better if you never saw the sun again, never saw the same faces, the same grim lakes or the encompassing trees.

His roots were stuck in the town, in the soil and the rock on which the town was founded. Just like his father and his father's father, et al. Along with the rest of the people who couldn't see past their own menial day-after-day program. As though the universe was this one county and there was nothing beyond its borders.

They couldn't fathom that the consistent isolation and the repetition would breed someone like him, someone who wanted more. He dreaded the idea of being like them, of simply living here long enough that the pain of desire would numb him; become used to the days and nights, become rooted here, like the hissing aspens and the birches that groaned in the winter. People like his mother, who spent her days at work and got drunk or high with strangers on the weekends.

His sister had been the smart one – floating through high school and now working on her degree, supported on a pair of meaty scholarships. If he'd had any idea what he wanted to do with his life, he was sure he could have jumped on that same boat with her.

Where the hell was she? Damien turned back to the wall, hiding his burning face, pretending to preoccupy himself as the worry festered.

He'd started getting ready at five in the evening, when the sun was in its downward stroke into the brooding treeline. Shoplifted eyeliner and lipstick as red as spring cherries, red as new loneliness; makeup leftovers he found in his sister's room after she left and somehow he pulled off a nice look with it, he hoped; he put on his sister's jacket over a brown thrift store t-shirt dress that was a size too small and made him think of burnt chocolate; pantyhose just dark enough to conceal the growing hair on his legs and crotch; cotton panties underneath that, and he wished he'd practiced walking in these heeled boots before tonight.

It might have been blind impulse or it might have been desperation, but he knew he had to get out of this place, at least for one night.

A man had situated himself in the aisle near Damien. Black denim jacket, facial hair like a cinema werewolf – when their eyes connected, he felt like a rabbit caught in the middle of a road, paralyzed by an oncoming semi. He looked like he was the owner of the motorcycle Damien heard roll into the lot a few minutes ago. This wasn't like some evening fantasy of Damien's; there was menace in that face, in the air around him. Trying to hide his concern, he turned away from the fish-and-leech-smelling water and wandered down a different aisle.

The evening was cold for the fourth of July, the sky in folded layers of pinks, blues, and oranges. Cold enough to take refuge in the single gas station in the middle of your hometown when you knew damn well it wasn't the safest place for you to be. It was the kind of evening he always associated with Judas Priest's gentler songs, with worry and disappointment. In this town of five hundred residents (assuming the new town sign that had been placed there on the side of 210 back in 1971 still retained any accuracy) there was hardly much else for a seventeen-year-old to do other than blindly hope to not become your parents. Nowhere to go, no people to talk to…

Hope had a taste that became bland after too long.

He checked over his shoulder to see if the man was following him. No, just shelves of junk food and canned goods. His nerves were forming images in his mind, what he expected the man with the black denim jacket to want to do to him, what *he* expected *Damien* to do.

When his body bumped into something in the aisle, he thought he'd been stupid enough to walk into the shelves, but a pair of hands steadied him. He whipped around and looked into Tom Green's oily face, old acne and pimples scratched away and already become pockets of scar tissue among valleys of fresh acne.

"Didn't you hear me, faggot? I said get out before I kick a bigger hole in your AIDS fuckin' ass."

He struggled – when he daydreamed about this night, about his first night out dressed up and hungry for fun, he imagined something like this would occur, and he imagined being tough and fighting his way out of it like Pris in *Blade Runner*. Tom's grip was like a hydraulic press around the front of his jacket, twisting into his skin. He tried to shove Tom away but the momentum only managed to move him into that clenched fist.

His head reeled back, the fluorescent lights like burning stars in his eyes as Tom dragged him across the store's laminated tile. Curses and expletives were chained like rosaries on Damien's lips, promises that he wouldn't keep any more than his sister had. A lump formed in his throat and kept anything but a few grunts from coming out. His boots squealed on the floor, and he could smell gasoline and candy.

He saw the man in the black denim jacket, more starving man than wolf now with his dark brown eyes, more animal while he watched Damien being dragged away, like someone had taken a steak and was pulling it on a string.

Each time Damien made an effort to strike Tom wherever he could, Tom gave him a furious shake or a twist. He tried planting his feet on the floor – something, a knee or a knobby fist, jammed into him and ripped away all the air in his lungs. He doubled over, felt a calloused hand grab the back of his neck. Door hinges squealed, and a small bell painted to look like brass jingled with its own metallic laughter. Cold air rushed around him, fondling him through his clothes.

Tom hurled him and he rolled on one of his heels; the ground rushed up to meet him. Dull thwack of the cement foundation banging his head and bright nova bursts of color flowered in his eyes. Before he could react, even be aware that the pain won't come for another second, he felt Tom's work boot stick him squarely in the stomach. For just a few moments, he had become raw sensation, all cold and agonized meat.

There were no parting words, no final goodbyes or empty promises, not in this town. Tom's silence as he walked back into the station was a clear enough message.

Bruised flesh on fire, Damien coughed and looked up at the lights behind the door. He was caught in a pool of it, in the dust silvered by the light and the pale glow of the bitter half-moon. He pushed off the cold walk, half wanting Tom to come back out so his rage had somewhere to go. He tottered on his heels. One of them felt loose. He supposed he had to be reminded that there was nothing else for him here. For one more act of disrespect, the wind blew his hair across his face, getting into his mouth and covering his eyes.

"Fuckers," he muttered. His lower jaw tensed, and he forced his lower lip to keep from bobbing. He leaned against the store and looked down at the dirt and abrasions on his clothes. He cleared his throat, tried to clear away the apathy there. Nowhere to go, nowhere around here he wanted to go.

There were moments when he was getting dolled up that he thought every part of his plan was dangerous, that it would inevitably lead to something just like this happening. That he shouldn't be doing anything that he was doing in front of his bedroom mirror. Now, he was much more aware of what he was wearing, where he was, how much he felt he needed something for protection.

The bell jingled again, the pool of light around him widened, and for a second Damien thought Tom had decided he wasn't finished. Or that the man in the black denim jacket had followed him out. Instead, he saw Blair step out and check her purse, and he felt loads better.

He hadn't seen Blair Halonen in a year and a half, but he knew it was her by the way she glanced up to see where the moon was in the sky on her way out. He'd always found it weird and charming.

He took a breath while he watched her and any hope of salvaging the night walk away. He hardly heard himself say "Hey, Blair," until the words were already in the open air.

She turned. Was there something in her eyes? It might have been something he would associate with adulthood; deep dark eyes staring, defensive, like a dog that's learned that biting is sometimes the best answer.

Her expression knitted, pale brow pulling into confusion. She turned the rest of her body to face him, her black chiffon top soaking up the light. "Is that you, Damien? Holy shit!"

"Yeah," he said, not sure what else to say. An apology hovered on his tongue, but he stifled it.

"Whoa, man. What're you friggin' wearing, and why?"

Damien saw the young moon grin on her face when she said it, and he tried not to let the disappointment show. He returned her smile and shook his head. "I dunno. Just for fun, I guess."

Her face softened, or maybe he just wanted to convince himself it had. "Well, you look good, I guess. Wait, so was that you those guys were hassling back in there?"

He mumbled another "Yeah" and lifted his shoulders.

"Assholes. In that case, I'm glad I swiped this."

Blair dug into her purse and underhanded the bottle of autumn-colored liquid toward him. He fumbled it twice before catching it by the neck. The proud, smug face of a bawdily dressed pirate captain stared back at him, one jackboot resting on a treasure chest bursting with treasure like an overripened peach.

"I didn't know you were into rum," he said.

"It's decent. Better than some things. We just needed to grab something before we headed out for tonight."

Blair must have seen the look on his face. She motioned toward the grubby Jeep Comanche behind her, and Damien felt a tad more impressed at his good fortune. Dark blue paint made several shades brighter by all the dust and dried mud on it, jagged scratches around the keyhole, a small toy skull crowning the radio antenna, a pair of big clunky boots resting up on the dashboard. All the signs that Skunk, for yet another year, hadn't made good on her promise to set fire to her double-wide and finally leave the county.

He liked Skunk, even though she had a tendency to be a damn downer at the best of times and a crass bitch at the worst. She always struck an entertaining medium between the two when she was drunk.

"What're you two gonna do tonight?"

Blair made a sound between her teeth, exasperation or hesitation. "Hell if I know. What is there to do around here you can't make yourself do, you know?"

"Yeah, I know."

Blair grabbed the rum from his hands. She smiled at him as she sauntered away, sucking up the light from the awning as she stepped to the Comanche's driver's side. He watched her go, along with whatever could be salvaged from the night.

Panicked anticipation clinched his throat when he said "Hey, can I come with you guys?"

She looked over her shoulder, the rest of their night lost somewhere in her eyes, sharing space with moonlight. Damien blushed, wanted to take back what he'd just said. But Blair uncapped the bottle and motioned for him to follow her.

Seventy miles an hour, and the night was blowing through their hair like the intimate fingers of some empathetic wet dream he'd had on some tired night. Cool and luxurious. Damien sat wedged in between Blair, who was keeping her moondrowned eyes on the blacktop and her hands on the wheel, and Skunk, seat fixed way back, propping up her sturdy frame on her elbows while her knees were stuffed against the dashboard.

They'd been passing the bottle of spiced rum up and down the line and he was starting to feel warmer, lighter, though no less anxious.

"What a shitty night," Skunk growled. "Every year I think I'm going to get out of this rabbit hutch, find a nice guy, lay him, move into his mansion and spend the rest of my life in leisure, and here I am. Stuck with you two idiots. This place is a bad Twilight Zone."

Blair laughed high and loud. "Where do you bitches want to go tonight?"

"We could go to the Volcano." Damien had known about the single gay-friendly nightclub in Asenath for the better part of a year, and as far as his own freedom and individuality were concerned, The Volcano was a star in his mind, a jumping off point to bigger potentialities. Someplace where some tall-dark-and-handsome, man or woman, would carry him away from this leech wound of a town and show him the real world.

He couldn't keep his heart from falling into his stomach when Blair frowned and shook her head. Skunk booed like a foghorn. "No goddamn way!"

"That place has glitzed itself up its own ass so badly it doesn't even know what it is anymore. It feeds on its own rep. You don't wanna go there, man. Trust me."

"Oh. Okay." He pouted, knew damn well he was pouting and tried to appear masculine while he was doing it. Sighing out his frustration, he took the bottle from Skunk and swigged, feeling its sweet bite in his throat as it landed in the bottom of his stomach.

"Ooh, take it easy, Demon," Skunk chuckled. She put a meaty arm around Damien's shoulders and started playing with his hair. "You're a...you're a little thing, aren't you? You have to learn how to go with the flow sometimes. Me, I...I never did that, and where did that get me?"

"'At the corner of Nowhere and Mayberry,'" Blair said. "You've told us this same shit a thousand times last year alone. Besides, life isn't just disappointment and shit. I don't know what else it could be, but it's not always that."

Damien snickered. Skunk glowered at the both of them, flipped her dark blonde bangs out of her eyes. "Yeah, I was a smartass, too. Then life knocked me around a bit before I had to learn that everything's so fucked up and there's no way you can get out of it."

"Thanks, Skunk," Damien muttered. He knew what they were both doing, or more likely what they didn't know they were doing other than bickering, but he liked to think that they were trying to make him feel better in their own off-putting ways. He stared into the night, at the signs flying past in a colorful blur. He knew this road, knew that in a few more miles they'd be crossing the county line – one of those invisible yet infallible walls Lee hoped he would cross and never see again. To the left of the road, a field was transformed into a marshland by a rainstorm. On the right, the train tracks that he occasionally dreamed about following.

He'd had been contemplating the night so strongly that he didn't hear Blair. The rum contorted what he wanted to say into a garbled "What?"

"Why do you want to go to the Volcano? You know something we don't?"

"Maybe he had a date, Blair. Think about *that*? Do you have a date waiting for you, Demon?"

The blush was threatening to burn the faux fur on his jacket. "No, I don't really…"

"Aww, that's too bad. Hey, come over here."

Skunk caught him in the crook of her elbow and drew his face to hers. The world became all sweat and diesel and clove cigarettes when she pushed her lips onto his. He felt her force her tongue into his mouth, ungraciously accepting its eel-like invasion. Delight and aggravation seemed to fight for dominance inside his mind. He wanted it to stop. He wanted more. Outside, the trees were shooting past in a sickening blur, and he had to shut his eyes.

Blair snorted a chuckle. "Jesus, Skunk. Give him some air." Damien was only barely aware that the volume on the radio turned up.

Then, Skunk was pulling away and ruffling his hair, laughing. "How was that, kid? Measure up to your dreams?"

Damien was smiling, but he didn't feel much like smiling. He felt like Skunk stole something that wasn't hers to take.


Damien and Blair were watching the fireworks in the rearview mirror. They'd parked the Comanche in the back of an old laundromat, looking like it had been abandoned for the better part of a decade before it was disemboweled by a fire. Skunk told them she'd be back in a bit, and that was a little while ago – they watched her stumble into the old building, kicking rubble out of the way, her black shirt becoming a part of the dusty darkness.

They'd asked if they could follow her in, but she brushed them off. With an animal glare in her eyes she told them to "Stay in the fucking truck, guys," and mumbled pieces that sounded like "my problems" and "you wouldn't know." When they heard the sincerity cutting through her buzz, they knew better than to ask.

He wondered where they were. Hibbing was half an hour behind them, and he was wide-eyed when they passed through the array of buildings and streets, the store signs and flickering lights behind windows made spectral. It wasn't as big as Asenath, that pale growth on the nose of Lake Superior, but it was brighter, humming with possibility. He'd wanted them to stop, see what shops or restaurants were open, but Blair seemed like she couldn't hear him. Damien yawned, the rum smoothing out his mind nice and clean while the night breeze sighed through half-open windows.

"What's it like, Blair?"

"Hmm? What's *what* like?"

"The world. Getting out of that stupid town and doing things on your own. Actually knowing that you exist, being someone."

Blair gave him a dark look, a look that said if he were anyone else, she would have knocked him out of the truck. She was quiet for a long time before she said, "Just stop it."

"Hmm?"

"You know exactly what I'm talking about. You have to stop being such a fucking wet blanket, Damien. Whiny little bitch…it's no wonder you haven't gotten away from your mom and gotten out of here. You just keep pissing and moaning about how dark things are that you don't just stop and figure out where the light switch is. Everything after high school is hard work, but it's a lot harder if you don't grow up first."

A red star lit up in the rearview mirror, and for the smallest instant, the world was bathed in scarlet. Damien covered himself in his jacket.

"Everything sucks," Blair proclaimed. "You just have to learn how to adjust and adapt so that it doesn't hurt you so much when you see it coming. The world doesn't wait for you to catch up, no matter how much you want it."

The wall could have fallen apart for the scowl he was throwing at it. More than anything he wanted Blair to shut up, wanted the fire to stop spreading across his pale cheeks. He looked at the open shadow where

Skunk walked through and expected to see her walking out, cobwebs and ashes stuck in her rust-colored hair.

"God, Blair. When did you start thinking like this? Was it Michael?"

She looked at him, brow furrowed. "*Michael?*"

"Michael Garrison? I thought you left because of what he did."

"Why? What did he do?"

It was wrong, maybe, that gibbering of delight he felt when he realized her ignorance was entirely real, but he took it happily. He wanted to feed it more. "After you two broke up, he started falling apart. He wrote a note and shot himself with his dad's shotgun, out by Beaver Lake."

Blair stared at him, eyes brighter than moonflowers. Her lips parted and then snapped back shut, so she looked away. Silence in the truck, while the night sky continued to blow up in shifting chromatic flares, sparklers screaming. The world smelled of sulfur, cordite, and cool earth. What little was left in the bottle passed her lips and was gone.

The fireworks came and went, Skunk hadn't returned. Damien supposed that in all the open fields and hills in Minnesota, the crowds would be dispersing, families heading home or to small diners that were still open tonight, while couples or singles would be making beelines back to bars or wherever else they could smell a chance of continuing the celebration. His stomach loudly reminded him just how hungry he was.

Then he heard a loud pop, and then another.

"What was that?" he mumbled.

"That was your stomach, princess."

"No. It was like a popping sound, just now."

"Maybe the fire crews just found a box they'd left over. And there's always some jackass stocked up on M-80s or bottle rockets out in the woods."

Damien shook his head. "It sounded like it came from…"

Pale yellow light speared the corner of the building, the thunder-rumble of an engine felt like it was splitting the night apart. Blair's eyes went wide, and Damien whipped his head around so he could follow her gaze out the window. "What the hell's that?" she shouted.

A big Ducati motorcycle pulled out slow and heavy from behind the laundromat. Damien thought the headlights made it look kind of like a wolf – a number of loud thuds against the side of the truck vibrated up his seat and into his bones, and he wondered what that sound was, wondered what the guy on the bike was doing and what he and Blair should be doing. Even when another pop vibrated in his ears and the glass flowered into a thousand shards in front of his face and Blair pushed him down beneath the dashboard and screamed "Get the fuck down, man!" and his head banged against the rough black polycarbonate so hard he saw more fireworks or fireflies Damien wondered what he should be doing.

"Whuh…" He wanted to say something else, but his stomach gave a jump and he threw up a little in his mouth.

"Oh, shit, Damien." Blair was gasping. He could feel her moving her head around, felt her hair as soft as the night against his neck. Bile burned in his throat, and the pain made him a little more present.

"Stay down," Blair hissed into his shoulder. "Just stay down."

The door flew open, hot summer night rushing in. Blair screamed bright and loud in his ear and her weight suddenly left him, her heavy boots scraping the floor, kicking the dash. Damien lifted his head, trying

68

to make sense of the scuffling sounds he was hearing and why his nose hurt.

Outside, Blair was being thrown side to side by a shadow that gripped her by the shoulders, a thin and grim shadow, with eyes like the moon's twin sisters. Her hair whipped around her face in a black rope, and the sound of tearing cloth was like a bonfire spitting.

A flower of rage bloomed in Damien, sliced through his buzz. He clumsily climbed out of the truck – his legs seemed more inebriated than his head, and his stomach was somewhere it shouldn't be. He sank to his knees, gripping handfuls of the cold damp grass and dirt. He felt too heavy, the ground twisting around too quickly. No, get up…get up, you stupid bitch. He tottered to his feet, mouth dribbling sweet rum.

Blair and the man were just a few yards away. She must have tried to run but he'd caught her by her shirt or her hair, brought her down into the dirt, lying on top of her. She screamed again, and Damien saw a pale hand rise and fall, a resounding thunderclap each time. The man was grunting, like a stray hound. Damien lurched forward and kicked out, planting one of his heavy boots between the tall man's shoulders. To his chagrin, it seemed to startle him more than hurt him; the man twisted around, and in the glare of the bike's headlights Damien and the tall man locked eyes, and with a tingling in the skin of his arm and lower back, he fell deeply into those lunar pools, paralyzed, beguiled.

"Another sweet, stupid whore," the man said, growling. His stubble looked like black moss, hair a sweaty mess. He stood, the grim shadow, and Damien wanted to do something, run away and hide, or grab something and hit him. One of those options. But he couldn't command his feet to move. As though the thought could only remain in his mind, couldn't reach all the way down.

The man was leering, spittle in the corner of his mouth. In the light, Damien could see a little serrated knife in his hand, shining like a garnet. A little sound escaped Damien's throat, a moan or a yelp, and he leaned toward the truck.

"Are you going to cry, bitch? Are you going to keep your mouth shut, and cry for me?"

Fear is ancient; it is powerful and all-consuming. It is an emotion that transcends its psychological trappings and scientific explanation, known to everyone and everything. Some could argue it is an intrinsic sensation to all life on the planet, perhaps, should it exist, life across the cosmos. It has traits that can be seen in humanity and other animal species: a fight-or-flight response; vocalizations through the mouth or nose; rapid and heavy respiration; even tachycardia.

Damien remained frozen, deer in headlights. The sensation of his heart cycling and recycling blood throughout his body so fast, so hard, his breath rate rising, the breeze murmuring against his sweat-stained clothes, it all made him want to throw up. His vision was blurring into cottony silhouettes, ghosts.

A hand reached out and gripped his shoulder, dirty nails digging through his jacket and shirt and scraped his skin. The man's own jacket – a button on the left lapel read "I'M YOUR BAD HABIT;" one was a pin with the image of an apple with a bite taken out, a green worm crawling from the wound and grinning a razor-toothed grin – smelled like coffee and sweat, and something else hiding underneath, something sweet and rotting. The grip tightened, and Damien whined again, still lost somewhere in those eyes. The other hand, the hand with the knife, went lower, under his shirt. Damien felt the cold metal stroking the jut of his hip.

"What does it matter? Right? *La nuit tous les chats sont gris,*" the man said, whispered into Damien's ear.

Fight or flight. The thought triggered the action a mere instant later; Damien had no idea it was even happening. He brought up his elbow and slammed it squarely into the man's face. The man shouted, knocked back a couple steps, covering his eye. Blood was already flowing through his stubble, staining his lips and chin.

The man looked at Damien, snarling, and the things that swam in the depths of those eyes made him want to run, desperately run away. He even tried, turned on his boots and slipped on the broken heel, skidding onto the cool ground. The man said something in French, something skewed by his own blood. He advanced at a run, knife held out and hungry, finger hooked into rakish claws.

Something came up behind the man, a glint in the mismatched patchwork of light and dark, and an empty bottle of rum ascended, bottom upward, then crashed down onto the man's skull with a hard, hollow sound. Damien expected it to shatter like it would have in the movies or on television, but it didn't.

The man fell to his hands and knees, grunting, and Blair swung the bottle again. This time, it did break. She swung it again and again, her hair black and wild, her face wild. She was snarling like the man had, Damien noticed.

Blair stopped. The man wasn't moving anymore. She got up on shaking feet, grass stains on her ass and legs. She pulled Damien up, and the momentum nearly threw him off balance again.

She was bleeding from half a dozen little incisions. One was one her belly, a few near her breasts. Her shirt was becoming darker and darker.

Damien touched her elbow, looked at her face. She looked tired. Scared. Angry. Mostly tired. "Are you okay?

Blair didn't answer, just gave him a look that said she wanted this night to be over and done with, to get away from this night forever. They walked to the Comanche but didn't get in, just leaned their bodies on the cold metal as if it were a salve. Damien looked at himself in the side mirror. Sweat was making his mascara run, forming black rivulets down his cheeks. He felt more sober, though he didn't want to be. Not at all.

"Hey, Damien."

"Hmm? What is it?"

Blair looked at him from the other side of the Comanche. The passenger side. "Come take a look at this."

No. I don't want to see. I want to forget about this and just get out of here. But Damien didn't say that; he dutifully stepped around to the other side to see what Blair wanted to show him.

The window that had been half-open was now a bright crystalline mess; one tap and that would be all it would take for it to fall apart. A bullet was lodged in the glass, small caliber, stuck like an insect in primeval amber. It took a moment for Damien to see what Blair was showing him – he'd been sitting there, staring out the window; if the bullet hadn't gotten stuck...

Then Damien threw up, mercilessly, mercifully. He fell back to the ground on his hands and knees. Blair held his hair back.

Later, Blair tried to stand on her feet, looking like a tree caught in a heavy wind. Spluttering, she hobbled to the entrance of the manufactory – Damien managed to unstick his eyes from the mirror long enough to notice, and soon enough was following behind her.

72

He wanted to say something, but he didn't know what to say that would bring up any answer to the confused muddle in his mind. His head was filled with cotton, heavy cotton, as he kept up with Blair's shadow.

The floor of the building was a mangled mess, a garden of phantoms left to toil in memory. Dust and grit covered the floor, stricken timbers and old equipment pounded down into a landscape too hazardous to traverse. But Damien saw a path through the rubble, probably tossed around by Skunk. He kept up with Blair, close enough to smell her earthy perfume while he worried at the lining of his sleeves.

There's only so much room in a heart before it starts to feel crushed, entrapped, compacted. There's only so much space in a body before it feels it has to get out no matter what the cost. Damien saw the cost looking at him as he followed Blair through a different room and followed her stare. Deep brown eyes that couldn't see them and never would, no more guilelessness in a bitter face. Blood darkening Henna-brown hair and spilling down the hill of one cheek, blood making intricate lines on her bare thighs.

Quietly, they walked back to the truck on heavy feet. Once inside the safety of familiar smells, they wept. Blair reached over and pulled him into her shoulder, and the feel of her fingers in his hair, the warmth of her skin, it made him cry even harder.

In time, the Comanche was eating up the highway as Blair and Damien gave voiceless whispers to themselves, trying to listen and be lost in the radio. The road here was suffering badly from sublimation, deep depressions and rising humps like dunes in a distant mystical desert, but Blair was sticking to her speed, not budging an ounce one way or another.

Twice Damien tried to open his mouth to give voice to the storm in his mind, twice he shut it again. What was there to say? He supposed sometime, some faraway time and place that wasn't here, they could talk about it. Until then, there were only the paltry comments or sundry musings passed back and forth, like pilfered rum.

They bought clothes at a thrift shop Blair was familiar with, and they filled up the tank at a gas station that seemed more high-brow than they were accustomed. They were silent, but more was spoken when their hands occasionally sought each other's.

Eventually, it was Damien's turn to drive.

# Primordial

"Here you go, Jeffrey. Enjoy it." When Aubrey hands the spindly Ichabod Crane of a child the plastic cup, hardly any air passes between its rim and his lips. The cup is drained, and the child mumbles his thanks as he walks away toward a group of smaller children, stoic as a brass lion.

Next in line, a little girl with cherubic cheeks and hair like sargassum kelp pouted. "I want grape. Grape is my favorite. Why can't we have grape?"

"You'll get what we've got, Shirley, no more or less than anyone else," Aubrey said, as if she weren't only a few years older than the oldest kids here in her bastardized orphanage. As if every word wasn't a step toward some new lost expectation of her role. There was a wary sharpness in her blue eyes today, conscious of every moment, every youth in the living room.

She handed out drinks with maternal automation, watching the children as they played and ran through the rooms, relishing in the openness and freedom they couldn't find until finally fleeing the city. Aubrey bit her cheek, trying to remember when she hotwired Ioseph's blue Lexus and picked up a boy with a shattered femur poking out of his flesh on her way out of ruined St. Paul. Long ago enough, she supposed, to become acclimated to the quiet of the hills without realizing it. It crept up on her.

"Would you finish up here, David?" Aubrey gestured at a dark-skinned boy of fourteen. "I just need a break, move my legs a bit." He nodded, kept ladling the cherry drink into plastic cups. It was early in the morning and he was bleary-eyed, skinny insomniac child, but she was happy he was so eager to be helpful. There was something in his face, though. Something was on his mind.

Before he could open his mouth to say something, Aubrey was already walking away, saying "Don't forget to save some for yourself."

She went from room to room, dancing out of the way of children who were still playing. She patted Julie, a tall redhead who smiled up at her and went back to her book, plastic cup propped against her knees. She'd rescued eight from the streets, and there were a few who hitched up with them like grit in a snowball between the Twin Cities and this long, undulating green field, somewhere in Koochiching County. They were a ragged assembly, like dolls recently found in old attics or secret backyards, but at least they were alive. And they could pull their weight, the ones that wanted to.

It was a miracle that the shack was equipped with a working shower. Whoever owned it must have had a pleasant life here.

She wove her way toward the kitchen, where garbage bags were piled up in white and black carbuncles in the corner. Now that it was summer again, the stench was like walking through fog. The youngsters wanted to toss them outside, set them up on the crown of a distant hill and have a nice evening bonfire. But she wouldn't let that happen. Holding her breath, she reached into her pocket and pulled out a small clear bag. She

76

folded it, crumpled it, and shoved it into the trash pile where it wouldn't be found.

Then, she walked back into the living room and sat down in her favorite lounge chair – handcarved cedar, green upholstery, very lush. It sat facing the large wall window, where, after a few yards, the field dipped down from view and spread out into forested valley, hewn by a small blue river. In the distance, a low mountain range rose up like shattered spinal columns, dark basalt and granite birthed from the womb of the Laurentian Divide. Aubrey settled into the cushions and closed her eyes.

Ioseph would have enjoyed it, too. He would have adored the sound of the grass rustling in the wind instead of vehicles squawking by; the chirping of chickadees and jays in the trees instead of damn gulls bleating for food. The image of his spectacles glinting in the sunlight, his freckled face broken by an uncommon smile flashed behind her eyelids. Aubrey smiled, pretending that it could have been a possibility.

No. Ioseph would have hated it.


Cold grey November afternoon, skies outside the window the color of damp linens and white rot, and Aubrey was lying on the long cedar-plank bench in the historical wing of the Hosmer library in Minneapolis, trying to sleep. It was the only place she could get some rest after the cops chased her out of the park, after maintenance crews started repair work near one of her ideal spots after botching up a previous attempt in the spring. The world smelled of autumn and mildew, of Time frozen and left undigested.

She was four, maybe three steps from the gentle morphine of sleep when the voice said "What are you doing in my chair?"

Her green eyes opened like rusted flaps, and she saw him standing by the dark iron banister. Her messenger bag was pregnant with spare clothes, a perfect pillow, and she eased off of it, red-blonde hair catching on the fleur-de-lis clasp.

The man staring down at her was nothing to look at; black hair covered by a brown wool beanie that said "North Shore" in blue; the black hair on his face looked like a dark bushel, conflating the sharpness of the blue eyes peering out from behind his wireframe glasses. Plaid jacket, blue jeans. She swore she'd seen him around the library before, but couldn't place the face.

"What d'you want?"

"My chair. I'd like my chair, please. If it's not too much trouble."

There was already a year and a half separating her from that rat's nest called Driftwood, Iowa and Minneapolis. A year and a half skulking in shabby motels and abandoned apartment buildings. Everybody here looked the same to her. But some sort of bell was going off inside her mind. Was he just a face she'd seen passing by the windows, or was he a regular at the library?

She also knew that that "Minnesota nice" mien was all shit. If she bit, he was just as likely as not to bite back.

She sat up, put her arms across the backboard. "It's a public building, jerk. That makes it a public chair."

A brief glare from behind his specs. "Look, I don't have time for this. Isn't there someplace else you can go?"

The notion was grating to her. The library had been the first place with any heat she'd been to since the governor shut down the homeless encampment by the Kellogg Mall, on the pretentiously kindhearted basis of shoring up defenses against viral infections. She also didn't like the pompous inflection the man used with his last question; it was something you said to a mangy dog that has overstayed its welcome.

Rather than say any of this, Aubrey politely told him to go piss up a rope.

He glowered down at her, then shook his head with a low mumble. Instead of walking away to get the security, he threw her off guard and sat down next to her. She scooted to the edge to glare at him, but he was already engrossed in a thick book that was marked with a dozen post-it notes. She smelled a thin cloud of cheap cologne and something mossy, fungal, probably coming from the book.

The moment he sat down with the book in his lap, it was like he'd become oblivious to everything around him. She snapped her fingers by his ear, to no reaction. She leaned in closer to see what he was reading. Every fourth word seemed to have at least five syllables or was in a different language, or both.

"That's a pretty old book," she said. No reaction. "Smells like it's old. Bet you could sell it for some good change."

"You don't pawn books that have cultural merit."

"Why not?"

Another tired glower was his only answer. She puffed, feeling irate now. "Pretty high and mighty about your books, aren't you? Seems a stupid, pointless thing to feel big about. What book is so damn important, anyway? Smartass. How smug would you be if I ripped up all those pages?"

"You can if you want, it wouldn't really matter to me." With a mild amazement and annoyance, Aubrey saw that he was actually smiling. "Maybe I'm borrowing this book from a friend and I'm reading it for the first time, or maybe I've already read it so many times that I already know the pertinent facts. It wouldn't matter what you do, really. You wouldn't be doing anything productive. You'd just be making residue."

She paused, considering if that was an insult or not. "I don't get it."

His smile grew. "Basically, that's all that human intention does. It's just residue on the canvas of time, *conductive* residue that attracts, charges, and promotes energies. Let's say you're driving up the highway to your favorite store when someone cuts you off—

"I don't drive," Aubrey said.

"—so fast that they scrape off a good portion of the paint and send the mirror on that side flying. What would you do in that situation?"

"I don't know. I suppose I'd do what everyone else would do and lose my mind; I'd shout and flip 'em off."

"There you go. You'd do what everyone else would do. Now let's say, by some twist of the universe, you have some precognitive knowledge of what would happen whenever you acted. You knew that by shouting at them, you would in some way be steering everything – everything – to some awful end. What would you do?"

She frowned, not sure where this was going. "If I knew that would happen, I'd probably just stay home."

"Right. You'd stay home. That's your intention, and it would send out ripples to help usher reality to its end. The end result is the same. Whether your intention is action or inaction, you're still sending out those ripples. Popping bubbles."

Aubrey didn't quite understand that last bit. She was still struggling to comprehend the rest of what the man, whom she now considered to be a weirdo if not wholly unhinged, had been saying. She pursed her lips and shook her head. "I guess I don't get it."

"I can show you, if you want."

80

The look he gave her was kind, and laced with curiosity. "I don't know. You got a place to stay?"

That was how she'd met Ioseph Johnson. If there had ever been a person she'd ever actually loved, Ioseph had been the one. For the first couple of weeks she had assumed – logically, she felt, having become accustomed to the wheelings and dealings that occurred in parks and smoky back alleys – that one of the stipulations of her living with him meant keeping his bed warm. Each time she offered, he would turn her down. Rather than be confused or angry, it made him yet more curious.

He was a perplexity. If she'd ever told him that, he would have accepted it as a compliment.

His apartment was on top of an antique store he'd inherited from a family friend, a squat blue little thing that always smelled of a mixture of cleaning solution, dust, and jasmine. If nothing else, it was a warm place to stay when the trees turned the color of amber, the streets became pale and treacherous, and the buildings rustled with the sound of pipes struggling under ice. A place where some guy didn't demand she call him "daddy." He even hired her as a part-time employee.

Still, to say that her time spent there had been uneventful would be a gross understatement. As days and nights petered to a slow trickle of inactivity - well, there was the sleeping and eating, and there were plenty of dusty books to read – she began to feel more and more like a parasite.

She expressed this to Ioseph one dull evening and was flabbergasted when he began to laugh. More than laugh, his thin frame was shaking so hard his spectacles kept slipping from his nose. She stared at him with her hands on her hips and a look that could have sent sap back into a pine tree. "What's so goddamn funny, may I ask?"

He waved away her irritation, trying to compose himself. "No, no, I'm not laughing at you, Aubrey. It's just…well, that's the whole point of everything. That you think it's such a bad thing being a parasite. That's what's funny."

It's easy to pick a road to drive down when you can surmise that the whole stretch is fine – no potholes, no downed power lines or trees, no black ice. It's easy to ask a question without thinking of where its answer might take you. When Aubrey asked Ioseph what he was talking about, he told her. He told her just about everything.

Mostly, he talked about bubbles.

Big is a word that does not correctly describe reality; it would be like trying to wrap your arms around a mature red oak and believing that you're embracing it. Reality is immeasurably immense, but it has limitations, borders, dark matter membranes fixed in place and holding everything. There is no Ultimate Nothing beyond this membrane, but other titanic bubbles encompassing other realities. Existence, he told her, was not a single fixed state of reality, but like a large mass of frog spawn or sea foam.

For all their endurance, however, these membranes are permeable. Just as light can pass through a prism, energies at certain frequencies can chew through these membranes and, with enough applied force, pass through entirely. The word Ioseph used was *vermiculation*. After some research she found its etymology lay behind worms, the way they chewed, digested, and passed dirt.

Shit like time travel, faster-than-light speed, bulk optics or quantum photonics, all that science fiction jargon that scientists were slowly making strides toward, it was all just worms chewing through and between realities. Things that he referred to as *synchronicity*, like déjà vu, forgetfulness, or even the concept of empathy, were comparative to the first stages of an illness, end products of a cosmic ozone layer becoming riddled with holes.

"But how'd that shit even start?" Aubrey asked, feeling as if she was understanding it and still light-years from the point. "You can't just say that's the way it's been without a frame of reference. What was the starting point?"

"Shub-Niggurath," Ioseph said, and he wouldn't say any more. Nine days after this conversation, she finally found the odd words in an old leather-bound notebook from 1905. Squinting to read the yellow, coffee-stained papers, it told of *something*, some indescribable force or entity that gave birth to equally indescribable, titanic children, and the placental outpouring, writhing with its own existence, became reality.

Or as Ioseph would see it, foamy *realities*.

It was bullshit, of course – it had to be. Ioseph was just another weirdo whose social inequity and isolation in a half-assed museum had spawned a funny neurosis, focused on some psychotic logger's journal.

But she wasn't in any danger, was she? He hadn't made any advances or given suggestions that he was violent, and as for sex, he seemed about as interested in that sort of thing as a woodchuck with a car. Besides, the skies were pregnant with the first snows, and the drastic drop in temperature was already raising hell around the city. For the moment, she thought, she would stick around, make some cash. See how things played out.

In the meantime, Ioseph was happy enough to teach her all about the inner and outer workings of the world. She felt she was getting a crash course in something that was at once religion, anti-religion, magick, advanced physics. Even if it was a novelty, it was a secret they shared.

Soon it was the first of January. Aubrey and Ioseph spent it by closing up the shop and lying on his bed, not quite as high as the NEOWISE space telescope but not far away. *Tarzan Escapes* was on the television, bathing the attic bedroom in flickering greyscale, the volume turned down low so they could hear the city outside. Her arms were wrapped around his torso, her eyes shut, hearing the bus whip by in the street outside, tossing aside slush the color of nutmeg into the curb.

She wasn't quite asleep, but she felt like she was dreaming. Her skin was warm and tingling, electrified.

"She's going to die, too, you know," Ioseph said softly.

"Hmm?" She opened her eyes and tried to move her head, but there wasn't enough strength in her. "Did you say something?"

"She's not eternal, much as I'd like Her to be. All that stuff about divine beings and unending physical or spiritual continuation is just philosophical fantasy. Things die, Aubrey. That's something both spiritualists and physicists can agree on. Matter falls apart, and even energy in all its changing forms can be dulled down enough to be nullified. Everything's going to end. Even Her."

She didn't know who he was talking about. She wasn't even sure if he was actually speaking to her, that maybe she'd lapsed into a between-state, neither in the Land of Nod nor out of it. After some time, she said "What about jellyfish, Ioseph? What about funguses?"

He frowned, his specs pushing forward on his scrunched-up face. She thought it was cute when he did that. "Genetic immortality is still biology, it's just matter. It fades away."

84

"I don't think so," Aubrey said, but she didn't elaborate. Life seemed too grand to just fade away, if any of what Ioseph had been telling her was actually true. Maybe things aren't truly immortal in the antiquated literal sense, but that didn't necessarily mean Life as a whole was temporary. Something to be blown away when a strong existential wind comes around. Even if *She* would eventually die, there would be others. Saying this aloud would have stripped it of its grandiosity.

When she closed her eyes, John Weissmuller was leading a scantily-clad Maureen O'Sullivan and a group of adventurers through a twisted, smoking landscape, full of quicksand pools and growling iguanas. When she opened them again, everything was in a painful blur of color. A red bar on the bottom of the screen said BREAKING NEWS, the scrolling marquis beneath that too small for Aubrey to read but the bright yellow lettering conveying the necessary urgency.

She watched a group of men floating, hovering, flying over a golden-brown desert, their bodies wrenching and jerking in the air like baubles on a string. In moments, she was asleep.

Aubrey woke to an afternoon just beginning to bleed into evening, the sky still blue but tinged with rheumy pinks. For a while, she did nothing but sit there, scanning the Dada configurations of clouds, listening to the forest-rustle of her breathing. Inhale and exhale. She tried to time her breath to the sway of the willow trees in the distance.

The shack was silent. Some of the children were reclining on the furniture, but most were resting on the floor, their plastic cups beside them. Aubrey waited for a time – time has a funny habit of working improperly in a comfy sunlit chair facing the window. Afterward, she stood and walked to the kitchen, stepping over small sleeping bodies.

The little girl who wanted grape was lying in a pool of sunlight, curled up like a puppy with her hair splayed out like a lady's fan.

A clatter came from the kitchen and she almost yelped. A little girl, probably six years old, sat at the table, eyes bright and awake. Aubrey stopped, stone still, one foot intruding into the kitchen, the other stuck in the living room. At the sound of her shoe striking bare tile, the girl looked up and wiped at her wet cheeks. "Aubrey? What's going on? What's wrong with everyone?"

She almost wanted to strangle the little girl, see those teary eyes bulge, lightning-crack vesicles spill blood out into the sclera. But that was the old Aubrey, the one who had yet to understand the way of things. She breathed in, out, knowing that one little girl wasn't going to ruin what was to be.

"They're sleeping, Juniper." Aubrey said, putting a finger up to her lips. "It's naptime right now, so we have to be quiet."

"Is it like when it's storming out, when we have to be quiet then?"

"Sort of like that, yeah."

"How come I'm not asleep?"

*I wonder.* She knelt down on the warm floor and looked the child in her scared young eyes. Sharp blue eyes, like Ioseph. "I'm not sure, but you know what? I've got a few things to do around here, and I don't know if I can do it on my own. Do you wanna help me take the trash outside?"

The girl sucked on her bottom lip, giving it serious thought. "You said we weren't supposed to bring the garbage outside."

"This is a special occasion, Lilly. It was going to happen anyway. You have to have big muscles to haul the bags over the field, though. I don't know if you quite got what it takes."

Lilly scowled. "I'm strong!" she hissed.

Aubrey smiled, stood back up. "Sure you are. Now, grab a bag, and remember…" She held up a forefinger to her lips. The girl mimicked her perfectly, with a thin smile. She reached up and grabbed one of the bags, and as she did it sent one of the smaller bags tumbling down onto the floor, sending its contents scattering across the tiles.

"I'm sorry! I'm sorry," Lilly began repeating into a mantra, a child's ward against punishment. Aubrey wished it were that easy. The girl looked like she was going to break out into fresh tears.

Aubrey put her hand on her shoulder, still smiling. "Don't worry, kid. It's not the end of the world. It's just garbage, right?" Lilly nodded but her brow was locked in a frown, browbeating her own clumsiness.

Together, they put the bottles of generic Gabapentin and Ambien back into the bag and continued hauling them out the door. Aubrey stopped to grab a lighter from one of the cupboards. A bonfire would be nice and festive. It would smell like Hell's septic system blew out, so she'd have to hope that the wind took a turn and was blowing in from the east, but it would look nice. There was a pretty spot to the south, a few yards past the corn and sweet pea crops, where a pair of old pines stood watching over the field like sentinels.

Her head was feeling fleecy. Full of cotton. Ioseph would have called it comprehending her own ticking clock. Aubrey, the old Aubrey, would have told him that was a cheap way of saying you believed in that destiny shit without saying it.

Afterward, sweat-stained and stinking under the noon sun, Aubrey lay in the tall grass by her rock garden, watching the fire trace black sigils in the sky. She didn't know where the little girl went to – probably playing through the grass, or maybe she'd gone back inside, try and sleep with everyone else. Burning wood had its own alphabets, from the way it blackened and sent worms of fire through its flesh, to the snapping and popping made when inner liquids vaporized, to the smoke it generated. Aubrey watched and listened for a while, accepting it, until she looked away.

Her rock garden was pretty, would have been prettier if there was any water around it like all the photographs of rock gardens she'd seen, but she made do with the rocks found around the valley. She'd made an arch of large banded agates found by the river, and that was enough to make it seem less like a cairn.

Eventually, she rested her head on his sweaty shoulder and shut her gummy eyes.


The phenomenon began in what had been the Fertile Crescent region of the Middle East. Mesopotamia. One of the progenitors of human civilizations Some unseen force was indiscriminately plucking people and animals and carrying them through the air at a rate between twenty and sixty knots per hour, at an altitude around twenty- to thirty-thousand feet. There were theories, but theories could only carry so much weight until reason snapped.

Families who worked double shifts to pay the bills and keep their kids going to summer school didn't want to keep seeing the same tired-eyed or frantically-speaking scientists, not when they kept offering half-hearted and worrisome statements. People believe what they want to believe; in the end, that's what it comes down to.

The news had an awful lot to say, especially the ones transmitted by the usual demagogues, who saw the phenomena occurring in the Middle East as religious or even political vindication for anything they wanted to deliberate. The first occurrences happened over Gaza, but the first footage that was made international was shot across the Persian Gulf ("That's not so far from where the city of Ur was built," Ioseph remarked). Scientists could try to soften the blow of the images with explanations and facts, but madmen with mouthpieces and computers were powerful.

Some people thought they could see faces or shapes from the way the bodies swarmed in what was now being referred to as The Cloud. Familiar forms you would think you see in birch trees or cliff faces. Some saw the patterns as less chaotic, too perfectly even, like photos of artificial nanostructures. Some physicists claimed the way the bodies undulated and spun appeared to be a form of convection. Forming spirals in spirals.

Ioseph was ecstatic.

"Don't you see what's happening here, Bree? Sweet shit, are you even seeing this!?"

"Yeah, I'm seein' it." They were in the bedroom, watching television again. Aubrey lay on the bed on her side, half under the covers and drinking a rum and Coke while Ioseph was pacing by the window, gesticulating wildly. It seemed that was all they did these days, and it was beginning to irk her.

"Something exposed the membrane and tore through. It makes sense; the membranes are thinnest where communities have existed long enough to live and die over hundreds of generations. Souls, ghosts, psychic emanations…they don't go anywhere; they make a ceiling of vermiculating energy across a whole region. Now, some kind of energy actually ate its way through! Imagine the energies, Aubrey. The sheer, titanic energies of that thing. Stretching and arcing across the globe, growing and growing…Are you even listening?"

"Yeah."

In the corner of her eye she could see him scowl. "Don't tell me you're not scared."

Huffing, she put down her glass and spluttered. "Yes, Ioseph, I'm scared. To be really honest, I'm fucking terrified. But you know what? What's happening right now is happening *over there*. It's a whole world away, Ioseph, and it seems to be pretty much contained. Life still has to go on here."

"I thought you were paying attention. If nothing else, I expected you to have some common sense. Fuck! It's not going to be contained if it gets any bigger."

"It won't get any bigger, Ioseph."

He stared at her as if she'd slapped him. Ioseph's adherence to rationality – his rationality – was ironclad, and her defiance must have sounded too sincere then. She'd drunk enough to sound as sincere as Death and barely remember a word. "I can't believe I'm hearing this crap. From you, of all people. The world is experiencing something it has never experienced before, and looking at where all the arrows are pointing, being in a heavily populated area is going to be severely detrimental to our fucking health! We have to get out of here."

It was noise, everything just noise that seemed to scratch at her skull. She leapt out of the bed, the booze and her book hurled onto the floor. "If you want to leave, then just go, Ioseph! *Go!*"

It didn't surprise her that he already had a suitcase stuffed in the closet, all set to bug out. He hauled it out from under the bed and walked out the door. Didn't look at her, no final glare, no hint at having been betrayed by someone that might have been the closest thing he'd ever had to a relationship. Doors below slammed shut like the final thump of a heart.

For a while, she rested on the bed, watching television and pretending what had happened hadn't happened. He would be back. He'd had tantrums before – during a particularly bad spat he'd thrown a glass against the wall and it exploded into a thousand sere drops, scattering across the floor. But he would always apologize to her later, sniveling like a puppy.

She knew the type; he hated being alone, and would do or say anything to repair whatever damage had been done. She fell asleep, and when she awoke, Ioseph wasn't there. She expected him to call, to send a text, to send an email, to give some sign that he was alive. But Ioseph was well disciplined in silence.

Days went by, and she waited. Two weeks, and there was no Ioseph.

A month later, Aubrey heard sirens pealing through the city.

Pareidolia. Hidden writing. Quantum photonics. Anomalous synchronicity. Events begin to feel like infant steps toward an inevitable conclusion. A cosmological encyclopedia, written and rewritten in broken, faltering sentences across global ecosystems. Was it simply the climate acknowledging its own steady collapse, and produced some entity as a countermeasure? Was the biosphere reacting to something in the air – maybe the thousands of tons of microplastics that filter through the atmosphere and settle in the ocean or on the land? Or had a lumberjack two hundred years in the past have one whiskey dream that would end up being prognosticative?

Ripples. Dreams and intent, sending ripples throughout time and space.

What do you do when you know the river will take you down into its depths? Do you stroke vainly for shore, or do you go as far as you can before filling your lungs with its cold waters?

Aubrey wished she knew.

It could have been anything that woke her when the sun began its downward stroke; the grass slapping at her face as the wind began to hitch up; an expiring dream that shunted her out too soon; a psychic synapse firing. Her hair pawed over her face until she brushed it away, looking up into the mask of the blue sky. Behind all that pretty blue were billions of stars, and how many of them were already dead, sending light into the abyss?

To her surprise, a wave of calm washed over her, the kind she'd only experienced after taking a pull off Ioseph's crystal bong. Behind her, in the distance behind the valley, she thought for a moment that she could hear distant sirens, like a choir of wolves or wailing woodland sprites, until she realized that Hibbing and Virginia and Pine City and everyone around the Iron Range were all gone, no one to operate the early warning systems. And then she smiled.

Because a wish a little girl made when she turned nine was coming true.

The wind carried the sound over the valley, the cacophony of a million, a thousand million disparate and terrified organisms, stitched and stretched. Some were humans, some were animals, deafened and blinded by their own captivity, careening into each other without rest or interruption. A twitching shadow stretched across the valley while she waited.

*Imagine the energies, Aubrey, the sheer titanic energies of it. Stretching and arcing across the globe, growing and growing...*

A colony. A home that would never leave or drive her out. She'd failed with the children and the cabin, but in a way she hadn't; she'd formed a community, a pool of lives, which brought the cloud screaming across the world. She'd done her part, offered a few crumbs to a giant, and maybe, whomever or whatever would take up the mantle that humanity used to control wouldn't be burdened by this thing. She could only hope.

Behind her, wooden beams and glass splintered as the shack was rent apart, its contents pilfered, as if by giant unseen claws. A single tiny scream pierced her ears – a thread not yet woven into the tapestry – until it vanished completely into the overlaying ocean of sound.

As Aubrey felt her feet leave the soft grass, she stretched out her arms so that she might embrace all of life itself. As she was born up into the deafening cavernous folds of entangled bodies, she added her own voice to the music as she began to fly.

# Sacrament of the Moths

Eagle Lake West is not a gaudy cemetery; there is no wall or fence of stone with a graven plaque, no tall wrought-iron gate to announce to the surrounding woods any guest, not even a groundskeeper's storage shed nearby. The headstones here are simple slabs of granite or limestone, if there are any, which are watched over by the chickadees and crows. Although there is a sign which says "60 mph," those familiar with the area and heading down 210 know to go slow around here, if the infrequent corpse of a deer, turkey, or fox is ever noticed.

An old man returns to this cemetery on the first day of the third month of every new year. Sometimes he bears bouquets of lilies or the lupins lining the road, sometimes cheap plastic remembrances that the caretaker will remove the next morning, but, in every instance, he carries with him an old Coleman lantern. Sometimes the sky is clear, and sometimes it rains, but this time the sky is the same charcoal shade of his coat. It was his grandfather's coat, and now that he was a grandfather, he felt it suited him very well.

He looks out for a slab of pale hornblende granite, smoothed to a glassy surface, his wife's name engraved on its face. He had the placement memorized the day they set her coffin into the cool damp earth twenty-two years ago, and his legs went to the spot by muscle memory. But a memory is always in orbit around other memories, circling deeper and deeper into reminiscence, and Micah Jacobson felt the chill of the air a little bit more than usual.

There is no despair in Micah's sobs. He'd been taught that weeping was a woman's weakness, so he learned to pretend it was happiness that was forcing his tears.

Occasionally, there are kids around to mock and toss jokes at him. Hey, buddy, you forget the hospital bathroom again? they'd ask, or something equivalent, huddled together while sipping their parents' beer. He'd ignore them, although sometimes he'd glare at them, and the light of age in his eyes would be enough to drive the monsters away. The kids were awful, but they weren't terrible. There were terrible things, oh, yes, the old man knew about terrible things. Things like the ravages which Time can wear on a man, the miseries of falling in love and having that person taken away from you because of something you couldn't prevent or fix. Spending nights awake, exhausted and haunted by regret.

No gawkers today, no one to hear the soft conversation Micah gives to the headstone and the chilly grey air. He feels small in his coat, small and tired, as if he's never done this twenty-one times before. As if he was a mere virgin dabbler to this ritual.

The clouds change position but don't leave. The unseen sun slips away beyond the farming prairie as if eager to evade witnessing what will happen. Micah stands, sees stars while his joints pop – sudden pain, sudden relief – and breathes out a sigh. The land flares orange in the lantern's glare, flecks of mica in his wife's headstone becoming stars, constellations, a galaxy etching hope.

96

Reaching into his pocket, his mind goes blank and he grins, drawing out the dried husk of a wood nymph moth and setting it on the edge of the stone. He closes his eyes and speaks his small prayers, evocations to things forgotten by the sun and the moon. He doesn't open his eyes until he is sure, until he's certain what has been done has truly been done, and when he does she is there, reclining on his wife's grave. Her skin the color of birch bark, thin angular body covered only in a green muslin dress, eyes filled with the light of his lantern, of countless other lanterns.

Micah knows very little about the fairy woman – questions like who she is, where she is from, why she resides in this cemetery, why she gladly offers concessions to the bereaved and the knowledgeable, and others have no truck with him. That she is here and willing to offer a modicum of relief is enough to satisfy Micah Jacobson.

He floats in the fire of her sharp-toothed smile, and when she stands he has to look up. "You, yet again," she says, and the twigs and leaves in her hair bristle. "The misery addict. I should learn to expect you, but there are so many who want to see me."

"I can only imagine," Micah says.

"Ah? Can you also imagine some other way for you to achieve your desires? I'm bound to nothing; I could refuse you on a whim, you know. Just slip back into the night and let you resume your selfish anguish."

"No," Micah says, perhaps louder than he intends. He shuffles on his boots in the shameful wake of that word, in the acceptance of her accusations. Her smile grows wider, balanced on lips the color of henbane petals. "I'm sorry, I...I just want to get this over with."

She waggles a barbed railroad spike of a finger at him. He's gone off-script, he knew it as well as he knew what comes after autumn. "I don't think so, Jacob's son. I think you enjoy this too much, our little tête-àtête in the night. I say you enjoy annoying me because it makes me want to hurt you, and you think that's fitting punishment for being alive. Ha! Perhaps you prefer me to your betrothed?"

Micah hangs his head, stares down at the dewy grass, his dirty work boots, the small deer hooves peeking out from under her dress. For a fragment of a moment, he thinks the moon is about to come out and save him, but it flees. Instead, he thinks about his wife's face, the curve of her black bangs infused with worry-grey, her blue eyes, hard Norwegian cheeks and a small French nose, all the little jokes centered on those features. His smile is fleeting.

"You think this knowledge is a strength, but it's as much a weakness. You're weak, as all of your species are weak."

There is no point in haggling; she knows each time exactly what she wants to take as payment, and he has never once asked what it is he has lost.

There is no hesitation this time, not after securing this payment so many times before, no more second-guessing or fearing what might happen afterward. He steps into her embrace, and when he does, he feels himself lifted up into the cold night, simultaneously jettisoned out of himself and drawn so deeply into himself there was no chance of ever finding an exit. Her fingers become razor-bladed thickets entwining him to her, drawing blood that doesn't leave his skin, as his flesh melds into hers as finely as twin pools of water. There is no pain at the conjuncture, not much of anything outside of raw, undiluted sensation, as Micah stops being Micah and becomes something other. Consciousness becomes a shredded, vividly microscopic thing as he feels, and only feels. He is certain he ejaculates, even though, in that moment, he has no body to propel the action.

It lasts forever, it lasts not long enough. When he opens his eyes (and he is relieved that they are his eyes), he's kneeling on the ground at her feet. His clothes are lying in chaotic lumps on the wet ground between them, and he never knows how his clothes leave him. There is no pain on awakening, only a sensation of having been emptied.

He's only guessed what it was she's taken as payment, when he was still expectant that one day she might tell him. Was it something intangible, a special memory, or a dream, a fragment of hope? Or was it something as simple and clichéd as blood? Semen? A few of his aging cells? None of these things really mattered all that much compared to actually finalizing the bargain. What was left of him to miss, anyway?

"It takes less of me each year," Micah grunts, speaking more to himself than to her. Speaking to know he still has a voice. He bends down and begins putting his clothes back on.

"You grow older each year," the fey says gravely. Her smile is gone, or at least flattened into a smirk. "Frail, scared old man, who can't even bear his own pain. While others suffer worse, you have to come to me and scratch at the wound. Amazing how star matter coalesced and, given four hundred thousand years of evolution, managed to breed you. You're a waste of time and matter."

Micah nods each time, familiar now with this part of their dance. No point in saying otherwise. He puts on his shirt and buttons his coat. When he looks up again, the fey woman is gone, and his wife is standing there instead. She is not ravaged by worm or rat, not as gaunt as the dead ought to be; she appears as she was when he had last seen her, after winning two bouts of stomach cancer, after four surgeries, after she had been taken from him by a simple patch of glare ice on the road.

As twenty-one times before, he starts the conversation by saying "I love you."

# To the Pines Go a Maiden

I was nine when this happened. Don't go mistaking that fact as a chance to grab pity from you, or that it's being just my way of makin' the story shockin'. It's just one of those things I sort of held onto when it happened, when the events became a memory. One that will never go away.

Summer solstice – the point of the year when the day is at its longest, the old start of summer before the calendar was Anglicized. When the sun is at its peak in the northern hemisphere, and everything is so green. Not for us, though. I think us kids would have gone out of our minds if we had to wait for the twenty-first of June to get out of school. Nope. By that time we'd already been raising all kinds of hell for a couple weeks, the way all kids do when they got nothing better to do.

It was just three of us back then – Jay Goodum and Minnie Overhauser, and then I brought up the rear being the youngest. We used to run around through the woods behind Minnie's house, climbing up as high as we could in the sappy conifers and the birches that were way out there (this was way back when the birch trees were about as thick as damn elephant legs, not like the scrawny things you see today), brushing bark out of our hair and spiders off our clothes. Sometimes, if the spiders weren't so big, we'd try to chuck them at each other just for the fun of it. Minnie was the kind of girl who'd find the biggest one and hide it with a handful of tree bark, then try to place the whole mess under your shirt while trying to hold back a wave of giggles.

There was so much happening that day, and there wasn't no way of knowing everything that was happening, no chance of translating it into paper with any reasonable precision. The woodlands smelled like earth and growth, sweet flowers and vernal warmth, and when the wind blew in from the east you could catch a whiff of old Leppo's cattle farm. I thought the wind was just about the best thing because it made the tall foxtails and switchgrass in the fields nearby bob and dance like an ocean wave, making whispery noises that joined the trilling of the willow leaves. A short way to the west was a faint brook that you could hear only when it wanted you to hear it. It started in from Little Sleep Lake and washed down like a tear down a person's cheek until it finally bled into the Mississippi. The squirrels were out making a big rumpus, waging little squirrel battles in the undergrowth.

Not that day, though. Our time was more invested in what Jay found by the shore of the brook. Minnie and me were throwing pine cones at each other, putting bigger welts on the welts we had, but we stopped when we saw the look on Jay's face. He was hunched down in the wet sand, crouching with the backs of his legs almost touching the hilly rise behind him, mouth hanging open like he'd forgotten what he was doing. His hair was hanging in a funny curtain over his forehead like a lot of the boys around here – there wasn't any haircutting places around here, so all our mothers would cut our hair, usually with a clean mixing bowl perched like battle helmets over our heads.

"Whatcha got there?" Minnie said while we walked up to him. I looked over his shoulder and saw something gleam.

"Nothing," Jay said, immediately getting onto his feet and stuffing the nothing into one of his shorts pockets.

I said "Come on and show us," practically shouted it. Jay gave me a dark look, blue eyes sharp and hard like his dad's. While he was distracted, Minnie moved bird-quick and jammed her hand into Jay's pocket. Jay balked and Minnie ran away laughing, ran across the brook with Jay on her heels. They both splattered me with mud and water but I fell in behind them, already laughing.

The forest caught their voices and tossed them back at us, quick attack and counterattack:

"Give that back!"

"No! It's mine now!"

"I'm the one who found it!"

"Yeah, and I'm the one who took it!"

You can tell when the woods start to get different, older, maybe. The earth becomes a bit softer and riddled with roots, and the air smells like an attic, like ancient dust and yellowed papers. Jay and Minnie ran on and on, deeper into the older sections of the woods. I kept up as well as I could, wondering how far away from home we were getting, if we were getting close to Little Sleep Lake, or even Leppo's farm. Maybe the highway was just over the rise on the left, just past the trees.

I was stumbling by the time Minnie and Jay broke over a thin hedge and into a broad clearing. I stopped to catch my breath – I've always had weak lungs, even though I never really been around anyone who smoked – while their repartee continued to flow around the trees. It was getting so my lungs felt like they were being squeezed by the ribcage that housed them. I got my way through the hedge, while the branches left little red scratches on my skin.

The clearing was vaguely circular, with a tapestry of old pine needles and leaves, and in the center was a big pine tree. I was old enough by then to know the difference between the kinds of pine trees around here, and this one looked like a Norway pine, a really old one, as big around as a front-end loader. I was struck by its oddness, the way it hadn't grown straight up like the ones around it. It was cleft in several places around the middle like lightning couldn't keep its paws off it, with some of its daughter trunks each rising up at different angles, but I didn't see any blackening of the bark at those clefts. Thinking back on it, damn thing could have been just under ninety feet tall if it was an inch, but when we were that age, it might as well have been a thousand.

Jay had chased Minnie around the pine and had almost caught up to her when he faltered over one of the breached roots, giving Minnie a chance to find her footing on the trunk. She climbed up through the branches, quick as a field mouse. She was already halfway up when Jay swore and started kicking the tree. I walked the rest of the way toward the spectacle, grabbing a thin idle tree branch that the wind had taken care to blow to the ground.

Jay kicked at the tree again. The scuffed rubber hardly seemed to make a sound here. "Gimme that back right now, Minnie! Gimme it or I'll hit you!"

Minnie was smiling into the next county; she twisted around one of the higher clefts and sat herself down on one of the outstretched branches. Her red hair caught the sunlight and twisted it, made everything about her glow like hot gold. She held up the thing she took and looked hard at it.

"Tough titty, Jay! This thing's mine now. Oh, man..."

I just watched as Jay fumed, feeling the laughter start to boil out of me. The sight of him standing there all frustrated and inept, he reminded me of Yosemite Sam going "Ooh!" after being foiled by Bugs Bunny. That and what Minnie said made me laugh even though the ache in my lungs became a little sharper.

Jay reached over and grabbed my stick. He pulled all the way back and hurled it up into the sky, missing Minnie by whole yards. She didn't even react, she just looked at the little object, glinting red in the sun.

"Wow. This thing's got little marks on it."

Jay was growling like an animal at this point. He rushed the tree and started grabbing at anything that looked like it could do damage, and started up a barrage. He threw with the precision of any fourteen year-old, but he had plenty of ammunition, and some of them managed to find their mark. A rock nicked Minnie on the shoulder and she fumbled on the branch. I think I stopped laughing then when I saw the look on her face. Another stick struck the branch near her knees, and she just then found the impetus to get back on her feet.

"Jesus, Jay, would you stop that? You're gonna do something I'll make you regret in a minute!"

I stepped back while Jay went crazy. I mean, she was in the wrong, but she was vicious, and could give you an ugly bruise if you got on her bad side. I looked at her face and then at her balled fist. This wasn't fun anymore.

A rock thumped hard against the trunk nearest her hand. Another one caught her bare knee, and Minnie made a sound somewhere between a grunt and a scream. Maybe it was the pain, maybe it was the shock, but her leg twisted out from under her and she lost her balance. Her arms shot out and she caught herself before she could fall all the way down, but I saw what the branch did to her thigh. The rough bark was like a cheese grater on the softest flesh of her leg; pink turned to red real fast, red and wet-shiny in the sun. At least Jay had stopped whipping stones at her.

Something landed at my feet, a dull ping in my ears, but I wouldn't bend down to look at it until I was dead certain Minnie could make it back up. For a second, I played with the idea of being the hero – I could catch her, her sudden death averted by my swift and masculine hands. But I realized that even if I tried, I'd only be as helpful as blanketing her fall with my limp, broken body.

Minnie's grunts were animalistic as she hoisted herself up. I could see tears in her eyes, teeth bared like she was going to bite down on the branch. She brought up one knee, straddling the limb, and she sat there for a long time.

We saw her lips move. Jay shouted "What are you saying?"

"I'm going to kill you, you little shit!" she screamed.

I had to step back, her voice was like a vortex of rage. The surprise of hearing a girl swear like that also caught me off guard, and the realization that I'd forgotten the thing at my feet made me remember it.

I bent down and picked it up, rubbed the wet soil out of the creases. It was a stone, about as big as a 42-milimeter marble, and just as smooth as one. Years later, I'd read about amber in the library, Baltic amber, and the stone was colored like that, but Baltic amber doesn't have starry lines in them, floating and glimmering with their own light. Those must've been the funny lines Minnie was talking about, little lines trying to form an overlapping image. It made me think of the branches of trees, swaying in a cool summer wind.

I wasn't able to see it any longer before Jay tried to snatch it out of my hand. I could make out something bordered by a circle before I had to play keep-away.

"Gimme that rock, Tim! Give it to me or I'll break your leg!" I felt a fist connect with my chest, knuckles grinding into the bone. The pain was deep and fiery, but I tucked myself inward and brought out my leg. Jay tripped and went down to the forest floor. "You stupid snot," he growled, and I ran a few yards closer to the tree.

Minnie was already scrabbling across the tree like a pale spider. "I'll put both of you in the ground!" she screamed.

This wasn't how the day started. This wasn't how summer for us kids was supposed to go, not ever. It was because of the stupid thing that Jay found, that was never seen until he happened to be by the river. I know that sounds a bit superstitious, but isn't superstition just a different kind of truth when you're a kid?

I threw the stone at the tree. I wasn't giving it to Minnie, I wanted the stupid thing to get lost so we could get back to the way we used to be. I wanted to play tag in the woods, or king of the hill, or go back to Jay's house to play Hearts at a dime or quarter a point – because Minnie's mother didn't like boys hanging around her Winnebago. I didn't want us to kill each other over something that didn't matter, gold or not.

The stone thunked into the bulk of the tree, not very high up, I wasn't very strong; it tumbled and spooled down, throwing light all over, until it reached one of the clefts where the daughter trunks emerged from the base and was lost to view.

Jay and Minnie weren't none too happy, I can tell you. They just stared at where they'd last seen the stone, plain flummoxed and still as statues. Minnie was the first one to wake up, unleashing a wave of expletives that would have made her mother have a conniption.

My body jolted back and I was staring into Jay's fury. His mouth was set like he was going to take a bite out of my cheek, and that made me want to cry. "What did you do, Tim!? What'd you do that for!?"

I didn't say anything. I wanted to say that they were going to kill each other if they kept going at it, that I was tired of them yelling about killing. I wanted to say all that junk about how I wanted things to get back to normal, but it all got jumbled in my throat. There were tears already welling up but I tried to keep them concealed, because tears around here meant a talking to and a punch in the arm.

Minnie was reaching into the cleft, scrabbling among the branches, ignoring what they were doing to her bare arms. She seemed to forget that her leg was bleeding like mad. I wasn't going to tell her that it was the wrong one. She was almost whimpering until she suddenly stopped, flinched backward. She was staring at her hand, and I had to guess that that was bleeding, too.

Jay let go of me. We both waited for Minnie to get down – her leg was all glistening red, and so much more awful now that it was closer. It was because of that wound, so much like an angry scratch, that she didn't run, but lurched like some kind of monster. She stopped so close to me, I could smell the used-up oil and fat that her mom recycles at breakfast. She didn't say anything. She stared at me with the same betrayed vicious expression Jay had a moment ago.

I could have run. I wanted to run, it felt like the right thing to do, but I wanted to stay there with them. Running away meant being alone in the woods. Maybe that wouldn't have been as bad as having them beat me into a pulp, but I'd already weighed my options.

From some universe that wasn't this one, I managed to squeak "Stop it, you two."

Minnie squinted at me, like she had trouble seeing me. Her lip twitched and she seemed to snap awake, if you can wake up when you're already awake. She turned away, stared at Jay, and they both looked at each other for a long time. They looked tired, incredibly tired.

"Sorry," Jay said.

"Uh-huh," was all Minnie would say. Her head was down, staring at her leg.

"Does that hurt?" I asked her. I wanted all of my concern out there so she could hear it.

Minnie frowned, reached down and rubbed at the wound. I saw that the blood was already soaking into the top rim of her sock. "No, it doesn't. I can't even feel it."

She touched the one on her hand, and her frown deepened. "I can't feel this one, either."

The woods stopped being fun for us. Right then, we decided that being somewhere else was the best idea. We walked away from the grove with the big old tree at its center, not saying a word. When I looked back, my eyes tilted up to the branch where Minnie almost fell. The blood there was gone.


The next few days went by in a slow flicker of activity. We collected beer bottles and brought them down to Calvin's autobody shop, a feat that got us around eight bucks in all, which we spent at an ice cream place that used to be a cabaret joint back in the twenties. We biked around the town and peddled along the train tracks, grabbing fancy rocks we could sell to folks passing through. Our town was one of those hub-like locations that seem to exist for the sake of being a through-way to somewhere else. We biked around town, hunting for fun that was so fleeting.

It was never stated outright, by any of us, but you could sense it when we were together. No matter how busy we made ourselves, we'd think about the woods. Our eyes would make a quick jerk to Minnie's leg, which she kept covered in thick overalls.

Five days after what happened in the grove, Minnie stopped showing up at our usual hangouts. We laughed it off and said it was just girl problems, but we kept thinking about her injuries that she couldn't feel. Jay would scowl and I could tell he was thinking about the stone and the war they had over it.

In the evening of a too-hot Thursday, we went to the Overhauser trailer to see her, but her mom met us on the lawn. She gave us both a dirty look from behind her spectacles. There was a cigarette glued to her bottom lip that bobbed up and down as she spoke.

"You boys want to know where my Minnie is? Well, that's awful nice of you, sure as rain. But I think you boys know how I feel about that sort of thing. And besides, Minnie ain't here."

"What? What happened to her?" Jay and I were flummoxed, and a teensy bit scared, frankly. Joanne Overhauser was an old Christian woman who used to be a school librarian in the next county, the kind who didn't like to repeat herself.

She took a deep drag on her cigarette, turning half an inch into ash. She stared hard at Jay for a while and then said "You're the Goodum boy from up Red Oak Road, ain't you? Well, I don't see how any of it's your business – boys your age oughtn't be nosing around little girls' houses –

but I sent her away. She's staying at her father's apartment over in Bemidji."

"Oh. But it's just that she wanted us to help her with—"

"I don't believe it. It's a sin to lie, boys." And that was all she would say until we were gone. She watched us go, her hawkish eyes pushing us as fast as she could.

We walked as far as the road, where a hedge of low-hanging willows blocked us off from the Overhauser lawn, then we doubled back in a broad circle. Minnie's mom was a mean old woman, and she'd lie out of her ears if she thought she was helping out her daughter. We left our bikes there and passed through the brush to their backyard. I've never done this before, but Jay told me that Minnie's room had a red heart sticker in the corner.

I looked inside first. I don't know what there was to expect; a cupboard, a tiny dark space like a basement, but it was just a room. There was a bed with a heap of grey sheets on it, with a knot of dark hair. Jay brushed me to the side; he tapped on the window, gently at first and then harder. I kept looking over his shoulder and turning around in case her mother began to wander over.

Jay rapped on the glass, and the heap on the bed moved. Minnie turned her head up to us, and I wish that the glass would have been dusty enough or coated with enough pollen so that I couldn't see the deep blue-purple lines under her eyes. Her clothes looked sweat-stained, like she was waiting out the flu or something rank.

She got up and went to the window. She walked slow, like all her joints were decades older than she was; she opened up the window and leaned out, her hair brushing along the bug-infested sill. She looked ready to puke the moment the air hit her face.

"What're you two butts doing here? If my mom sees you, she'll knock you out and cook you."

"We know, we snuck by her," I said. I wasn't sure if I should have mentioned our conversation with Madame Overhauser, but I decided not to press it.

"Is this where you've been for that last few days?" Jay asked. "Were you just sleeping here while Jay and me have been raising hell around the countryside?"

Jay laughed at that, but Minnie didn't laugh. She gave me a look that was both tired and sad. She mumbled "Wish I could say no, man. I haven't been sleeping too good lately."

Jay snickered, made a sound like a caterpillar was caught in his nose. "What? You get nightmares or something?"

Minnie stared at him, and the look in her eyes was something I wanted to forget, wanted with all the power a nine-year-old can muster up, but couldn't. Even now, I still remember that far-off look when she looked at us, like a Dust Bowl victim.

"Yeah," she muttered, rubbed her eyes. "Yeah, something like that."

"Well, come on out. We got some money off Cal's, and there's supposed to be a neat new movie playing at the drive-in tonight."

The drive-in was something special in our town. Instead of the high-end industrial places where you have to pay for just about every little feature, you paid for nearly everything in advance once you got your ticket. The canvas was set up on a flat farm plot that used to be owned by David Kinkle, but after his son wanted nothing to do with raising animals, he decided to make it into an entertainment center. Around that time, he was raking in about two thousand dollars every combined spring and summer.

And the best part was that he hired Todd McGewan. Todd was just out of high school, which technically made him an enemy to us in the educational food chain, but he was cool; he wouldn't hassle you if you looked like you weren't old enough to see the picture, and if you were smart enough to chat him up or help him out when he wasn't working, or give him a smoke when he asked for one, he wouldn't charge you nothing.

But Minnie shook her head, sweat-greased bangs clinging to her skin. She looked like she was going to throw up. "Sorry, guys. I don't think I can go out tonight. Just thinking about being outside…"

We all heard a door squeal open and shut around the other side of the trailer, and Minnie's eyes went wide before she shut the window as softly as she could. We watched her stumble away to her bed and slip back under the covers, little more than a ghost of the girl that was running with us through the woods near a week past. Jay and I glanced at each other, secretly knowing, I think, that we would have hit a dead-end, but not something like this.

The day became somber, even though there wasn't a cloud in the sky. We backtracked to where we'd put our bikes and peddled back to town, trying to salvage what diminished fun we could out of the day. I suppose that, being boys from a small town, we weren't too quick to say that it was Minnie that gave meaning to our own friendship, but the bare fact was that that was the truth. Without Minnie, Jay and I didn't have much of a reason for doing stuff together. Suppose that's why the rest of that summer we just drifted away, like lily pads torn from their moorings.

I didn't want to talk about this part. I thought I could jump right to the end and nobody'd have to worry about the in-between, no matter how connected it was. No matter how culpable it was. There were points, or dots there, forming a path to the rightful conclusion – and I was nine years old. I didn't want there to be any points or dots or goddamn paths. I just wanted things to be how they used to be.

There are things you try to block off from taking hold in your memory. Sometimes it works, but mostly you just help it dig deeper. The memory becomes an anomaly; you're never certain if it was true, if it was merely dream or something you fabricated to give yourself something to worry about. This would be another week after Jay and I visited Minnie and unsuccessfully tried to haul her out into the light; three days after Jay and I stopped being friends.

It was a dream. That's all it was.

I want to believe that's all it was.

In the dream, the forest opened up for me. I don't think I was naked, but my feet were bare, and the feel of night-damp soil and undergrowth wormed between my toes and made me shiver, even though the air in the woods felt warm. Warmer perhaps than it should be. I walked with a purpose, that kind of unknowable purpose you get in dreams, like you're living in an automaton that looks and feels like you.

I wasn't scared of the woods at night; long as you're smart and you don't get yourself lost, the woods are just a fine place. But the night has a way of changing things, making the trees taller, elongating and twisting their branches.

A brook was murmuring not far away, and there were roots that peeked out through the dirt. While I walked and breathed in the world I realized I was following the path we took back then, when Jay found that stone.

There were footsteps in the dirt ahead of me, grass that had just been pressed and were slowly stiffening back up; I politely stepped to the side and followed beside them. My dad was superstitious and always believed you shouldn't step in someone else's footsteps. A soft mist hung low, draped along the land and curling around the tree trunks. It felt like pale wet satin. There were sounds in the woods, small animals running through the brush, no light strong enough here to reflect any eyes if they were looking at me.

There's no point in trying to guess how much Time passes or regresses, how much just fails to pass, in a dream. Time is just replaced by a series of passing images that you recognize as being before and after, reference points that might be helpful if you want them to be, if you consider your placement in dream-time a priority. I don't know how long I was walking, how long the dream wanted me to walk, until the girl appeared from the trees.

I couldn't see her face but I recognized that long reddish hair, that height and shape. She was dressed in a thin white gown that was glowing against the mist. Truly glowing – a dull orange glow was illuming the translucency of the gown from the inside. It was coming from between her thighs. She was strolling deeper into the woods while I followed.

The landscape was different now: I recognized the path evenly enough, but off to my right was Little Sleep Lake, shaped like a wilted pumpkin and as smooth as black glass, even though it was a good few miles away from where it should be. I watched it only for a little bit; Minnie was walking faster and faster. That pulsing light inside her gown was growing brighter, as well.

I knew exactly where we were going. We were going to that grove lorded over by the old Norway pine. My feet wouldn't listen to my brain;

that's the worst thing, when you're lucid enough to be aware of your environment but you're still unable to react. The hedge was now much thicker, much higher up, like a wall of knotted bracken, but Minnie seemed to pass right through it. When I neared it, I had to rip and tear and pull at the branches for a little slice of eternity until I'd made a gap big enough for me to crawl through. The thorny branches still tore at my skin, and raked at my face with bitter claws. There were hard things in the soil that weren't rocks, weren't twigs; I recognized them as the delicate bones of small animals, and there were plenty of them in the hedge.

The tree. The tree wasn't there anymore, but Minnie was. She was in the center of the grove, crouching over the flat loam. Her butt strained against the fabric, looking like a pearl. Her shoulders worked up and down, and it sounded like she was grunting.

I didn't understand what was happening, but blood rushed to my cheeks anyway. The orange light grew and grew, blazing a corona against the trees. A star was inside of Minnie, displaying silhouettes of her bones, her organs, her arteries like honey glass. Until suddenly it fell. The bead, orb, whatever it was that seemed composed of molten light, fell from her crotch and into the ground, slipping into the old pine needles and mossy dirt.

I waited, huddled in the cold earth – it was like waiting for the clap of thunder when you see the lightning bolt on a muggy August evening. Like waiting to see the mountain lion after it's disappeared into the long grass. And then it happened.

Like a slow explosion, the earth itself seemed to heave as every blade of grass, every needle, every branch on every tree became infused with that apocalyptically orange light. The light lurched, and crawled, and slithered along the bark of the trees, conscious and thirsting for purchase. The grasses strained and swayed, tree boughs stiffened as the canopy rose into the endless night, and I wanted to scream, but if I opened my mouth that light might get inside. The woods were cheering.

First the lightning, and then the thunder. The ground in front of Minnie bulged, pushed, and the tree, the titanic Norway Pine, tore its way through the dirt. Some of its limbs looked like branches, just like the trees surrounding it, but some were bent and knobbed in ways that looked like the arms or legs of animals. Feet, claws, spines, hooves, fins, falling into its body and disappearing, reappearing at some other point on its trunk. Ancient dust, stones, and things long since buried rained down in billowing clouds as it thrust its sinewy bulk into the night. Minnie made no reaction; did not scream, did not run.

Something happened in my head when I looked up at it, something that gave way and made room for something bad to take seed. The pine stood there, but it wasn't a tree. It was colossal, a thick and coiling knot of something black, gelatinous, spasming, reaching up higher than the forest surrounding it. Maybe it was the whole forest, its roots stretching for miles beneath, its branches tangling in the canopy above, clawing for the stars.

The clefts I'd seen before spasmed and formed glistening folds; narrow conical teeth as long as my arm sprouted from them when they pulled and stretched. Minnie was still standing in front of it, just standing there, not moving, staring up with a dreamy smile like it was the most beautiful thing she'd ever seen.

A slit formed like a dirty gash in the center of the trunk. It parted, spewing semi-transparent goo onto the ground that steamed and spat. The eyes, gathered close together, looked like a mass of frog spawn or fish roe, each one dark and staring with a broad horizontal pupil. Its branches wavering as if searching for something, something more. There was a dull hum or vibration in the air, coming up from the earth and rattling through my bones.

Part of me was only just aware that I started digging into the dirt, tossing away handfuls of the damp dark soil and the little bones when I came to them. I wanted to hide, and I don't know what made me think that digging into the dirt like a mole would hide me from a tree, or something that could imitate a tree. Survival kicks in, and you scrabble for whatever you think will help you get through it.

Minnie was reaching up toward her own survival, or escape, or absolution, and I saw that her mouth was moving. Maybe; I had tears in my eyes and everything was getting fuzzy.

A corded bough slipped down from the darkness and embraced her. Her body lifted up into the air, higher and higher into shadow, until she slipped into the gnawing fold—

When I woke up, I didn't want to move. My parents came in and asked questions, became worried when I wouldn't say anything. I stayed in my bed, the only thing that was wholly sacred and impenetrable to a child, where I knew nothing bad would happen. My room seemed less safe than usual. It seemed like at any second the ceiling would fall in, the timbers would collapse and bury us all.

I glanced outside the window, staring at the road and the trees beyond it. Daylight had taken on a faded look, ominous, dangerous. I considered calling Jay, but I thought better; he wouldn't understand, wouldn't get it at all.

I wouldn't leave my bed until it was noon, and it wasn't two hours later that I would hazard a walk through the house. It was a weekday, which meant both of my parents had gone to work. The refrigerator harbored a lunch and a dinner, and my dog Dan, a big black Labrador, followed me around and helped take away some of the horror from last night. But still…

Dreams leave a residue, however ethereally thin. Sometimes it goes away after a few moments, but sometimes it just doesn't want to go at all. For a very long time, I felt like I hadn't woken up, that the house had just become another part of the dream.

There was something I had to find out. I had talk to Minnie about the dream; something told me that she would have some kind of idea what it meant. At the very least, it would be a big help to have someone to listen.

Once evening came around, I finished my small dinner and grabbed my bike, and headed up the road to the Winnebago. I wouldn't mind going through her mother if it meant knowing that Minnie was still safe. Probably still sick has hell, but safe.

There were a thousand things going through my mind, a thousand possibilities that played and replayed in the dirt under my wheels. I don't know what I was expecting once I got there, but a row of police sedans with their red-and-blues flaring against the willow leaves wasn't one of 'em. Fear kept me from getting any closer than the other side of the road, but while I watched the men milling around the lawn, I looked around for Joanne Overhauser. I was hoping to see her sitting in the same lawn chair, talking to one of the officers, that cigarette bobbing on her lip with every word. Minnie would probably be beside her, standing off to the side and looking as adult as she can.

But neither of them was there. In fact, there was no lawn – the Winnebago was a crumpled wreck, glass and wood and sheet metal littering the vicinity in a wide circle. At first, I thought there'd been an explosion, maybe Joanne had left the gas running on the stove without remembering and had herself one last cigarette. But there was no smoke, nothing charred by fire and heat. An explosion wouldn't have flattened the Winnebago into a distinct rectangular shape, wouldn't have made not merely one deep, circular pit in the earth, but half a dozen in a wide, even space. Some of the cops were shaking their heads. As I looked over the destruction and into the woods, at the quiet forest humming in the breeze, I started shaking my head, too.

Fifty years – a long, wide span of time to pass by after that day, a lot of things to tell myself, plenty of delusions to try and convince myself of. Things that I try to make myself believe but can't. Things like how that was just a bad nightmare, and that those deep, even-spaced circular pits on the Overhauser land didn't look like gigantic hoof prints.

# Painted Night (Transmissions)

Lydia drew the paintbrush from the can, not bothering to wipe off the excess darkness. It was messy—some of it got onto her hand, making tiny pits and rivulets on her bone-pale skin, dribbling down onto the dead, dying leaves in long ropey ribbons. She didn't care. All that mattered was the job at hand, and she was almost done. A gust blew through the trees and underbrush, whispered along her bare legs like snakes, like worms, and she shivered.

She had started early in the afternoon several days ago, had managed to neglect everything around her, keeping all of her senses tuned to the painting of this shoddy little shack. Because monotony, a rainstorm, and the creaking of her joints had all repeatedly interrupted the process, Lydia had managed to take in her surroundings more suitably.

This was a strange forest. There were those strange forests you read about in fantasy stories, in fairy tales laced with morality and blood, but there was a difference between reading about one and being in one.

The dark did something to this forest, as though the warmth of the trees and the tranquility of its atmosphere was just a mask it wore underneath the sunlight. When the sun dips down into the horizon and begins to bleed yellow-magenta into the sky, animals wander back to their burrows and nests, though she's seen nothing just yet. Only noises. There were some coyotes wandering around down by the brook a couple days ago, but they were cowards and had hightailed it when she clapped her hands. Sometimes at night, a mist will come down from the neighboring swamps in Beltrami County, blown on a silent easterly breeze, crawling like spectral fingers through the pines and oaks, clutching at the fungi and brush. When autumn comes like an elderly but asthmatic gentleman, the leaves do not merely lose their pigmentation; they lose all their color entirely. They turn grey, cracked and crumbling, as though they were all survivors of some massive inferno that might have ripped through the forest like a monster in ages past.

Lydia liked the forest and all its strangeness. Just being here for a couple of days had washed away her concerns, kinks smoothed out. It was also where she had met *them*.

She couldn't see *them*, not entirely, but *they* were always present here, forever watching and speaking to whoever wanted to listen. *They* told her to come here, long ago, but she didn't listen to *them*, not then. But two broken marriages, a falling out with bitter parents, and a daughter later, and everything seemed to bring her back here to these woods, to this one spot in the forest.

Paint it black, *they* told her, and everything will be alright.

She hummed and sang brokenly as she painted, words coming to her from some dim niche in her mind, a thousand songs trying to be spoken at once.

She looked down at herself, absently wondering what her mother would have said had she seen her like this, remembering that her mother died of lung cancer in 1997 and wouldn't have anything to say about it.

She looked like a dirty piebald cat; sand and twigs were stuck in her reddish-brown hair, her face smeared with a week's worth of sweat and grime in some places and clean in others, punctuated here and there with paint. Her dress was torn near the bottom, the fabric frayed and unraveling, and it was covered in so much refuse from the forest floor, one could no longer see the soft floral pattern. One of the straps was falling off her shoulder; the dress was already a size too large, and why shouldn't it be? She hadn't eaten anything since…Monday? No, Wednesday.

The house was a house only in terms of proportion. To look at it, one would have expected it to be a three-room building with a small attic, but inside was nothing, absolutely barren, an old chrysalis left to rot. The structure was a holdout from old days, when all of the nearby towns were still wriggling in their economic infancy and now floundering. Nobody knows who had built it, or why it had been built, and it really doesn't matter anymore. Hobos, vagrants, runaways, whole generations of animals have probably found temporary solace in these walls at one time or another. But they wouldn't anymore, not after decades of decay had slowly crept in.

Moisture had made the wood warped and crooked, making the angles strange and obscure. The interior was devoid of any walls, and she guessed that someone in the past had knocked them all down. She had found an old hatchet with a rust-eaten head lying inside, but that couldn't have been whatever was used. That hatchet now rested on the ground beside her feet. When she had found the cabin, the only inhabitants were a community of grubs, wood lice, spiders, and a family of over-nourished rats. Now, there was nothing, except her and her daughter.

She brushed in long, vertical strokes as more words flowed out of her mouth. She didn't know what exactly she was saying, but she hoped that *they* were listening.

Her family hadn't understood. She tried explaining *them* to her husband, but it only frustrated and angered him. "You don't know what you're talking about, Lydia," he'd said just before grabbing her arm so hard that his fingers left scarlet marks on her skin. "You have to stop this right now. Look at what you're doing to us, what you're doing to your goddamn daughter."

*Your daughter*, he'd said, as if he'd had no part in her creation. As if she wasn't trying to help them all see, as if all of this was some silly diversion that John was quickly finding unpleasant. He'd said a lot more, his sourness growing with every second, shooting down each of her attempts to speak.

Lydia was furious, and the aggravation of her nightmares and John's unwavering failures as a husband had all found a home in her right hand, clenched into a fist and driven squarely into the center of John's face. Spittle flew through the air like shattered glass, and before she could see the red flowing from his nose and mouth, she turned on her bare foot and ran out the door. The satisfaction she felt later was more for his silence than for anything else. She stayed at her sister's home for several days, listening to more complaints and revulsions of her family in response to her newfound passions.

After she returned, John was waiting with a lawyer, come down from the city. He tried to take their daughter away from her, but he soon stopped trying. A can of beer and arsenic does in eight minutes what lawyers attempt to do in as many months.

She took her daughter and fled on that same night. Her husband's body had not yet finished seizing on the kitchen floor when Lydia closed the front door behind her, her daughter's small soft hand in her own, the rest of their lives ahead.

There...soon enough, she was done. Lydia took a step back, brittle twigs snapping under her feet, looking at the final result that had taken her a week to finally accomplish, and even though it was full dark with the half-moon hidden behind a thin veil of blue-grey clouds, she could still see it. Or rather not see it. It was a large black void shaped into the likeness of a crooked house, just as *they* told her was needed. Paint fumes had been wafting into the atmosphere and mingling with the still, silent night air, creating a violently exotic concoction. She doubted those fumes would egress for a very long time. She hadn't allowed a single space, inside or outside, to not be touched by the blackness.

"Momma? Are you over here?"

Lydia turned and looked at Sophie, her little Sophie. She was tall for six years, but she supposed she got that from her father's side. Norwegian genes. Her chestnut-brown hair fell over her deep blue eyes, and the parts of her that were not concealed by the measly clothes Lydia had managed to steal for her were slightly pockmarked by bug bites. She was a real child of nature.

She smiled, leaning down and grabbing the hatchet beside her, concealing it behind her back. She whispered to Sophie in the dark, telling her to come over, to come into the house. The girl's bare feet made no noise as she stepped over decomposing logs and dingy toadstools. She smiled at her mother, and Lydia felt something tear inside of her, grown taught and snapped. The moon broke through a vent in the clouds, and when Sophie looked up at her the moon glinted in her eyes, twin pools of liquid silver. Beautiful, a little Iphigenia.

Sophie reached up with one small hand and Lydia took it in her own. Her daughter smiled, she smiled, and together they walked into the house.

For the barest of moments, Lydia felt like she was walking through a dream, that everything around her had the febrile, malleable consistency of a nighttime fantasy and nothing more. If she were to even think too hard on it, then everything would tear apart. There would be a rip in the space just in front of her eyes, a lightning crack that would grow wider and wider, consuming everything around its jagged Jack o' lantern maw. Including her. Including Sophie. But there was no chance of that happening –

The floorboards creaked.


Time passed, though no time existed here. The moon had completely vanished underneath sheets of black, had run away, not even a phantom of its alabaster face showing. No cold light from the voyeur stars, no fireflies, no phosphorescent lichen or fungi to expose the slightest trace of Lydia's surroundings. She kneeled on the rotting floorboards, walls of black all around her, her hands wet and sticky, cooling in the night air. She made the gestures with her hands exactly as *they* told her to, exactly like the dreams. Everything had to be exactly like the dreams. Soon enough, her efforts would be paid for in full.

The science of it was baffling to her, at first. Paint is by nature a liquid that over time becomes a solid; its composition remaining concurrent throughout its curing process, and yet its nature is entirely transformed. The paint by its own substance was the conductor of energies; the color used was little more than assurance.

There was a whisper in the leaves outside, the smell of night breaking through the paint fumes and sweet copper. A sandy scratching on the walls around her. Her heart wanting to break out and fly away into the dark, into some other dream, but her body stayed firmly where it was. Slowly, apprehensively, Lydia opened her heavy eyes.

She saw *them*, and *they* were so beautiful. *They* surrounded her, adulating in soft mutters. Nebulas whirled in *their* faces, stars dying out and resurrecting, decaying in the fading light of different suns, infinity in all *their* eyes. *They* flitted and meandered around her into peculiar shapes and strange geometries – Fey from some distant reality. Lydia heard *their* whispers and she smiled. She felt like dancing.

An inexplicable warmth welled up inside of her, pushing away the chill. She felt the floor leave her knees, and when she felt her body become weightless and soft, she began to laugh. She continued to laugh even when her voice floated away from her, becoming lost somewhere in the dark and she was rising, falling, wafting outward from herself. She moved her body in an indeterminate sway, an oblivious dance of Nothing. Every part of her was fragmenting into what nothing aspires to be. And when you become Nothing, what else is there to be afraid of? To require, or want?

She never stopped dancing.

# Gardens in Island Lake

## I

A machine can be broken and yet still function – perhaps erratically, with minute skips and twitches, but it can still be a token of what it used to be. Helen found it astonishing how readily people refer to their possessions as junk, forgetting the sentiment they had when they purchased it or was given to them, just like *that*. She leaned out over the rusty railing overlooking Island Lake, staring into the morning mist that bloomed in bright pale flowers along the water, wondering how people could be so inconsiderate to themselves.

It was a ploy, really, a stalling tactic she used every time she came here. She wondered if it was just a matter of pride, or simple laziness, but she could never quite put her finger on it and gave up after a few moments of trying. At the end of every summer, the streets and water mains of Asenath would be torn up by construction crews to be remade, maybe better this time, and the blare of angry motorists filled the air like violent geese, and the smell of the factories by the harbor would mingle with all that diesel and raw sewage and fast food into a smell that Helen abhorred, and then she'd finally appease the needling voice in her head –

she'd hop in her Silverado and drive the seventy miles back to this little town, cul-de-sac'd between the woods and Island Lake.

She'd always park in the same place – the empty gravel lot in front of the bar & grill (after a slow decline in patrons since the late 1990's, the actual bar & grill was torn down in a controlled fire in 2010, replaced by Thomson's, though many people in the town still referred to the lot and the new building standing there as just the Bar & Grill). Maybe later, she'd get gasoline at the Quick-Fill across the street if she needed it, and maybe she'd get something to eat in Thomson's, but never long enough to attract attention. Never long enough to enter a prolonged conversation with someone's relation who'd forgotten her.

Helen scented the morning air, knowing it wouldn't be morning for too much longer. She savored the coolness, the satiny feel of the mist as it bled away, the sere glimmer of dew on every blade of grass and leaf. The smell of the lake was best of all; it was the smell of Time, of memories past and memories still gestating.

Pretty ripples spread over the dark blue waters beneath her. There were basaltic stones and snails clinging to them, consuming the nutritious scum blooming in the shallows. Minnows and small perch darted in and out of her vision. A few years back, she used to return to her Asenath apartment with treasures from the lake, a piece of water-smoothed jasper or granite, a broad-lipped spike mussel or a Chinese mystery snail, when she had an aquarium taking up most of the space in her living room. This was long before she learned that the mussels were endangered and the snails were invasive, and the rocks were becoming cumbersome. She couldn't see any clams.

A loud *Ping* drew her attention behind her. A truck was passing by; maybe it had clipped the railing, or one of the hubcaps had dislodged after hitting the pothole. It was as big around as a coffee tin, big enough to cause a mean bounce. When it passed, its driver gave her a bemused look.

She heard the sound again, crisp and clear as it rolled over the lake like a church bell. Looking across the road, across the train tracks, she scanned the houses along the shoreline until she spotted a small Lund boat the color of cherry skin. It was anchored some distance away, hardly moving at all, even as the two men who crewed her shifted around to the starboard side. She thought one of the men was holding something in his hand, and when she heard the sharp crack again she knew that he was taking a hammer and chisel to the hard brownish stone near the boat.

Helen stood there, watching, until the sound of metal striking rock began to grate on her. She started walking along 210, heading back into the town, keeping her scowl aimed down at the pavement.

The Earth turned the sun higher in the sky, the pinks and purples all fading now to that familiar blue. By the time she made it to the Thomson's lot, the town was starting to wake up; vehicles were either gassing up or already heading east toward Cloquet, toward Asenath, where their jobs were; Thomson's was open, the lot already speckled with old timers or couples. The bright yellow glare of a school bus darted by like a fat largemouth bass, little faces staring dazedly from dusty windows. She looked away as a wave of nausea struck her.

Later, she would ask herself why she didn't just get back into her car, drive back to the city and the concerns that had become so familiar there. She hated Asenath, but she hated it a little less than this little old town. There was no answer, none she could say to convince herself that she even had an option, even with the availability of hindsight. So she grabbed her purse, checked herself in the car's mirror, then walked into Thomson's.

The inside was Midwest chic, made to pay homage to the lumber and railroad barons that hacked and blasted out chunks of the forests and mountains, scattering seeds across the land that would become communities. Everything was made out of bright cedarwood or darkly varnished oak. The hardwood walls were covered in old farming paraphernalia and framed blown-up photographs of logging camps and trains, black-and-white or sepia, public heirlooms.

She sat up at the counter, away from the windows. It felt to her like she hadn't sat at a window in twenty years or so. The young woman behind the counter walked over, smoothed out her leaf-colored apron, smearing Rorschach stains already there. "Morning. Get you anything?"

It wasn't her hard red hair tousled into messy curls, or her sunburnt skin, or her eyes the color of swamp water, or her sharp and concise language skills that made the memory form in Helen's mind; it was the scuffed little cross hanging from her neck. It was tiny, fifty cents-worth of aluminum-nickel painted gold, with a little diagonal scratch on the vertical post exposing the real metal. Tuesday Langenbrunner's mother wore the exact same one. Her daughter must have inherited it when decades of sucking on the nicotine teat finally struck her down. Helen could practically smell the sage and Marlboro high-tars in the air.

"I'll just have a sandwich for now," Helen said.

"Gotcha. Coffee?"

She shook her head. "Water, thanks."

Tuesday nodded and gave a thin morning smile. "It'll take a while, just so you know."

Helen nodded, thumbing through the chintzy menu. While she waited, she listened to the growing sounds of people breaking fast around her, chewing and scraping utensils on ceramic plates, clinking glasses. The smell of wood, meat, coffee, and orange juice. A mother had brought her young child with her, who was insistent on not behaving right. Old friends and families were bartering stories across tables.

She wondered, as she occasionally did when she was tired and bored and needed something to think about, if her name ever came up during these idle discussions. Were those two elderly chaps by the window talking about the girl from around here – what was her name again? – the one that had been caught with some mayor's aide during a school basketball game? Had someone warned that woman over there in the corner, the one bouncing a toddler on her knee, to keep her child safe because Helen Walker was looking for another baby to kill?

Helen looked at the clock on the west-side wall, an old Kit-Kat clock with swinging tail and searching eyes. It was almost ten minutes too early, yet in perfect working condition. She started playing with the pepper shaker and waited. When Tuesday returned and dropped a plate in front of her with her sandwich, Helen grabbed at it – half of it was gone by the time she realized what she was doing. She hid her embarrassment behind her water glass.

"Wow. I don't think we've ever had anyone in here come in from a famine before."

Helen ignored the statement. She chewed and swallowed, feeling the mass of bread, lettuce, and bacon fall into an empty stomach, like tossing a stone into a bucket. Tuesday began to spray down the counter and wipe it up with a rag. Helen grinned, remembered a little girl fussing over the cat hair on her bedspread, the unseen speck of sand on her carpet, and, later, the way the fuzz curled on Isaac Brody's blazer.

*I should be going*, she thought. *I should get back home. There are things that have to be done in Asenath, not piddling around this tiny place again.*

She said "I saw some guys over in the lake a few minutes ago. They were hammering away at the rock."

"What?"

Helen motioned toward the lake behind the wall. "Some guys in a red boat, chiseling at the rock in the lake. They from the university or something?"

*You're scratching at a scar that doesn't want to heal. It itches and you tear away at it, so it just itches even more. Just stop it.*

Tuesday made a dramatic turn of her eyes toward the ceiling. The rag dropped onto a puddle of soapy water on the table. "Oh, damn it. Probably those Holt brothers again, digging for something they can sell off to tourists or museums for beer money. Those damn bums."

She turned to look out the window as if to catch the culprits in the act, but the lake was blocked off by the business district of the town: the salon, probably still run by the mother of one of her school peers; the old warehouse, where railroad workers used to store their equipment, though these days, it was used more as a private storage unit; the grocery store in its third or fourth incarnation; the bar, its own name scratched out by generations of wind and rain, and the tall iron fence surrounding a tiny square where people can drink and enjoy good weather; the clinic, looking like a little brick box when you drive into town.

Helen ran the name Holt in her head, feeling something jar loose. She remembered babysitting a pair of scraggly young boys with that name, boys that were always shiny with sweat and dirt. They'd had a particular penchant for playing off-color pranks, for getting lost and then stringing guilt out of people, and stealing stuff out of people's yards. She didn't babysit them for long.

"The rock is on the Marigold property, as well," Tuesday said, "so what they're doing is an offense. Monsters should have been locked up a long time ago."

"Do they still live over by Wright on South Finn Road? The old blue heap by Miss Muttinen's house?"

Tuesday narrowed her eyes and her smile faltered before righting itself, like a boat in a rogue wave. Helen watched as something inside her clicked into place, something that made her expression harder and guarded.

"The Holt boys, you mean?"

"Mm-hmm."

The woman flicked her eyes to the clock and said "Sure. You from around here?"

Helen wanted to laugh, or cry, or scream and throw her water in the woman's face. She wanted to do all three, but she calmed herself down and just said "No, not really. I just know some people around here."

"Yeah, I guess so," Tuesday said, and then gave Helen a look reserved for strangers, or newcomers, or outsiders. The expression said *I'm starting to think you're a threat, and I know where the phone is.* Helen nibbled on her sandwich and gulped her water, feeling her breakfast hit her stomach like a punch.

After she finished up, she left a ten dollar bill on the counter while Tuesday had gone into the back. She dodged out of there, feeling like she'd stolen something and had just missed getting caught. In her car, she put her shaking hands on the wheel, closed her eyes, felt her heart threatening to break out of her chest.

Stupid. Real stupid. Helen turned the key and pulled onto the tarmac, feeling eyes everywhere, training on her the way hunting dogs will scan the marshes for waterfowl.

Here it was again – another opportunity to leave, to go back home to her apartment and her big lop rabbit she named Albert, sprawling on its side in her lap. But Asenath wasn't her home, it never had been. Home, she decided, was where she wanted to be right now.


## II

Since the town's official founding in 1896 by the Northern Pacific Railroad Company, the elongated slab of dark, iron-rich slate resting on the northern edge of Island Lake had always been considered little more than a strange thing resting atop a sandbar. An annoyance to fishermen or something to look at and ponder while chopping wood or bailing hay. In the summer, it stuck up two feet out of the bright blue water like the skeletal phalange of something drowned and forgotten.

It wasn't until 1989 when a young woman went skinny-dipping in the lake and uncovered a conchoidal shell of a Cambrian gastropod at the base of the rock that the grotto started to garner local interest. It was small, only nearly as big as the woman's thumbnail, but it was evidence that the hulking rock was more significant than the town had believed it to be. It was named the Meridian Slate, after the woman who first found the tiny snail – since then, colleges and universities as far as Texas have sent people to study it and the fossilized lifeforms locked inside its dense body. Vacationers from the cities descend on this spot every summer, not only to try their hand at appearing like their rural counterparts but to shill out twenty bucks to the families who live on the lake for a boat trip out to the shallow grotto. By now, all the fossils that could be found in the portion above the water had been pilfered, leaving its surface pockmarked and cracked by hammer and chisel.

Helen had kept an eye open for newspaper articles related to her hometown, and the lake in particular, keeping a handful of them tucked neatly away in a teal plastic crate she bought at a furniture store. She already knew about the odd gaps in Minnesota's fossil record from those articles (the fragment of the earth that would eventually be called Minnesota experienced a series of intrusions and regressions by a Precambrian sea, which would finally leave during the Silurian Period. Flora and fauna that lived here at the time were simply eroded away by the environment instead of experiencing deposition. Strands of life petered out during the late Devonian period; no records of Triassic life have been found – more erosion. Seas would continue to enter and regress throughout the land over the passing eras. The Cenozoic would also be oddly spare of fossilized life, but the ice ages that occupied the Quaternary Period would provide a boon for preserved organisms), and although the Meridian Slate didn't provide any insight into those gaps, what it did provide had helped solidify the science that was already extant.

Helen thought about the articles as she drove out of the center of town, across the train tracks, down a nameless dirt road that tottered for the most part near the lake. It was an easy thing to focus on – the Meridian Slate was an oblong time capsule measuring some seventy feet by twenty feet by eighteen feet, leaning upward on its longest side like a capsizing ship. After excavating some length of the rock and sediment around the pillar, the treasure lid opened further: Ordovician mollusks the size of tennis balls, small Cambrian gastropods in communal clusters, annelids, whole gardens of sea fans and other bryozoans; some ten yards from the base of the pillar, the skull of a giant beaver was found, *Castoroides Ohioensis*. The flowers looked pretty enough, pressed between the sheets of slate.

It was the tooth of a Devonian shark, though, that seemed to clinch it for her. Even though all of the lakes and rivers in the state were the progeny of gouges and ice melt from Quaternary glaciers, the tiny shark tooth seemed to scream out to any nonbelievers that everything here had at one time been the ocean, wrapped in the arms of Mother Panthalassa.

The span of 540 million years was collected here below the waters, delicately coated in sediment and pressed with the weight of eons.

Soon, the barrier of birch, tamarack, and aspen began to thicken until the lake itself was obscured, and there was only the thin dirt road again. A cloud of russet dirt and gravel kicked up behind the car. Last chance to stop picking at this scab; after another quarter mile the road would branch out to the south, which led back to the highway and Asenath, and north to everything she left there.

A long time ago, Helen learned that it was just easier to dwell. She nibbled on the inner wall of her cheek and waited, listening to the perpetual music that wheels on a dirt road can make.

The trees became even thicker, wilder, leaning against each other like coworkers too exhausted to move. When she was a little girl going to the school here, she used to dream the pitted winding roads here were made by gigantic worms.

Helen gasped – her mouth filled with the salty-sweet taste of pennies. It felt like she must have pinched a nerve, as well.

A house, shadowed and empty since her mother died in a car accident somewhere on Route 73 four years ago. Helen had to sell the property to the state to pay for the expenses a lower-middle class family can accrue, and so the house just became a cavity, a home to spiders and squirrels and any small unseen thing hiding in the walls. Helen knew that it couldn't and wouldn't be seen on any real estate listings anytime soon.

An old granite boulder in the ditch marked the property, better than could any mailbox. The house appeared from behind the trees, a single-story stump of a building with missing roof tiles and slats hanging like bones. The windows weren't broken as she had suspected, but they were covered in four years of dust and pollen. The land behind the house opened up on a backyard that overlooked the lake.

That goddamn washing line. Helen put the car into park and stared at the washing line in the corner of the yard. Two rusted poles with a length of nylon rope somehow still connecting them. Old pine needles and leaves had by chance landed on the line and stuck there between the earth and sky. There were other symbols here, like a tire swing, or a toolshed, but it was the washing line that brought it all back to her. Springs and summers spent helping her mother putting up the laundry, beating out dirty rugs, or hanging festive sheets and spreads from it for Halloween and Thanksgiving.

She winced at the way her stomach tightened at seeing the house again. She had hoped that this time her body would refrain from acting on its own, without regard for her, but it had, spilling another wave of nausea. It wasn't a good omen. Not to say that Helen believed in omens, but it was difficult not to consider that twitch as prognosticative.

Helen got out of the car, sighing with the breeze as it touched her with the simple caring of maple leaves; she avoided the porch and its overlapping verdigris of white and black rot, walking around to the backyard. It was broad, but cluttered, and the grass was high enough to brush against her calves. She wondered if any of the neighbors ever considered mowing here. There was a garden with shallow cement walls, conquered long ago by crabgrass and foxtails. It didn't look like there would be any rescuing it, no point. A canoe listing on its side sat against the back of the house.

She walked to the edge of the lake and sat down in a dirty patio chair. There wasn't much point in looking at her watch; the sun told her it was already noon. She watched the way the lake stole and passed on the sunlight, listened to the way it whispered as it nibbled from the shoreline. Her mouth hadn't stopped bleeding.

The grotto was barely visible from here, but it was still out there, a grey-brown bump sticking out of the water.

Every moment – every infinitesimal portion of infinity creates a mystery or modifies an already existing one in Island Lake, in *every* body of water. The thought made her shiver as she closed her eyes and let the world take her to a dreamless sleep.

III

Helen didn't start showing until late September, while she was still in her sophomore year at high school. By then, she was certain that her widening belly wasn't the result of nerves or overeating. She was a local star in track and volleyball and often kept an eye on what she ingested. When her classmates began to notice, much of their concern was centered on jokes about *what* exactly she'd been ingesting.

At this time, she'd been convinced that it was Luke Olinski, the mayor's son, who'd put the bun in her oven. Her boyfriend had been someone else, a point guard on the basketball team, but, as it goes, things happened. A moment of something in summer camp, instability or curiosity, a secret shared by her and him and another lake.

She had convinced herself that being a mother, and the pregnant period beforehand, would automatically place her in an ancient and mysterious sorority, that avenues in life which were previously inaccessible to her would open up. After a few weeks, the reality of what her parents called her *condition* started to crash down on her. The school principal and several teachers made her attend a discussion concerning her, suggesting repeatedly that the process was more than an imposition, and her fault to boot. It didn't take long before she began to wonder if it really was.

When the message was relayed to the mayor, the word changed from *condition* to *allegation*. She had to talk to him and his son, who firmly denied he even knew her. Her mother told her that he would say that, countering every naive opinion she had. The nights were the worst, when she was alone with her thoughts and conflictions. Her friends had all left her; not all at once, that would have been something akin to mercy. Instead, they just petered out, their interest and concern for her fading as every day passed.

It didn't stop the town from knowing about the girl who'd got herself knocked up by any of a dozen boys. That was how it was passed on, and any of her attempts to correct it were instantly rebuffed.

There had been threats – over the phone and in her mailbox, anonymous, vicious. Some were blatantly kids trying to be mean, spurred on by dares, which hurt no less than the ones she'd get in the evening, the ones she imagined were made by fat slovenly men who breathed through their mouths and had animal heads mounted on the walls of their farmhouses or hunting shacks. Threats and promises to be delivered when the sun went down.

There was nothing more sobering than the realization of your position in life, the weight of this hungry thing you were born into, and into which you were about to push a whole new life. It was overwhelming, and caustic, with every second of her existence feeling like it was eating pathways into her flesh. How could she condone it, releasing a child into the world she knew wouldn't show them any affection or consideration? She was alone, and her baby would be alone. It was unconscionable, merciless.

She had made sure nobody knew, not even her parents, who were under the impression she was contacting a midwife or an orphanage, when she began calling the clinic over in Asenath. The two important buildings in the town, the two that actually made it seem like a town, were the school and the Lutheran church, and the word abortion seemed to her something filthy and grotesque. Something that good, well-meaning girls didn't think about. But she had been thinking about it until finally the pressure grew too great for her and she finally made an appointment.

Then she learned that the only way to keep a secret was to conceal it, deep under layers of neurons and grey matter, where there was no chance that it could be found out. It was easier.


It was already night when Helen awoke, shivering in the breeze. She stood up, listened with some delight to the staccato percussion of her joints popping back into place. A jaundiced half-moon dominated the sky, bright enough to cast a fairy ring around itself, and though the lake seemed quieter, it was still mumbling at the rocks along the shoreline.

Fireflies were about, dancing and blinking in their almost musical patterns.

She knew she ought to be getting back to Asenath by now. Albert would be worrying, perhaps enough to leave a fresh cluster of pellets on her bed. There were still job prospects she needed to investigate – she'd been living off the money she'd made working for the paper mill just off the harbor, and she quit that a few months ago. If her account wasn't reaching for the red already, it definitely would be within a few more months.

*Curiosity and cats. You can't afford to keep doing this*, she thought to herself; *you can't keep coming back here if you want to put all that shit behind you and finally move forward with your life.*

But maybe I don't want to, she countered. She'd been told a long time ago that arguing with yourself was a form of insanity. Even though she doubted that that was enough for a diagnosis of psychosis or schizophrenia, surely it had to be of some concern. Regardless, she knew something had to be done. It was like a drug, which, she supposed, some memories really are, and they were just as hard to remove.

She started walking back to her truck when she noticed that something wasn't right.

The crickets were out in full symphony, generating a livid hum that bounced through the trees, making every leaf and needle resonate. She felt it in her skin, vibrating into each cell. Sweat broke out, and the void in her stomach began to expand. She paused, taking deep gulps of the night air.

It was the lake. Something was wrong with the lake. The sound of the water pressing against the rock was different, heavier. It was crashing against the shoreline, tearing at it. The air became heavier, too – heavier, deeper, and unbearably hot. It was like breathing through steel wool. The music the insects were making was changing, chewing at her eardrums, making her whole body hum in nauseous throes.

Helen doubled over as everything she'd eaten at the bar & grill surged up through her throat and spilled onto the lawn. While she wiped her mouth, things with shiny black segmented exoskeletons scrabbled through the grass to lap and writhe in the sick.

She leaped back, a choked sound erupting from her mouth. She began retching again. She turned her eyes away and noticed that the stars were gone. No, there were still a few marking that black tapestry, but they felt wrong, unfamiliar.

A bright flicker in the corner of her eye drew her attention back to the water. It was far out, about some fifteen yards, a pale fabric undulating on its black surface. At first, she suspected it was the moonlight, but the moon had faded to a dim vapor in the sky. She stared at it and its pale floral print, yellow like forest buttercups, afraid it was another illusion, afraid it was real.

She watched as it bobbed up and down on the wave, twitch like a fishing bobber, and then disappear into the water, a part of her heart following it down. Something, impulse or concern, drove her to walk back to the house, drag the boat across the lawn and into the water, scattering dust and cobwebs from the single oar as she scraped against the strange waves – love or despair, terror and confusion, though she had no lack of certainty that it was some secret alchemy of all those emotions.

The water was not as rough as it looked, but it wasn't still, either. Her thin canoe seemed like a toothpick in a river. Each time she felt she'd gotten the boat under control it would buck and tilt. The water rippled without the wind, and she tried not to think about the things that might be cavorting beneath her.

It was amazing and profound how the night managed to distort perception, turning the imagination toward something it didn't want to see. Helen kept her eyes on where last she saw the cloth; she was sure now that it was a cloth, the same one in which she'd wrapped her baby years ago, or yesterday, or millennia in the past. Each time she stopped to turn and see where she was heading, she spied the grotto, standing up out of the water. It seemed taller, lighter, and there were things capering about its cracked and pitted surface. Things with armored bodies, searching antennae, and fluttering mouths.

Was the air getting even heavier, as well? Yes, and hotter, much hotter than a spring night in Carlton County ought to be. But Helen stopped believing that it was spring, or that she was in a little town in Carlton County anymore. Any trace of that past conviction was behind her on the shores of a property that didn't belong to her any more than she belonged to the town. Helen paused to catch her breath, breathing deeply the deepening air. It felt as if she was trying to breathe underwater. She twisted around to mark her bearings, seeing that the grotto wasn't far away now – just a few yards, and the cloth was firmly wrapped about its girth.

All lies, the good ones, are the ones that are spread from carrier to carrier and fail to immediately set up any red flags, that do not make someone cock their ears and say "now wait a minute." Persistence and proximity are the loyal footsoldiers of any pathogen, and little towns make excellent petri dishes. When the secret somehow found its way back to the gossipers, it merely became the lie that Helen gladly allowed to grow.

After meeting with the doctor at the clinic in St. Paul, he informed her that he couldn't perform the operation without risking harm to her own body because of how young she was. He refused, even when she offered fifty percent more of what the operation would have cost, money that a seventeen year-old from Carlton County clearly didn't have. She returned home, angry and terrified of what exactly she would be releasing her child into, and like all plans that seemed more like a step toward something indefinable than a mere decision, a thought gestated.

She had the child in her home, alone, wracked with pain, slick and stinging with mingled sweat and blood. Her parents were attending a wedding for a relative in Virginia, believing her when she told them she would be fine alone, that she had friends who would be with her. The sheets were red and steaming in the November cold. One of the things that she would always remember was the way the steam rose up from her body, like phantom orderlies. She used her father's old Stanley knife to cut the umbilical cord. She didn't know how much time had passed until she'd noticed that the infant wasn't making any sound. Dragging herself higher onto her bed, she saw the twisted loops of the umbilical cord and what it had done, saw the purplish skin.

She wept, and when she was done crying she grabbed a large cloth, white with buttercups on it. She walked to the edge of the lake; it was nighttime then, a new moon, black moon, caught for the moment turning its back on the earth and the sun. She tentatively waded into the lake, the waters catching her dress and making it billow around her like the bellum of a jellyfish, cleaning what had already dried on her thighs. It was an incredible weight, everything, and she allowed the waters to carry it away and down.

Her hand reached out through the dark, trying to hook the cloth with her fingers. She lost her footing and slipped, almost dipping into the water, but she steadied herself onto the grotto. A segmented thing she recognized as a trilobite crawled on its myriad claws around the top of the rock and onto her hand. It was roughly the same length as her forearm, and the mixture of sight and touch was enough to make her scream. Her cries carried on the water, dissipated like mist at noontide.

The trilobite, shocked perhaps by the sudden vibrations in the air, scuttled back around the other side of the grotto, down into the water. Wringing her hands as if she could clear her skin from the crustacean's touch, Helen fixated on the cloth, ordering it to come back to her. If this was all a dream, then it was her dream, and it would obey her command. But the cloth was resolutely fixed on the rock.

She glared at it, at the communal movements of the tiny glassy-shelled snails, at all the insects that were still making that awful hum. It was making her head vibrate and ache.

*Just get it over with. Just do it and be done with it. Be angry and scared later, after this nonsense is all gone and you've got proof of what happened.*

In one violent motion, she scrabbled to the edge of the kayak and ripped the cloth away from the grotto. An inch-long tear opened up, but she only heard it, and having heard it, forgot it. She no more considered the cloth in her hand than she did the snails, or the trilobite that had returned to feed on them, or the bony-mouthed fish that darted under and around the boat, long and dark enough to be mistaken for a crocodile.

She was fixated on the thing embossed in the rock, preserved well enough for her to see where every bone, organ, and skin tissue had been, even after each organic cell had been replaced by mineral.

For a moment she couldn't tell if the two were overlapping, or if they were in fact one and the same. Surely it was the former, absolutely had to be. But the torso looked like it was strained, perhaps almost gelatinous at the time of its internment—

No, she was right. It was a baby, a human baby, and it was crawling out of its spiral shell.

Curiosity and cats. With one hand she reached out to touch the fossil, so alien and familiar, while she pressed the other onto the stern of the boat. The weight was enough to tip the boat over, sending her into the water.

Helen's head struck the grotto, brilliant nova flashes pulsing in her eyes. The pain that had been growing in her head exploded into a fantastic bonfire of anguish, and then it winked out. Helen felt herself tumbling, her concept of direction and equilibrium snuffed out. Her hands scrabbled for the grotto, for the lake bottom, for anything that could give her a sense placement, but she could only grab fistfuls of water.

Soon, she felt her consciousness begin to fade, dissolve into the old water. Fish and snails were an audience to her finality.

As if it were any consolation, the last thing Helen saw before she drowned was the jealous yellow half-moon.


Helen struck the lighter and knelt down, touching the flame to the trail of nail polish. She watched it race down the porch and into the house, bright yellow led by a slash of blue. It searched, it hunted, and it devoured. It found the little swath of beige fabric and old pillows and from there it spread. Across the lake, houselights flickered on as people gathered on the docks to see the conflagration.

By the time the fire department had been called, Helen Walker was already driving up 210, the night carrying her to the city. She felt lighter, calmer, like the black waters of a midnight-soaked lake. For the first time in a very long while, she decided to drive with the window down.

# We Will be Stars

"So, what is it supposed to be?"

For a minute—a minute longer than she would normally allot herself when her work was called into question—the troll woman says nothing. She scowls at the slab of raw biotite mica and the thin radial veins of quartz and pretends that she didn't hear what her friend asked, that all she had ever heard speak was the lake as it hammered at the bluff, and the groaning of the ash trees and trembling aspen behind her. She doesn't stop kneading the rock. Even though intense heat is transferring from her fingertips into the stone—500 degrees Fahrenheit, 1,000 degrees, surpassing the solidus and entering the liquidus as the atoms of the rock destabilize and it becomes like rough wet clay, like dough—she isn't hurt, doesn't feel the sting even when the molten rock flows between her fingers and down her ample wrist. Droplets land at her feet on the rough outcropping of shale and limestone to spit and steam until they are just pebbles.

"That ought to be apparent," she finally says. She pauses long enough to brush away chords of onyx-black hair out of her face, and then she's back to work.

"It ought to be," her friend says. The woman sniffs, adjusts the strap of her dress so that it rests higher over her thin freckled shoulders. She taps the base of the rock with her birch rod, as though touching it with what she understood might just give her the knowledge she wants. "It ought to be, sure, but not to me. And not to you either, I think."

Stifling the dozen retorts in her throat, the troll woman nods without conceding, nods just to show she heard. It was all just play, really, another round in the same game. Her friend was bored and needed to entertain herself by being analytical. After a moment waiting for an answer that wasn't going to come, her friend silently turns back to the bluff.

There are no clouds today, only the immensity of the blue sky above and the lake below, floor and ceiling like sheeted blue jay feathers with a horizon the barest thin line of shale grey. Behind them, the trembling aspens and silver birch muttered to each other as a gust came up from the southwest, making the woods revel in the late spring. The troll woman can hear all the things that are whispered about in the woods, the word-of-mouth gossip from the jays and red squirrels and the occasional nomad porcupine. As much as she wants to join in on the conversations, she withholds herself to keep to her project.

It had been three weeks since she'd found the slab of dark rock, three long weeks of staring at it and nothing coming to her but uncertainty and seeping clouds of grey. She knew she had to let the positive in and shut out everything else, but there was something in the back of her mind, wherever the precursors to odd and disreputable thoughts start to gestate, that seem to keep out everything that made her an artist. It hung over her and echoed to her, like a voice from the other end of an impossibly long corridor.

It was a decent system they'd had going for all these years, effective in its simplicity and efficient in its design. The troll woman would mold the stone and raw material into shapes that were beautiful and ornate, or imposing and intimidating, and her friend would bless her finished designs with magickal life. Her friend liked using the word "life," although the terminology was different to the troll woman, who understood what she meant anyway. The stone would not suddenly become sentient and begin to indulge in intense philosophical discussions—their existence was already made profound by merely *existing*.

But recently her designs had started to become not so beautiful or ornate. Detail and form were starting to, to use a word borrowed from her friend, to decompose. To her, they seemed to become unsightly, almost detestable, and she didn't know where it had started. Were they representations of her confusion over what to make next, or half-assed excuses? She didn't believe that – she'd never had a problem conjuring some grand new piece. Was something the matter with her hands or fingers? Surely not.

"I think you're making fun of me," the troll woman says. She makes sure to invoke as much intention in her husky voice as possible; if her friend heard it as a question, then that was her mistake. The woman glances back at her, looking as if she'd tried to make a joke that hasn't panned out, pausing only long enough to deliver that lingering expression before she resumes her elaborate dervish.

"What makes you say that?" she asks. "What would make me presume to mock you, that I should be so foolish?"

"Clever people can be foolish," the troll woman says, hearing the petulance in her voice and almost wincing.

"Are you complementing me or insulting me?"

The troll woman keeps her mouth shut, allowing her irritation to collect and steep. She keeps her silvery eyes on the rock for a little while, until she finds herself casting them at the woman in the yellow summer dress, summer yellow like marigolds or honeysuckle. Still dancing, still pooling and casting old magick into the stones, like she hadn't done anything wrong, like she hadn't slipped a little razor blade into her own words. She scowls, her scowl unheeded, then she hefts another slab of stone onto her lap, beginning the process again. Her eyes, sharpened as they were by her art and the centuries she'd spent honing it, search the melted stone for unique minerals that had latched on like barnacles. She doesn't expect to find any, and she doesn't.

Winds blow up the bluff and throw her friend's tarnished-pewter gray hair around her face. She ignores it and sweeps her birch stave through the air, drawing lines in the ground around the last art form the troll woman had created to open up the correct channels of power. The troll woman stops to watch her friend move and dance against the wind, and then with the wind, around the disgusting thing she has created. She looked at it and tried to fathom why she'd made such a thing. She recalls wanting to make a tree, some tree from a wonderful and wild dream, but what she had molded from the brittle felsic rock hardly resembled a tree any more than does a mole.

She wants to say Stop it, just stop that right now. You're not doing either of us any favors doing that. You were a mild amusement before, but now you're becoming a distraction, so just stop it. She doesn't dare say this because it would mean the human woman would leave, and this is a cold and lonely country.

154

The troll woman sighs against the wind and keeps molding the rock, making an effort to shape it into a form that is at least equal to what she saw in her mind. Her friend continues to dance and sweep her birch stave in mystical formations. The troll woman wants her to stop it, stop giving strength to the horrid things that she'd been half-baking under the moon and leave her alone. Deciding that internalized loathing is preferable to utter despair, she narrows her silk-silver eyes and resumes kneading, molten rock hissing and spitting in the air.

It was easy to mistake despair for joy during those long, long nights by the bluff. At least, the troll woman thinks so. At least, it was easy for her to believe that during all of those cold summer nights, when it seemed like every animal in the world had chosen not to sleep, and the abandoned mine where she made her home echoed and augmented all of their conversations. It was easy, yes, to pretend that the hollow and hollowing feeling inside her was just mistrust about her own happiness. The whispering of the lake and the night sky filled with stars offering light millions or billions of years old were her only companions, the only ones she needed, and they were so exquisite and beautiful that when they told her she didn't need anyone else, she damn well believed it.

The woman first came to her several years ago, seeking the solitude and sweet-miserable solace of the bluff, the lake, and the stars. The troll woman had been so close to begging her to go away, of stomping her feet on the solid ground, making a noise, making a spectacular show of playing the monstrous and possibly psychologically maladjusted hermit. Over the course of those several years, she'd tried to put a finger on why she hadn't, why she'd allowed the intruder – and what else was the woman? – into her life. No answer she told herself really came close to hitting the nail on the head; no matter what word she used as a substitute, it was, in plain English, just loneliness. And when she heard a voice that wasn't the lake and wasn't the deep yawning night, or the bitter-pale light of the moon, she was as grateful as she was wary.

It was an unpleasant afternoon, the sky dark and alive like the wings of moths, eager to remind everything living near the mountain range that early summer was a time for discontent. It wasn't raining, not yet, but violet lightning tore gouges out of the sky. Lilac-colored gashes, reflected over the lake. It smelled of a proper summertime storm. The woman had probably noticed her gathering rocks and boulders about her home, stomping to and fro before the rain made islets among the rocks and washed something nice out of her reach. She approached, blue jeans and denim jacket with deerleather fringe dangling like store chimes, and the troll woman didn't know what to do, and less of what to make of her.

"What's that? Is that a cave or something?"

The troll woman followed the other woman's gaze and shrugged "Just my home," she said, astounded more by her own curiosity than her neighbors.'

"Mind if I take a look inside?"

"Yes."

The woman paused at the fortified sound that had bolted out of the troll woman's voice. "Why's that?" she asked.

"Because I didn't invite you," the troll woman said, pushing off a layer of pyrite from the sizeable hunk of milky quartz in her arms. She held it like one might a newborn. She found that thought amusing, since she figured both she and the quartz must be about the same age.

"Oh. Well, can you tell me about it, then?"

She supposed she had felt confused, and a bit angered, at having a stranger ask her about the history of her house. It wasn't her place, and it wasn't her business, and the ghosts that nestled in its recesses belonged to the troll woman and no one else. But she wouldn't think of that until later, much later, after they had become friends and she couldn't bring herself to say it aloud. She told the woman about the old mine, instead, and the blue-grey lightning-scarred lake that people call Lake Vermillion, and before that, *Onamuni*, but which had a different name. She told her that a report about gold being found on the shores of this range of shale and basalt caused a broad influx of would-be prospectors in the 1860s, but what gold there was had been depleted by the time news of it even reached the papers. Instead, what the miners found was a rich supply of copper and iron ore, long veins of it striated down into the womb of the rock, and another leading south toward what would be called the Mesabi Range.

The troll woman told her that the dozen or so villages just south of the range were spawned in the blood of that ore, and when the last of the Vermillion mines closed in 1967 – "For a group of reasons, really," she explained, catching the almost canine expression of curiosity in her companion's face; "It had to do with the way they mined taconite, and the amount of it that was left in these mines. This area just didn't have enough, and like wolves slowly following a herd of deer, the business leaders wanted to relocate to where it was more lucrative for them – only a few or so remained to grow on their own, the rest abandoned or swallowed whole by other growing townships."

"What's taconite?" the woman interrupted. The troll woman considered explaining it to her, but she figured it would just go over her head, so she didn't.

The woman left an hour later, once the rain had finally broken and filled the range with its roaring whispers – the troll woman still hadn't invited her in by this time. She had presumed the other woman would forget all about her, that she would go back to the exciting and fast-paced and self-consuming world in which she was born and leave the troll woman alone, but she hadn't. She came back the next day, at nearly the same time, when the grass and stones and the lake smelled of the rough afterglow that a good summer storm always leaves in its wake.

Damn it, she came back.


Like all the other nights that had fallen behind her, she concludes her evening by staring out at the wide lake, wide and weeping the last of the sunlight in its center while the darker, blue-grey of evening begins to creep in from all sides, all the islands and outcroppings too small to be called islands humming their own sad songs. She contemplates the projects she had finished, those that she had yet to get started on, and all the ones she had either bungled or shattered into debris out of frustration. She tried to keep a generally good score, keeping one higher than the others. Today seems like neither a good nor a bad day. She would mark the last of the sun winking out over the edge of the world as a time of plan-making, compartmentalizing and consideration, but not tonight.

The passing day weighs down on her and she cannot pull it off long enough to think of anything else. She lurches back into her home, into the old iron mine that was left abandoned to the weather and forest in 1967, thinking about her friend. She takes a deep, deep breath; the smells of time and must and the small things that creep into caverns to live their own brief lives had always acted like a salve on her nerves, but not tonight.

An epiphany, no matter how misconstrued, was a great poultice, but it would hold only for so long. In time, the good feelings they would give her would vanish; sometimes gradually, like the water eating its way through soil, and sometimes all at once in a swift mass wasting. She can't remember how many realizations and leaps of perception she'd had near the bluff over the years, scores or hundreds, but they'd all been marked with intervals of depression, of staring out over the bluff or at some unique clastic formation in the mines in the dim hopes that it would show her the way out of her woe.

She would fantasize, from time to time, about being a star. Being a mere consciousness infused into a globule of plasma, gas, and stellar dust, and being allowed to go anywhere she desired, to do whatever she pleased, to be seen and acknowledged by incalculable living beings, to give birth to hydrogen and oxygen and other elements that brought life to an empty universe…that was a special desire she held deep in her heart, and that, for the time being, was where it would stay.

Just as now, there have been a few times – not many, but certainly enough to warrant circumspection – when the troll woman would pause and wonder if her new friend was nothing more than another period between woes, some sort of manifestation of this or that emotion or feeling, but that didn't seem very accurate. Were that true, it meant their bickering was nothing more than internal monologue, and to the best of her knowledge, she never used the same language and syntax as her friend. Rationalizing her friend's existence would prove more taxing than her mind would warrant, and she'd fall asleep more worried than relieved; waking up just means meeting the same worries and frustrations, and likely going back to the same rationalizations.

After another hour of convincing herself what was real again, she closes her eyes. It wouldn't be until next evening, waking up after the second owl's call, that she'd think life was just a series of opening and shutting eyes, falling into a rhythm of seeking light and then dark.

She doesn't want to think, she's tired of thinking, so she drags herself out of her mine. She sets immediately to work.

The moon is out, bright and vicious and mocking her with its smile, the lake mocking her back. It is dark, but not half as dark as some parts of the mine, not even close to what she might call dark. Soon, she finds an elongated chunk of vesicular basalt. It isn't very big, about the size of a young river otter, and filled with pockets of calcite and olivine. She could feel the age of the rock as it begins to flow between her fingers, all those many, many years homogenizing while the atoms are going bat-shit from the intense heat.

It's a little thing, pretty as all stone is pretty, and when she is finished working with it, she is pleased enough to tell herself that she has done a good job.

When her friend arrives that following morning, there is a cold demeanor on her face. There is no "good morning" or "hello" or any kind of salutation. She looks at the pile of odds and ends the troll woman completed since she was gone, makes a small tired sound in her mouth. Then, she goes to work with the brusqueness of a badger. The troll woman watches for a short while until their eyes meet, and then quickly turns away. For reasons she cannot bring herself to say, she doesn't want to be on the other end of the woman's gaze.

The day is calm and silent – the woods and the lake know that another summer is nearing its curtain call and autumn will soon announce itself in the air and the trees; day length would shorten, the green will fade

160

away, and soon it would be the autumnal equinox. A period that the troll woman dreaded, as it meant an uptick in her business, but not necessarily in demand for her works. For her, it meant mingling, rubbing shoulders and soliciting herself to those who probably wouldn't deign to give her the time. She was never any good at that sort of thing.

"Are you done with that yet," her friend asks, sharp and concise as the violet head of a thistle, causing the troll woman to look up from the section of finely layered oil shale. As she did, a large piece falls apart in her hands, sliding between her knees and onto the ground with a comical splat.

For a moment she could only stare at it, at the end result of the past two hours' work. It doesn't seem real, like another pessimistic daydream of hers. Within moments, it feels like all of the moments that comprise her existence begin to rapidly spin and condense like the accretion disk around a black hole, centuries of contempt filling her, and in need of a target.

From the outer edge of the mine, where the grass vanishes and the bluff sweeps down to the gritty yellow-brown shores some fourteen hundred feet down, the woman stares at her, her head dog-cocked to the side like she had two years ago. "What's the matter," she asks. "Need some help or something?"

The troll woman bites down on the inside of her cheek, tearing away some of the skin. "No. No, I don't. Let's just get these finished."

Her friend nods quietly, heaving a sigh against the wind, and the rest of the day passes just as quietly.

When she comes back the next day, the troll woman doesn't go outside to meet her. She remains hidden in the lost hollows of the hollowed mountain, busying herself with some small, beautiful piece of limestone. When the woman calls for her and makes the walls reverberate with her voice, disturbing everything that stays quiet and safe inside, the troll woman does not answer back. She waits, and waits, until there are no more sounds coming from that entrance, and even then, she refuses to go outside. There is plenty of work down here. Work, time, and her ambition.

She is rooted here anyway, and she has to keep herself busy. She can't be bothered with strangers right now.

# Love Song from the Asthenosphere

Time is bent, but not yet broken. I've walked through the mines of memories, but many are not my own, and it has taken a long time to piece together those which belong[ed] to me, pocketing the pieces and putting them together. I cannot perceive them as they once had been anymore, but the experience and the sensations remain as they were, like echoes carried on the wind, and that is what I am able to convince myself has happened, which had happened.

Thought passes to thought, jumping from niche to cerebral niche, and I can endure those shreds of my existence again.

Right now…

It's only on nights like this, long cool nights with the alabaster moon fat and high and the wind bringing the smells of the woods into the city, that I can let everything go and allow myself to calm down. I can forget about the pain, the pills, the friends and family members. On nights like this, the universe comes twinkling down and everything else seems so vague and ethereal, unimportant. Last time there was a full moon, I drove out into the uneven fields west of the city, took a walk through the tall grass in my jeans and bone-colored coat, and I howled like I used to do when I still lived in the country. When there was still a little girl who couldn't stand the little boy that stared back at her from the mirror, confined.

It was the most fun I've had in a long, long time.

Not tonight, not in mid-November with the temperature making a kamikaze dive and frost spreading pale fingers along the roads overnight. It was already beginning to cling to my window, and in the meager glow of the lamp on my nightstand I fancied I could see tiny illustrations in the frost. I slipped a two of diamonds into my book, an old copy of the collected works of H.G. Wells, and laid it down on my work desk, looking outside at the dim, wide expanse of Minneapolis. A neon beehive of concrete and steel. I grabbed and tipped the bottle of cognac into a glass and downed it in one, trying to fool myself into thinking that I had a sense of refinement or a cultured palate.

No howling for tonight, no nighthawking for me for a while. I had to prepare for a lecture at the university tomorrow, planning out the best way to tell college students of the atomic structure of rocks, the subtle differences in mica and schist, the dangers of sublimation, while trying to ignore the listless, indifferent looks of the proposed leaders of tomorrow, pretending not to see the sharp white-blue glow from their phones underlighting their faces, or that their sniggling whispers were not about my voice. I hated this teaching gig, but at least it paid, and I suppose I had to be grateful for the job. Even if it was a couple weeks each month.

I poured another glass, feeling it hit my stomach like a dying ember. It usually took two or three glasses for my nerves to settle enough for me to get to sleep. I would have taken an Ambien or a Benadryl if I felt I could handle the nightmares they give me, but I don't. I checked my papers, saw that they were all in order, placed in appropriate manilla folders and stacked beside my briefcase, the rock samples and tools (the dispensable ones I keep strictly for these horrid lectures) set evenly apart.

Rotating the glass in my hand, I spared another brief glance outside into the streets, the dark and imposing sky, before downing what was left in the glass and heading to bed. I set the glass away and stripped down to my underwear, threw myself into the cool shadows between mattress and blankets, waiting for the alarm to strike six.

Seconds after I closed my eyes, the phone rang. I sat there in bed listening to it, the effects of the cognac unraveling with each sound, hoping that whoever was calling had dialed the wrong number and would soon realize their mistake and piss off. But they didn't.

I grabbed the phone. "Hello?" I asked.

"Hey, kid. It's me, Frank."

I sat up, grunting from the pinch in my side. I was fond of my uncle Frank. I liked that after so many years he still referred to me as "kid," eliciting memories from when I was young and he'd sit for me, putting up with me playing scientist. "Hey, Frank. I take it you don't have a watch wherever you are?"

"Nope. Listen, uh, is this a bad hour for you?"

"Yes."

"I need you to come down to the hospital, as soon as you can."

That got me to sit up a little straighter. "What's wrong? Did something bad happen to…"

I didn't know who I was thinking of, or could think of. An ex-girlfriend maybe, a family member, someone I would sooner forget about than feel any concern for. But Frank sniffed on the other end. "No, no, nothing like that. This is a business call, really."

Was he drunk, or was I drunker than I thought I was? "You're losing me, pal. Look, I have to get up at six tomorrow…" I checked the clock on the nightstand. "Shit, six today. I have a lecture to give at the school—"

"Tell them you can't make it. Believe me, Virginia, if you knew what this was about, you'd know just how important it is."

"And why can't you tell me about it right now?"

There was a pause on the other end. When he spoke, I knew from the inflection that he was grinning. "Because I know how much you like mysteries, kid. Listen, Virginia, you know if I can't get you, I'll just grab somebody else."

That struck me as a lie. It struck me that he knew I wouldn't let him, and I knew that. It was the urgency in his voice, the dramatic flair.

"Which hospital did you say?"


I half expected there to be pandemonium at the hospital when I got there, a gathered crowd in full-on panic mode, black helicopters, people being shunted aside to make room for me, an escort to wherever it was Frank was holing up. Sometimes, I like to perceive the world through a film lens to make the doldrums a little brighter. There was none of that when I pulled into the lot in my blue Saturn, with the November air reaching down into my throat and tickling my lungs with every breath.

It became apparent that Frank had made plans when I got to the receptionist. She informed me of the floor where my uncle was staying and told me to go on ahead. When I asked her what was going on, she merely shrugged and seemed very grateful when the phone rang. I headed up to the fifth floor, the trauma center, wondering what in the hell was going on.

166

I had already spent enough time in hospitals and clinics to have developed a marked disdain for them, the free fusion of chemical and organic scents, antiseptic and sickening; for the eye-gouging fluorescent lights; for the equally eye-gouging white floors and ceilings; for all the grids and straights lines I see in every corner, for the attempt at utter perfection of detail in the face of imperfection of the patients' health; for the invisible hierarchy among the nurses; for the bad memories. None of it sat well with the alcohol in my stomach.

Uncle Frank was seated in one of the uncomfortable slate grey chairs in the waiting room, rolling his brown felt hat in his hands. With his wrinkled parchment skin, hard expression, and crooked plum nose, he was a dead ringer for Jimmy Durante. He claims to have gotten that distinctive nose from his days in "the ring," which in his case meant the countless nights of his youth spent drinking and brawling in bars down in Saint Paul.

When I got closer, he looked up at me, and in his bright eyes I saw that spark of action that I imagine heroes in pulpy adventure novels possessed, a tiny glimmer pouring out from a soul too rabid and vivacious to be contained.

He smiled a crooked nicotine-stained smile and hugged me, said "Great to see you again, kid!" Expensive aftershave hung around him in a thick cloud.

"Yeah, nice to see you, too. Now would you explain what this is all about?"

"It's something that has to be seen in order to be explained, kid. Believe me." He put on his hat and smoothed out his coat, looking like he should be standing beside James Cagney or Edward G. Robinson, and

I followed him to the reception area. The petite, severe-looking lady behind the counter gave Frank a dark look behind her spectacles.

Frank, gentleman from another age, took off his head and nodded. "Hello. We're here to see Miss Jennifer Azalea, please?"

One of the receptionist's eyebrows rose up high on her brow and rested there, her eyes glancing from me to my uncle. "And who are you, miss? Are you Virginia Pike?" she asked.

Before I could say anything, my uncle interrupted and stated I was the specialist, and yes, I was Virginia Pike. My eyes and the receptionist's locked for a second, and I tried to compose enough confidence to hide my confusion over this whole mad situation. After the receptionist scribbled something on a clipboard below the counter, she pointed us down the hall. "You remember the room, mister—"

"Yes, yes, I remember the room number. Thank you, Holly." Frank motioned for me to follow, as if I was a child and we were walking through the rolling hills, leafy bracken, and corridors of pine, fir, and birch back home, searching for agates.

I flattened out the collar on my coat, feeling more insecure than I should be. "You still getting into trouble, Uncle Frank?"

"You kiddin'? Trouble keeps getting into me. Alright, number ninety-nine. Here it is." He flipped the latch and stood back, holding the door open for me and motioning me in with a pragmatic flourish.

A doctor stood beside the electroencephalograph, scribbling in a clipboard until he saw me. Young fella, but the sternness in his eyes meant he had experience, or perhaps he was exhausted. His foggy hazel eyes darted from my head to my toes then back up to my eyes, and that damn feeling of being out of place hit me again. He held up a finger to his lips, and I nodded, stepping deeper into the room. I stuffed my hands into my pockets and looked at the figure lying on the bed.

She was very pretty. She couldn't have been over thirty, nor could she have been under twenty, with a healthy face that defied the chalky gauntness of the off-white light. She had long hair black as oil, black as country nights, though the top of her head was covered with a white handkerchief. Her eyes were closed, and I saw from the pair of IV bags hanging beside her that she was floating in a saline-morphine sleep. Her head was going to hurt like a monster bitch when she wakes.

Uncle Frank brushed past me and motioned to the doctor, making introductions. The young man, Dr. Boreson, walked up and offered his hand. "Are you the rock expert?" he asked quietly.

I accepted his hand and shook it. "Yes, I am, if what you really mean is mineralogist. Are you the one that can tell me what's going on?"

Dr. Boreson shot an inquisitive look at my uncle. "Oh, I'm sorry…I thought he would have told you already."

"I thought it would be better if she were here before we said anything."

"You do realize that this is a person lying in that bed, and not some kind of novelty item?"

"Well, I think we can agree that she's a marvel, in any case."

I shook my head and headed toward the door. Frank grabbed me by my elbow and pulled me back, muttering "No, no, no. I'm sorry, I'm sorry, Virginia…come on, stand over here."

He ushered me over to the side of the girl's bed, into the pool of pale yellow light. I didn't feel comfortable, standing over some woman I had never seen before, a girl lost in her own sleeping mind and oblivious to the machines she was wired to, and the three pairs of intrusive eyes. It made me feel like a burglar.

Strands of hair were hanging over her face, and I resisted the impulse to brush them back into place. "Who is she?"

Frank was about to speak when the doctor interrupted him, holding up an authoritative hand. "Look, I can't disclose any information if you haven't filled out the forms. I can't make any exceptions."

"We have, we have," Frank grumbled.

"No. You did, but *she* didn't."

They continued in this manner until I made another attempt for the door. Dr. Boreson huffed as he reached over and very slowly, delicately, pried the kerchief off the woman's scalp, the tape catching on some strands and giving a soft ripping sound. I stared, I think, for what must have been a long time; I was about to say "what is that?" but my voice caught in my throat and I could only mouth the first syllable, lips pursed.

"I'll be damned," the doctor said. "It wasn't that big this morning."

Nestled within the folds of her black hair was a patch of...something. It shimmered beneath the lights. The patch itself was fairly small, perhaps three inches in diameter, and consisted of numerous bumpy fragments that I assumed were bloody glass. I looked at Uncle Frank and he gave me a serious look, no clever grin that could have given away a bad joke.

When Dr. Boreson said "We were hoping you could tell us what this is," I immediately knew what I was looking at. Why else would they bring a damn mineralogist into a hospital?

I told them I needed my hardness testing kit at home, and after a short discussion of safety and procedure, I drove back home as fast as I dared to grab it, along with a couple other things. I also made a call to the university and told them I was feeling under the weather, which wasn't entirely untrue. I made it back to the hospital by six in the morning, and though the sun was hiding beneath the horizon, it was still shedding its light into the sky, though it was difficult to notice for the thick sheets of stone gray clouds pregnant with rain or snow, probably both.

The hospital couldn't spare an empty room for research, but they set aside a corner of the cafeteria, which was adequate enough. I laid down a microscope, measuring apparatus, my hardness testing kit, a couple miscellaneous objects for comparison, some paper and pens, everything aligned with a precision I picked up in the lab.

In the young woman's room, I waited and watched as the doctor, supervised by a couple nurses, carefully plucked one of the larger fragments of the substance from her scalp with a pair of forceps. The nurse held open a little plastic bottle, and the doctor gently set the object inside. While I watched, I kept rolling the woman's name around in my head. Jennifer Azalea…it was a nice name. It fit her. I thought my name fit me, but sometimes I have to reassure myself.

The nurse handed me the bottle and I took it to the cafeteria, handling this thing that measured ten millimeters in length, this thing that shouldn't have happened.

To myself, I ran through different scenarios, half-assed biological speculation: they were salt crystals that formed after the woman suffered a head trauma, the blood congealing oddly; they were sugars that bloomed in a bizarre form of putrefaction; maybe they really were just bits of glass.

Eventually, the day advanced in an arthritic crawl. I became aware of it only by the slight brightening of the hall outside. There was a bottle of ibuprofen still in my purse. I'd assumed it was empty, but there were two pills inside. I downed them both with a plastic cupful of water and went back to my work.

After a while, uncle Frank came in to see how I was doing. He was sweaty and tired, an old man trying to snatch back that energy of youth that was eluding him more and more. "So, what do you think?" he said, hunching over the table.

I focused the microscope, letting the crystal fill my eye. "About what? About the mineral, or the fact that we just picked it from some woman's fucking cranium?"

"Either one. Both, I guess."

I pulled away from the table and rubbed my eyes. The air in here seemed cloying, too medicinal. It was becoming difficult to concentrate. "Well, it's translucent, trigonal, with deep red inclusions on the top that might be hematite. You know, this looks an awful lot like quartz."

"Quartz?" Frank said, trying not to sound incredulous. Quartz was the second most abundant mineral on the planet, appearing in a myriad of forms, all of them beautiful. He leaned over the table to look at my papers, as if trying to find in them some discrepancy I was holding back.

I said "Yeah, a rock crystal cluster. I ran it through the tests, the ones I could actually perform here. Corundum wouldn't scratch it, but it would make a gouge in topaz; it's a seven on the Mohs scale. It's trigonal...shine a light on it; it has a vitreous luster. If I had the time to do a chemical analysis, I bet it'd say silicon dioxide. This shit checks out, Frank."

"Fascinating," he muttered. Silence enveloped us, broken by a couple of people wandering into the room to get something to drink, then left after seeing us. Frank cleared his throat, and his voice took on a conspiratorial note. "You remember what the doctor said when he pulled the bandage away? He said that it wasn't that big before."

"So what? So it's growing? I really, really doubt that, Frank. Are you sure she didn't just fall and smash her head on a rock?"

He shook his head, and we lapsed into another silence. I rubbed at my eyes before diving back into the microscope. I asked "Do you know if the encrustation is showing up over her skin or from beneath?"

"I don't know."

"Ask the doctor."

"Is it really important?"

"Probably not."

Uncle Frank stayed for a minute longer, silent. As he left, I looked away from the microscope, another thought rolling around in my tired mind like a loose bag of marbles. Were the inclusions really hematite? Couldn't they just as easily be droplets of blood, forced up and trapped by the mineral molecules? Or was my brain so tired that it has to grab at morbid ideas in an effort to make sense of this?

After an hour had passed and Frank had not returned with further information, I decided I couldn't wait for him any longer. I set everything aside on the stool closest to the wall and placed a long sheet of paper towel over everything.

I opened the door at room ninety-nine, expecting Frank and the young doctor to be in another quiet squabble, but I saw a head in my peripheral vision turn toward me, black hair billowing around her like grass in a breeze, the most intense green eyes I've ever seen, fixing on me like a snake.

"Who are you?" Jennifer asked, and almost instantly I felt blood fill my cheeks like magma, sweat seeping through the flesh on my brow.

Invading her privacy and being paralyzed by those incredible eyes, feeling like an idiot and wishing I could expunge the past ten seconds or so from this reality; to have babies reversed back into wombs and deaths undone, lives taken and lives saved, countless possibilities never realized, all that shit undone, if only to have kept this situation from happening. That was how I had met Jennifer Azalea.

These mines are murky, and I think I have some thoughts out of order. These sensations do not feel correct, not how they had happened, not just yet. Maybe I've been chipping at thoughts that aren't my own at all. As if it matters—I've started this narrative of memories, ownership notwithstanding, and I aim to see it through. There is a beginning and an end with no connection, two torn ends like a broken bridge. Or perhaps there is only the connection and the two points are meaningless.

The memories play like flashes of intermittent sunlight and tree shadows passing by on blacktop:

I'm in her room and she is awake, wide-eyed and looking at me. I tell her who I am. I tell her why she's in the hospital.

I am walking home from a concert, and a white Camaro idles beside me in the street. A man with shiny spectacles leans out and says "Hey, faggot!" I see that the driver is my cousin, grinning like a coyote on a familiar scent.

She writes down her phone number and hands it to me, telling me that she would like to talk again sometime. Our fingers kiss as I take the paper, scared and embarrassed and too damn tired.

The plane is traveling over Nebraska, thirty-two thousand feet from the misery of a job prospect that didn't go well. Drying eyes, thinking about asking for a white wine but deciding on the terrible beer.

The sky is darkening from one hint of gray to another. My headache isn't as bad as it had been, but it was returning. My mind was still upstairs…I was enamored with her.

Just as I was enamored with the others, I silently warned myself. There were other lovers whose voices still reverberated inside, and I was in no shape to add another voice to the pile. I was no stranger to relationships crumbling down quietly, relationships that burned up in heated explosions, agonized weeks spent trying to forget everything in alcohol and self-hate, every searing case my fault. It had always been me, for one reason or another, which ruined whatever we had tried to create; for my obsessiveness for detail, for my social anxiety, for my temper, for a hundred things that I just cannot get under control.

Some malformed seed of positivity was buried in this muck, though, because I really did want to see her again.

Throughout the remainder of that month and the whole of the next, I began visiting her in the hospital. She was a painter; she had just as much talent with charcoal and number-2 graphite as with nail polish, and the only time a sketchbook wasn't in her hand was when she was asleep and it had slipped from her hand. When she was lucid enough, we found common ground by talking about the trivial things in our lives and relishing that someone else would find them trivial. The development of a rapport this quick was a rarity in my life, and its strangeness was overwhelming, like standing in the headwinds of a nor'easter.

I was kept privy to the cavalcade of doctors and nurses that handled her condition, though I suspect my part was due to Frank's persistence that I could help. Not that I could apply any real answers; no one could figure out why minerals—the doctors insisted they be called foreign bodies— were growing inside of her. The affliction had ceased after twenty-five days, which was just as peculiar.

The minerals had suddenly stopped growing along her bone structure, but the fear that they were still there and threatening her internal organs pervaded every meeting. They had done several operations to remove the substances, and because she didn't seem to show any serious damage, she was allowed to leave after a few weeks.

"I can't say it's been fun," she said on the Thursday after her operation, "because it hasn't. I'd like to see the bill they're going to stick me with when I get out. On second thought, no, I'd rather not see it."

I sat in the guest's chair, watching her make a landscape painting using nail polish. It was a coastal scene, with sharp sapphire waves and pale sands, a cliff in the hazy distance. It might have been Pensacola Beach, or Coronado, or Carmel, or anywhere in the world that sends the imagination to someplace warm, wet, and fun. The room smelled of fumes.

"That's really nice. Where's that supposed to be?"

She notices my expression and grins. "I don't know, honestly. I had a dream that I was somewhere like this, and I wanted to put it on paper before I forgot it forever."

"Could be California, or Florida," I offered.

She didn't respond to that. Instead, she said "I used to be into freshwater diving, when I was younger. My parents had me doing all these exercises up in the Boundary Waters and in Lake Superior, and they took me to a thousand different beaches. They probably thought I wanted to be an Olympiad swimmer, but the truth was that I just wanted to look for sunken treasure. Secrets buried in the lakes, stuff like that."

176

I hummed in agreement, fidgeting with one of the nail polish bottles. It had one of those cheap-wit names that some people must think very clever. Diving Belle.

"I think I was six the last time I was at the beach," I say. "Not much of one, just a sandy patch near a trailer park, but it was close enough. I wish I'd learned how to swim back then."

"Maybe I could show you some time," she says. I try to hear a note of hopefulness in her voice, or maybe it was just me. "I live near a bluff over by Silver Bay, and I'm always by the lake. There's a nice view of the Split Rock Lighthouse."

"That'd be nice," I say, too amazed to say anything else. I smile, and when she notices, she smiles, too.

We saw a lot of each other after that. Halfway through November, Jennifer took me to an art exhibition at Monolith, a dark little club in a dark little part of the city that I have never gone to, nor had any reason to go. It was night, and the only lights on inside were the ones hanging over the paintings and sculptures, fog born from dry-ice flowing about our ankles. Some dark Euro-industrial music was pulsating from overhead speakers, Grendel or Einsturzende Neaubauten, something that made the windows twitch in their panes.

I walked around behind Jennifer, plastic cup filled with cheap-ass beer as we surveyed the abominable works. She stopped at one canvas, straightening her big bone-white sun hat. I told her she didn't need it, but she was adamant that her "condition" was continuing to grow, and she was determined to go to whatever lengths to keep her secret her own. I told her I understood.

We have our own natures, where we prefer to exist how we want. Jennifer was in hers, and I was a mere wanderer. Where she went, I followed behind, silent when she spoke, nodded when she expected me to. She took some photographs with her digital camera, and I waited for a moment I could dip out and find some peace and quiet in all this.

One piece showed a woman reclining in a dark and windowless room, nude, a sheen of sweat eking through her cappuccino skin to stain a rich violet lounge chair. There was a troubled expression in her face, eyes closed as though she were sleeping, if she was sleeping and not merely lost in thought. Above her, a monster with a woman's face stared down at her, pale eyes glowing, brow lined with her own torment. There might have been eyes in her ropey black hair, too, or it might have just been reflections of light. I followed the curve of her body as it trailed all the away into the shadows, the dissolve of pale skin into ashen scales. I looked closer, seeing there were cracks stretching over the smaller woman's body, like rich dark marble.

"This one's kind of weird, isn't it?" Jennifer remarked. "I heard the artist painted this after visiting a little town near the Aegean coast, during the winter solstice. Hmm...It doesn't have a title."

"Where's the light coming from?" I asked her, nursing the sour beer. "Why is there light reflecting off her skin when there's no source?" I couldn't see Jennifer's eyes, but I saw from the humorless smile that she was giving me an annoyed look from beneath her hat.

"Damn realist," she muttered. There were others we purveyed, alien facades or grim fantasies clouding scenes of everyday life, trace occult whisperings and ultra-violent erotica, Grand Guignol for Clark Ashton Smith acolytes. An asymmetrical mandala hung above the staircase, done in what looked like coffee and blood; I wanted to grab it and rip it apart with my bare hands.

One artist, an elderly Irishwoman who was only ever referred to as "Glynis", seemed to have an overdeveloped infatuation with H.R. Giger, with biomechanoid landscapes and glistening pseudo-sexual scenes. A number of her works were scattered around the second floor. It was starting to make me sick, but the patrons were oohing and aahing and just about orgasming in their fascination.

After a time, Jennifer and I became separated somewhere in the crowd. The migraine was violently blossoming in the midst of sweat-soaked leather and black latex as I tried to find her, but she had vanished. Even with that damned hat of hers, she had disappeared in the dark. I found the bathroom so I could throw up, then I went looking for her.

An hour passed before I saw her again. She was standing at the balcony on the third floor, leaning over the wrought iron railing and staring into the street. Nobody came up to her or offered her a drink, as if this scene were set aside just for me. I passed through puddles of light and intermittent darkness and stood beside her, wondering if anything was wrong. Her hat tilted to me, rouged lips raised into a small smile, then turned back to look down at the street three floors down.

I asked her if she was alright, but she didn't answer. Not immediately. She leaned forward a little more, and the railing squeaked "Be careful," I said, said again because I thought I whispered it. I was about to ask her again when she expelled a sigh and spoke so softly that I had to lean in to catch it.

She said "I wonder…if I fell, would I be diamonds? Or rubies?"

I put my hand on her arm and asked her again if anything was wrong. "I'm not having much fun tonight," she said. I wasn't about to tell her that coming here had been her idea.

"You want to get out of here?"

"Yeah."

I took her by the elbow, ignoring her decree that she didn't need any help. We made it through the building and into the lot, our boots crushing the first snowfall of the year, eager to feel the heat blowing out from the vents.

As she was about to get into the passenger seat she paused, head bent down into her furry coat and one hand clutching her chest. I heard her say "Ow," hard and sharp.

"Jennifer? What's wrong?"

She took a breath, short and slow, then a deeper one. She slid into the seat and buckled her seatbelt. "I don't...It's not anything to worry about, Virginia. I'm alright."

The moment that last syllable spilled out from her lips, she winced, bared her teeth, looking like she had been shot in the chest. "We're going to the hospital," I told her. "And don't you say a goddamn word about it."

It was a heart arrhythmia, I later heard from the doctors, once the initial worries were superseded by other concerns. We got to the hospital within twenty minutes, and by then her chest was causing Jennifer so much pain there were tears coursing down her cheeks in silky rivers. They rushed her to the emergency room, and I was left alone in that special kind of Limbo they call the waiting room, shaking, while pastoral paintings stared back at me.

This next I know is not my own, but it is relevant. The doctors had put Jennifer under and began the surgery immediately; many of those on staff that night were also present that first night back in October, and were acquainted with her case already. That didn't make it any less precarious. While they were performing the surgery, the doctor made an

180

exclamation, and the nurse gasped and twisted around. She bumped into the aluminum tray, fixed on its stand, the instruments clattering and skittering across the floor.

Because Jennifer's rib bones no longer looked like rib bones. They looked like gleaming arches of translucent celestine. No amount of wiping or suction would remove the bluish glimmer, and those present were forced to give in to their shock and wonder. The crystal was undiluted by any inclusions. It was pristine. No coarse druzy habit, but smooth, well-polished, as though they had been formed over centuries by Nature. The doctors assumed that the calcification—after finally settling on the most accurate word to use—began in two places within her skeletal structure, in her sternum and separately between the dermis and bone of her skull, and it was spreading like an infection. They were afraid that once it reached her spinal column she would be paralyzed indefinitely, or worse.

The increasing density was playing hell with her organs and surrounding tissues. This was the reason the doctors thought she was gaining weight when she was barely eating anything at all. Dr. Boreson, who was on call elsewhere, got the word from a colleague and he gave the word to me while Jennifer was still under anesthesia. I saw the attendant photographs. Before I could stop myself from thinking it, I wished they'd removed a sample so I could've analyzed it. I was drawn into academic professionalism to avoid thinking what was most obvious.

Later, much later, the first thing Jennifer said when she awoke was "Is there any water?"

Here's another memory, freshly plucked and set under the light of recollection. I don't like pondering it, because it's not one I'm

181

particularly fond of. That fight between me and Jennifer. It was one of only a few, drawn out over the course of several months, but this one was bad, explosive. The kind where every word was a bullet, every action meant to tear down the other. That spring was us learning how to hate each other.

Depressurization over a myriad of reasons…It was me, and it was her, we were both at fault, and so we blindly destroyed each other in an effort to derive some amount of base pleasure at being the victor in this confrontation. We wanted to be right, and we wanted to hurt each other. In the end, there was no warrior standing tall and proud and so fucking full of herself. Jennifer ran out the door, the bandages she wore about her face coming loose, her sobs cruelly muffled.

This was an old scab I had been picking at for years, and the blood was not unfamiliar.

Once the rage wore off, as it always did, I realized that I'd done it again. I'd driven someone away because I couldn't accept the idea of sharing myself. Couldn't accept anything good that comes along. I ran into the bathroom and slammed my fist into the face of the stupid bitch in the mirror, not even feeling the razor shards biting into my skin.

There were bottles lying behind the cabinet door, waiting. I grabbed at them, tore off the lids, and shoved a handful of capsules into my mouth, swallowing what I could and choking on what was left. Some bottles fell into the sink, the pills circling the drain. I didn't know what I had taken, and I really didn't care. There was nothing in my head while I did it, just a void. Just a sense that what I was doing was right, that all of this would magically reverse itself if I could hurt myself enough.

Silver bullets. The silver might exist, but the cure doesn't.

182

My vision blurred, condensed into a tunnel, fade to black. The bathroom melted away, like Time, or this moment in Time, were putrefying. There was a sense of waking, somewhere, and I could see myself lying on the floor. Foamed saliva pooling around my mouth onto the tile. The tile was cheap vinyl, made to resemble dark green marble, almost like malachite. I never liked that tile because it made me feel like I was standing in the middle of an ocean, a dark and alien ocean. The experience was terrifying, but the terror was numbed, and only an associate of the confusion. There was joy, too, joy at being free from the anger.

I walked away, away from that body. Cracks ran along the joints where the walls met, widening into black slivers. The house melted away in long sections, panels liquidating through open space as they rose and fell and twisted away in every direction. I took a breath, but I didn't feel the relief of breathing. I didn't know where I was going, if there was anywhere to go, so I just kept walking.

Yes, I was scared, and a bit ashamed, and surprised that I could be feeling emotions in this state. I made no sound while I walked, even when the nothingness beneath me faded and became a glittering sheet of agate. It was amazing, walking along a single slab of agate, seeing my own nude reflection walking partly in step with me. It confused me why I should look so good, but it was unimportant.

Soon, in the distance, there were towers of light, spires and palisades rising high. Cyclopean clusters of colorless rock crystal glowing with an immense, palpable light. Gems the size of mountains, ranges, canyons. There were figures in that sprawling distance, but just indiscernible shapes to me. Shapes, and light.

There for a moment, before I was falling away, falling into every direction simultaneously, and I was lying on the cold floor of my bathroom again, back in my broken and bleeding and ruined body.

There is pain, and there are scars that still cling to me, grim passions and regrets that are stuck deep inside like fissures in glass. There are memories I don't want. As I remember this, I can feel everything again, and it hurts. The ripples fan out across time and it hurts as deeply now as it did then. But I have to remember, because I have to finish what was started, what was started again.

A month passed after my overdose. I wanted to talk to Jennifer again so badly that breathing hurt. I didn't want her to become another face I can barely remember, another voice I hear in a bad dream.

I got into my Saturn, wincing at the sun – I hardly go outside anymore, even for work – and drove the hour up 61 to Jennifer's house. She lives in a tiny house out by Silver Bay, not too close to the bluffs, but close enough to hear the waves crash and scratch at the cliffs. Close enough that Lake Superior becomes a gleaming shard of light, stolen from the sun.

The poinsettias and chrysanthemums were still waving lazily in their red clay pots on the patio, but they seemed stiff, as though they could not escape the chill of a past winter. The huge cedar tree in the yard was cloven in two, its groin lightning-charred, bark split and hollow. Nothing was different. But why were the hairs on my neck standing up, like the air before a storm?

I didn't care about anything, I just wanted to see her again, and if she yelled at me, hit me, then fine. At least I would have heard her voice; argument was still a form of conversation. I knocked on the door, softly, then again, a bit harder.

A windchime was my only answer. She'd bought it once when we were together on a date, at some little shop in the Mall of America. She brought me there almost explicitly because she knew I hated crowds, and thought she could draw me out of my shell. The chime was a series of selenite cross-sections, seven full moons singing in the breeze.

Her car was in the yard, she couldn't have left. She doesn't take walks, at least not when the sun was out. I knocked on the door and called her name, not knowing what I'd say if I saw her. Isn't it funny how a plan collapses in on itself?

On a lover's doorstep, in an air of uncertainty, minutes feel like hours, hours like seconds. I stood there waiting, occasionally knocking on her door and infrequently calling her name. I told the door why I came, what she meant to me, why I was willing to take the rap for everything if only to see her again. There was no reply.

So then, I opened the door and stepped inside. The sun poured into the lightless house, chasing out the shadows that should have stayed where they were. Horror requires air and expectation in order to be executed. The air fled my chest as my eyes roamed over everything in the room, over every gleaming surface.

Some years ago, while I was traveling through Brazil with some friends, we had happened upon a cave system while hiking through the mountains, an entrance to the cold corpse of a volcano. Inside was an antechamber, and there were thousands of gorgeous and clever growth formations of a dozen different gemstones. Stalagmites and stalactites of crystal, twinning arches lining one end of the massive ceiling to the other, and gleaming structures embedded in the walls like eyes. Beams of quartz led like guardrails to deeper realms, the walls of the earth's womb.

It was like we had stepped into a geode. That was almost like this moment.

The interior of Jennifer's house was coated in a thick film of crystal, every visible surface and niche shining as if covered in glare ice. Every corner worn smooth. Columns rose up from the floor, some incorporated into the ceiling, spires that twisted into each other, into fantastic chaotic formations. Stars were encased in the crystals, fiery with sunlight and portraying a color spectrum that only seemed recognizable after a few moments, dissolving into colors that hurt my eyes, even when they reverted back to familiar, understandable hues. There were patterns so chaotic that they seemed organic.

What happened here? I sank down to the floor, my knees banging hard on a dais of banded onyx beneath me. Where was she in all of this? Did she run away before it became so prevalent? Or was she somewhere in this house, buried within all of this, the nucleus of this crystalline microcosm?

Did I lose her already? Was I responsible for all of this? I'm sure I was; I could have helped her sooner, if I hadn't spent so much time pitying myself. Tears were falling from my eyes and I held myself as if I might fall apart at any moment, knowing I already had.

After a while, I began to hear gentle, almost musical sounds behind me, a steady chime-like percussion. It wasn't the wind chime. I didn't turn around. I knew exactly what it was without having to bear the hell of acknowledging it. I wouldn't look at it. Forget the reason I came here, I didn't want to look at it.

"Is that you, Virginia?"

I shook my head, hair getting into my eyes and mouth and I didn't care. The chiming sounds moved around to my right side and stopped. I heard something heavy shift, felt the change in the air as something knelt down.

"Virginia, look at me."

"Go away."

"You said you wanted to see me, Virginia. You came all this way to hear my voice and see my face. So don't be so melodramatic. Hear me, Virginia, and see me."

I didn't. I did. I opened my eyes, the world homogenized through my tears. I wiped them away with the palm of my hand before looking at Jennifer. It was Jennifer, of course, but different, wholly different. She knelt there on her haunches beside me, naked as she was when the doctor pulled her from her mother's womb. A shape of multicolored crystal sat there, opaque in areas and translucent in others, shimmering. Her eyes still had the intensity of aeon-swept emeralds, her limbs like columns of uncut alexandrite, her nipples like chips of topaz. It even affected her hair, grown in thin dendritic strands of hematite.

I saw my face reflected in hers, and I couldn't hide a small smile. A light was flickering throughout her body, probably piezoelectricity— probably octarine for all I fucking knew. She knelt down and pressed her lips to mine, warm lips and terribly solid, but still comforting. I felt something pass through me, into me, a feeling or a spirit, something that was from her, connecting with my existence. Myself at all points in time.

I was hers. She was mine. We belong together, in every way.

I've never left this place, our little palace in the country. Jennifer has taken care of me as my body began to change, as liquids evaporated and organs gradually atrophied, solidified, useless filled space, and were changed. All of this hurt, of course, but it was a nice hurt, an agonizing tickle that lasted for months – a blink of the geologic eye, really. A single frame in the immeasurable band of time. When we kiss, I feel her becoming a part of me, and I a part of her, as if our bodies become inclusions of the other, twinning fragments of the same singular crystal.

We've been here for so long, forever together. We have witnessed the descent of rain, leaves, snow, thunder. An endless dancing cycle of nature as the earth revolved on its axis, and we thrilled as we knew we were a part of it, a fragment of the earth itself. Our consciousness traveled through the rocks and the secrets they possessed, accessible only to us.

You cannot describe it in any language. There is only weak metaphor, only humble comparatives that step in where raw sensation and perception is the dominant language.

I hear a knock on the door. We'll be here for a long time, I think, and it's nice to have company. Under the watchful eye of time, we'll all be together. Gleaming like stars held tight in amber.

# The Beguiled, The Leaves

It's all too easy to cut your finger on a memory. All too easy to stumble over the regret of the child you forgot you were.

Edith Lundberg was out in the field behind her house, helping her grandchildren fill up their buckets with blueberries before the bears got into the bushes, before the blue jays came and pilfered them before autumn set in, reprimanding Roger and Billy whenever she caught them sneaking a few into their mouths, when she thought about the grove. She paused, hand poised over the bucket, long enough for her son-in-law, Randall, to stop hanging Easter decorations on the porch and call out to her. "Hey, you okay over there, Edie?"

"Fine, just fine, hon," she said, even though she was miles from fine. She straightened back up and shrugged her shoulders until she heard a series of small pops, pleasantly like the spitting of a burning oak log.

She looked back at Randall just in time to see him shake his head at her daughter, who nodded in silent agreement. *I know, but what can we do?* that nod said, and Edith wondered what answer they might come up with. Yes, pity the old woman, two days past her seventieth now and having trouble remembering things, already ten years since her vision had started to go. She adjusted her thick glasses, taking a cold, shaky breath. She watched Roger and Billy playing in the fields, throwing burs at each other, the blueberries forgotten.

For a moment, she thought her specs had slipped across her nose, that maybe a bird had been spooked and she had another embarrassing moment of forgetting, but when the realization came, it came like a strong backhand. She was staring at the woods.

Be honest. You're not staring at the woods, old woman, not exactly. You're staring toward a place you used to live near a hundred years ago, and a place in the trees where the lindens grew big while someone made the grass sing...

That did it, the little phrase that frolicked in her mind like a fidgety little animal. Someone made the grass sing, and they taught her how to do it, too. A memory triggered, reproduced, producing more, until a well inside her that hadn't been tapped in half a century opened up and swallowed her whole. The grass here was tall and thick, and when she stumbled and fell into it, it wasn't any less like collapsing onto a hay bale.

And then, when she wakes, she hears a small male voice say "Is gramma dead?"

Her daughter hissed between her teeth, "No, Roger, don't say that. She just..." but she doesn't say anything more because she's not sure what's wrong with her mother. Edith frowned, tried to think of how to tell her that a mother is allowed to have no answer. She supposed Sally was already learning that with the divorce. Amicable or not, divorce stung as only a divorce can sting.

Damn, but her head hurt.

"Gramma, wake up," Billy, her granddaughter said. A small hand brushed her hair off her brow, and she decided to stop playing unconscious.

She said "Boo," and her granddaughter laughed. Sally gave a huff, pretending she's not mad at having her week ruined, the week she was supposed to be recuperating from the emotional conflict. A dozen retorts burning in her eyes, and Edith smiled in a way she hoped was apologetic, but she wasn't apologizing. Sally stood up and said "Come on, kids. Grandma needs to get some sleep." She grabbed Roger's hand, bruised with blueberry juice, and walked out of the room.

Billy looked down at her with the eyes of a six year-old and leaned in like a conspirator. "Do you want me to tell you a story?"

Edith grinned and hugged her granddaughter tightly. Blessed are the children. Feeling much better than before, she said "No, dear, you don't have to do that for grandma."

"Then will you tell me a story?"

"Ooh, I'm sorry. Not tonight. I just need to rest a bit." And Edith can only pretend that her heart isn't broken when her granddaughter heaved a great sigh and stepped out the door, closing it shut. For a long time, Edith only stared at the yellow bar of light peeking under the door.

Maybe, if Edith were a woman immune to regret, resistant to the weight of her age, she would have told her granddaughter a story that she hadn't thought about in decades. It would be a fairy tale, devoid of the glittered trappings the term *fairy tale* has become burdened with. Sacrifice. That's what fairy stories have always been about.

Maybe, if Edith had been a braver woman, she might have begun the story like this:

Once upon a little town, there were two sisters. They were a living mirror-image; the other residents of the town – not yet named back then, and wouldn't be for some time – were fond of commenting on how identical the two were, hard Swedish sentences appraising their long flaxen hair and high cheeks, simple farmer's girls' dresses with farmer's girls' scarred hands. The older emigrants smiled when they saw the sisters crossing the dirt roads or running through the fields about town, validated in their feeling that Sweden had come across the seas with them.

It would be too much to presume the sisters' similarities were any deeper than superficial. One sister's face was often pinched with worry, brow arched in contemplation while she stripped birch bark from the forest and bundled them in sheets with twine, or pulling the hide off of a moose her father had killed. Would this bark be too dry and burn too quickly in the stove? Would the wood be too wet to burn as well? Was the meat healthy? She was a nervous girl who grew to be a nervous young woman, prone to act only after careful deliberation.

Her sister was not so. The Castor to her sister's Pollux, and impulsive as a rabbit in summer, Edith was more inclined to dream of things she couldn't do, couldn't see, or couldn't have. Though she cared deeply for her family, she frequently caught herself considering what life would be like if she had any sway over it. Sundays found her at the Bethany Lutheran Church in Little Sleep Lake with the dozens of other Swedes and Finns who came off the Luccania Liner and settled here, in this town hewn out of the sea of timbers, but she had little patience or trust in the words the priest handed down to her. There seemed to be an awful lot of talk about what happened after you were alive, but she didn't see the point in that. Wasn't what was happening *right now* just as important, if not more so?

Everything began on the day the last of winter's snow melted into pools, flooding hollows and crop gardens. Their mother had insisted they go outside and gather up all the windfalls before they began reconstructing and adding to the fields. The past summer had been good to them, and they had good reason to feel industrious. While Dena had already begun a sizeable pile, Edith continued to wonder and wander closer to the trees.

Thomas Walker was a boy she went to school with, another boy from Europe whose birth name had been sacrificed for legal documentation, and he enjoyed teasing her with tales of fairies and elves, wish-granters and mind-readers, which soon would find out how lazy she really is. She recalled her own mother's warnings to never carry cream or take cakes into the forest.

She'd never let on to her family what was in her heart; religion and home life pressed passivity on her, but her impulsivity was constantly fighting it. The discontent with the farm, the desire to see other things, the want for her family to have nicer things, to see new places, the vanquishing of boredom, it was all a flood inside her, wanting out.

So – she told herself in one form or another – it was for her family when she snuck off and stole into the woods behind the farmhouse, her most treasured possession hanging from one hand. There was nothing but hope and shaky joy inside her, making every step through the warm loam silent, and the pine needles fallen from last year soft as moss.

She'd been walking for a while, following a skinny river, when a puzzling thought struck her. Who would know where one might find an elf? What traces does a tomte leave, if any? She realized there was plenty she didn't know, plenty she wanted to know but wasn't sure where to start. There was no specific destination she had in mind when she stepped between the trees, only that she had made the first step; the journey itself would lead her to an answer.

There were so many things she wanted to have happen, things to make everything so much better. If she had only one wish, she could change the world.

The land reminded her of the ocean, waves seized in motion, the trees singing in the wind – the stink of a cattle farm wafted in from the south. A thin brook wove through the trees, and she watched the small flycatchers darting in and out, grabbing at anything they could catch. A finch watched her with a black marble eye, chirping loudly and adding itself to an avian choir that grew in her wake.

Eventually, she came to a bend in the river, where the soil deposits had risen and thinned the river so that it was more like a shallow brook. She took off her shoes and stepped through the water to the other side.

Edith stared up at the big linden trees, amazed at the different forms trees could take as they grew, and at all the life that they harbored. It wasn't until she was many yards into this part of the forest that she realized not an ounce of sunlight could pierce through the tightly interwoven trees. Insects murmured in the air and something – a rabbit, she imagined – darted through the short underbrush. The air was thick and warm, seeping into her body. It was so calm, so calming, and that was a wonderful thing.

Lazily, like paint drooling through a brush, she wondered how far she'd come already. When she passed through yet another pair of trees, a grove opened up before her, spongy loam between her toes, the grass pretty with dew, a pond to the right of where she entered, looking bluer and deeper than a forest pond ought to be. Some of the tree roots arched over the pond's rim and into the water like elephant trunks. In her enthusiasm, Edith hadn't considered if the adventure would take longer than the sun's tenure in the sky. The sky was only dark green to her.

A breached rock tripped her up, and sent her face-first into the cool loam. Cool and soft, but she still saw fireflies flickering in her vision. Pine needles invaded her mouth and she spat them out, grimacing at the bitter taste that wouldn't go away.

"Oh!" In the grove, something was sitting on the root, staring down at the girl with big brown eyes and a smile that her mother hadn't made for a very long time. The fur on her cheek, tawny brown and freckled with white, rippled in the lazy breeze, and small wooden ornaments adorning her antlers, chiming. She was naked beneath a heavy brown bear pelt. As Edith stood back up on quivering feet, the fey beamed and laughed in a way that made the leaves dance.

"What a curious way to introduce yourself," she said. Her voice was like a bed of grass in midsummer.

"I'm sorry," Edith said, brushing herself off, feeling her heart flutter in her chest. She put quite a lot of stock in fortune, in that fabled coin labeled GOOD and BAD, and she quietly praised her current stroke of good fortune in having succeeded. She'd finally found one, and in her excitement she'd forgotten what she'd planned to say. "I just...I'm fine."

The teeth in that smile were bright and sharp. "I know, I can see that. It doesn't do well to convey the obvious, girl." Edith was about to say she was sorry for the second time before catching herself, instead looking at the object of her interest. The strange woman slowly stood, her pelt falling from her naked shoulders, giving the Swedish girl, who now felt very small, a sharp view of her goatish legs, the long bovine tail that hung between her knees. Her eyes lingered on the dense thicket of her pubic hair until she looked away, cheeks burning.

The faun paused and sniffed at her; Edith could smell standing water and exotic flowers. "What's that?" the faun pointed to the doll.

The girl stared down at her toy, at the thin red smile, the brushed rouge of her cherubic cheeks all but washed away by time, bright blue painted eyes of a friend; Ulla had been with her since she had accepted her father's gift for her fourth birthday. That day seemed a thousand years ago and 3,972 miles away in Sundsvall. Another world away, and Ulla had always been a better confidante and listener than her own sister.

So, it hurt her when she said "It's a gift." She proffered little Ulla up with benedictive hands, waiting for this moment to pass.

"For me?" She accepted the toy and ran a delicate finger through its Angora hair, brightening. "She's a pretty thing. You must think the world of her. How generous of you," she said, spinning around in a gleeful dance. She whooped and pranced on hooves black as topsoil. "This has been such a wonderful day! I ought to give you a gift in return!"

And the faun showed Edith how to make grass sing. She picked a long blade from the ground, held its edge against her lips, and the girl breamed when she heard the high fluting noise that rang about the grove. The sound was gentle and pretty, and drew the girl up, beyond the trees and into the bright blue skies. Sometimes her father would play records on the gramophone and, if he and mom had been sipping, would get up and dance, and everyone would have a nice time; but all the instruments on those records were nothing compared to the simple whistling notes she heard.

They both sang songs that they knew and played in the grove, and taught each other small stories and crafts. Edith had been having such a good time until she noticed how long the shadows had become, how much evening light filled the grove. She stopped chasing her spry new friend, lost in thought; there'd been no consideration that once she returned home she would be spared her father's hand, and the matter that had brought her here had been forgotten until now.

The faun paused on one hoof, still as stone, and looked at her with a cocked head. "Something wrong?"

When you have no time to waste, only unrepressed haste can get you out of a jam. Edith said "Uh...Can you grant wishes?"

The faun frowned. "Yes."

"Please. Can you grant me a wish?"

The frown became a smile. "Of course I can, girl. What is it you want?"

The chance to change whatever you want, shape it into whatever you desire. Surely not. The worrying thought entered Edith's mind that, maybe, the skogsrå was just a regular woman, skilled with makeup and theatrics, and malicious enough to play with a girl's dreams. But Edith felt the potential tingling within, nigh overwhelming, asking her to make it come out.

Too many possibilities, too many thoughts circling her. Finally, she seized on a vision of the lake. Families from all over the county were fond of taking fish from Little Sleep Lake. There were catfish and pumpkinseed fish that tasted wonderful, and Edith remembered how sweet the blood of the bluegills smelled when she was scaling and beheading them. Thinking how happy her family would be if the fish actually helped them out in the endeavor, she smiled and said "I want something that will make the fish come to us. Something that can draw them in so we wouldn't have to wait so long for a bite."

The faun nodded adamantly, and reached into the bole of a nearby tree. She pulled out a silver ring as big as a queen's crown, with funny symbols carved on the inside. "Put this into the water beside your boat when next you cast your lines. Your icebox will never be without fish now."

The girl thanked the faun and asked if she could come visit her again. The faun said that would be fun, cradling little Ulla like she was her own infant, and she watched the girl walk back through the woods. The sparrows' black eyes followed her all the way back home, silver ring cold as night clutched in her hand, head swirling with what had just happened.

Had it even happened? It couldn't have been a dream, not with the freezing metal in her hand. She was lost in thought, but her feet took her straight home. After stashing the object in the upper rafters of the barn, she crept back into the house and, as she'd suspected, her father did not hold back his belt. After delivering a severe rebuke about working hard before the winter came, she was sent to her room, hungry without a meal but full of joy. But the tears that traced her cheeks were happy ones.

That night, lying on her bed on the side of her that wasn't smarting, she told her sister about her new friend in the woods. Rather than share in her sister's enthusiasm, she only scowled and reprimanded, doubting the wisdom of keeping company with a doe that wears bear skins.

But the faun's promise was not a trick. Prior to the next time her mother took her and her sister out to the lake to catch some fish, Edith had affixed the ring to a length of chain and attached it to the rear of the spine. Joseph Langenkamp, who lived over on Hay Island, remarked in his own boat how he had never seen so many fish in all of his seventy years, while his grandchildren had been afraid for the roiling water.

198

Mother had exclaimed with pride when she reeled in the great catfish, then pregnant with her brother and somehow keeping her balance as she unfastened the hook from its jaw and deftly tossed it into the porous basket beside the boat. Even when the other fish, some of phenomenal size, began leaping out of the water and started braining themselves against each other, the family smiled at their good fortune.

And when father came home from the grain mill that night and saw their haul, he forestalled any of the questions he might have had and gave each of them a broad hug. "There's enough here to sell in town!" he said, triumphant that the squabbles over the property tax can now be put to rest. They could stop selling off their dwindling livestock and try to make a go at it.

The rest of spring passed like a cool breeze and turned to the sultry breath of summer. The farm saw all kinds of good fortune; they'd sold their oxen for a number of efficient young stallions (who came with a group of fine mares); they'd added to the barn so they could fit in the goats and chickens, which all added to their overall profit; and mother had given birth to her baby brother. And with her special ring, they saw no end to the number of fish they could catch.

Made confident by such bounty, her father had neglected to bring the boat in, leaving it anchored in the water. There was no fear of thieves, not in Little Sleep Lake.

On the first of July, a fire tore through the upper part of the county, chewing through the prairies and fields. A dozen families around the lake were affected. Crops were not spared; whole sheaves of wheat and corn became glowing lanterns, and it was bare luck alone when the winds changed and pushed the flames away from their farmhouse.

Father died trying to fight the fire. Mr. Holopainen, his supervisor at the mill, came by in his fancy buggy and told mother the news. He said he was sorry it had to happen to such a nice family, such a beautiful woman as mother. He said something else and mother screamed at him to get out. The sisters sat in their bedroom, staring at the far wall, not seeing it.

She wouldn't know until much later how much money her mother had spent just to have a formal Christian burial.

It took them the better part of two weeks to return the livestock that had fled and fix up the field. Edith noticed that the deer had vanished from the land, and that was a sad vision lost. Their family depended on the livelihood of the animals, and if there were no animals for hunting or husbandry, that meant endangering her family. So, on the last day of summer, she went to see the faun again.

She was sitting on a boulder in her grove, whittling, the tips of her hooves languishing in the pond. Edith didn't know what it was supposed to be, the long thing that was being fashioned from the twinned linden bough, but it did look rather interesting. The faun's tail twitched.

"Don't hide in the shadows, child, I can smell you anyways." She set down the curious implement and pivoted on her bottom, smiling her sharp smile.

Edith didn't waste time. "I need you to grant me another wish."

"Do you? I'm not really surprised. The knowledge that what you want can come true, even though it's at the behest of someone else, to bring a dream to reality, is a very powerful narcotic. It hurts when you can't have it, and you can never have it only once."

Edith didn't know what the word narcotic meant, so she merely nodded in agreement and waited.

200

A flicker of an ear, a pursing of lips. The faun gave her a studious look. "Magic is change. What do you want to change, girl?"

She'd come up with it that morning, and she was certain it was what she needed. "I want all the apple trees around our farm to grow and bear fruit, all year 'round, snow or not. That way, we'll never go hungry, and we can make more money, and the deer can keep coming closer to the trees and we won't have to go out hunting for them."

The faun narrowed her eyes. "A bit late in the year for apples, isn't it?"

"But can you do it?"

Did the girl see a glimmer of offense in the skogsrå's eyes? Did those brown gems become a warning shade lighter? "Of course. But this is a bit larger than the last one, which means a higher payment. What you want is life, which requires life."

"I don't understand."

The faun glowered. As she did, the vibrancy of the grove faded a little, the grass retracted into the earth, and it was awfully silent. No insect sang, no bird moved its wings. "Even intelligent people can be stupid, girl. You're not that stupid. Your mother just gave birth, didn't she?"

Edith nodded and said yes, a sickening feeling tightening in her stomach.

"Life for life, girl. Come back to me with your baby brother, and your orchard will know no end."

She nodded and thanked the faun, feeling hollow. She hadn't expected this, not at all. Up until now, she'd felt that she was in the creature's good graces, that the faun saw her as a friend, an equal, and this was a relationship she'd intended to cash in on. She hung her head, commanding herself not to cry.

On her way out of the grove, she saw something in the soil. At first glance, she took it for a tiny stick, but a stick wouldn't be shaved cleanly on four sides. She picked it up, ran it between her thumb and forefinger until the charred end at the tip crumbled. It was a matchstick, the kind you can purchase at Lonnie Dahlgren's store at ten cents a box.

She ignored it. She had other things to worry about.

The dilemma cost her two days. The fey's awful proposition had been a lot to think over, but she came to a decision in the middle of the night. If she really wanted a baby, she can have one, Edith thought, but not my brother. So she snuck out of the house, walking quickly up the horsetrail, led by a full moon as yellow as melting animal fat. The road along the way to town was a gash through the woods surrounding the lake, so she brandished a sturdy oak beam in case there were coyotes or wolves along the way.

Their neighbors were the Calhouns, another farming family that also came on the boat, but they were from Munich. Mrs. Calhoun and the girl's mother were friends, and she or her sister often took things to or from the two houses. Because they were farmers, she knew they were deep sleepers.

The big grey dog came bounding off the porch to meet her, wagging its tail and snuffling at her hand. It followed her up to the house, calmly sitting back down on its favorite spot beyond the swing of the door. She moved around to the east edge of the house and, as slowly as she could so the pane wouldn't make a noise, her chest hurting with the breath she kept locked inside, she pried open the window to the diner.

The Calhoun baby slept in a crib near the bedroom. She slipped in unheard, pretending she was a cricket or a spider. The father snored like thunder, and the mother had a nasal whistling noise that made Edith think of the sound an arrow made when fired. Mouthing silent commands for the child to be silent, she swaddled the infant in its thin blanket, and drew it from the crib. With a final glance at the parents, she crept away, choosing the front door, stroking the boy's small warm head. She thanked the dog and walked into the night.

She might have thought what she was doing was awful, profane. She might have considered the trouble she could get in was a more pressing matter than her dreams, her ambitions. But she recalled the grim stories her grandfather had told her, about the days when he was still in the Swedish infantry, the ones that put perspective on the significance of only one little life in the grand scheme of things, and her pace didn't falter.

The faun set her meal down on the grass and cheered at the girl's arrival, and all the lindens joined her. The girl expected the baby to mewl and howl, but it was smiling a toothless smile up at the flickering lightning bugs and starlight. The faun accepted the child with a nod and a grin, bits of bloody rabbit fur clinging to her bottom lip, holding it close to her breast. Edith felt sick, and couldn't stand to look at the baby anymore, so she stared at the bright veins of amber that wove through the faun's horns. Had they always been there?

"Very good, child," she said. She traced the baby's brow with one sharp finger. Writing, Edith thought. "As I've said, life for life."

"May I leave now?"

"You always have that choice, girl. I never said you have to stay here, and I never ordered you to go. What you do in your life, you do alone, and you share the responsibility alone. When you wake tomorrow, the apple trees will be full in bloom."

When the girl finally got home, the wind brushed cool fingers through her hair, bringing the sounds of frolicking laughter from the distant woodlands.


For a long time, Edith would not visit her friend in the woods. Even when the blue jays arrived, heralding the oncoming autumn long before the reddening of the leaves, even when the weight of farm work became rougher and heavier, she couldn't find a reason to go see the faun. Not even for a third wish.

There were other things to worry about. The lake had attracted plenty of attention for all the fish that had begun to land ashore in rotting droves, in heaped gleaming balustrades that hummed with black flies. The silver ring was never discovered, and Edie would never see it again. The dolorous stench festered, carried for miles on even the smallest breeze. Scientists from Minneapolis had been called in to try and explain why some fish normally found in saltwater were appearing in a freshwater lake of a landlocked state. Over time, it was concluded to be a stocking mishap (though no records were ever discovered, or even consulted), and permitted to be forgotten.

But life must continue, just as consequence must follow consequence, and the world wasn't going to stop for a Minnesota girl. The faun was true to her word. Every apple tree around the farm began to blossom and bear apples with an impossible rapidity. The fruits themselves were unusually hyperbolic in size and weight, bending the trees so that they resembled old men, and a bite into the rich flesh of one would yield the sense of fullness, regardless of how much one has already eaten.

For the first month, Edith's plan to attract the deer and other animals had worked – congregations of them returned after fleeing the fire, but where the prey go, predators follow; droves of wolves sent many away. It became dangerous to be outside, to gather firewood, take care of the farm animals, to walk to the outhouse. Nights were filled with their sibilant choirs.

For Edith, the nightmares only grew worse as the weeks progressed. She would wake up in her bed, sheets stained with cold sweat, but still she felt as though some piece of her, something intrinsic to her being, was still in the woods, dancing through the oaks and birches to strange, piping music. Dancing until the bones in her feet crumbled to splinters under strange constellations.

During the first day of snow, she watched the way her mother staggered from room to room as if in a dream, clutching her son close to her. She ran out all the things they had to do that day, and had small hope they would get everything done in one day, or one week. Mostly, when Edith had to go into town, she avoided bumping into the Calhouns, but it was difficult to ignore their haunted faces and broken voices.

So many unforeseen consequences to her dreams made her want to weep, but there wasn't time for that. She had to help her family, just as she had before. They were in trouble, but she knew a way out.

The sun was just breaking over the treeline, bathing everything in fire, when Edith slid out of bed to visit the faun one last time. Even with the windows shut tight she could still smell the mingling putrefaction of fish and apples; sweetness, meat, life, rot. She fell asleep with that smell in her lungs, and she dreamed she was dying, skin sloughing away from her bones like slush off the windows in February. She dreamed her parents were burying her in frozen ground. She had pounded on the coffin lid for them to stop, unheard.

The chores would wait. She left for the woods once more, bundled in her coat and hat, soft earthy brown like the eyes of a doe. She had in her hands a small box, carrying her mother's jewelry, heirlooms and tokens. Taken from its perch the day before. Her mother would ask what happened to it, and she'd come up with a lie on the spot. Her mother believed anything she said.

Late autumn had cleared the lindens of their leaves, leaving the grove skeletal, but hardly devoid of the sensation that it was alive, that it was still watching. Wolves sang in the distance – too far away or too close, the woods playing with the noise, making their placement indeterminate.

She looked around, hands clutching the pieces of her mother's jewelry she intended to use as bargaining chips. "Hello?"

Her hesitation dispersed the word, so she shouted it. "Where are you!?"

"Quiet, girl. I'm right here." The faun materialized from out of the lindens, shivering beneath her pelt. Small smile playing on her lips, though her body seemingly less than how it was. Her antlers were laden with many tiny trinkets, dripping honey amber. Tiny orange spiders scampered up and down her horns. Edith frowned; had the skogsrå always appeared so decrepit? The faun walked up to her, hunched and pensive. "You don't need to shout in my garden, I can hear you well enough. What are doing here, anyway, child? I suppose you've come back to gloat."

"Gloat?"

The faun shook her head, ornaments jingling like sacrificial bones. "Yes, of course you have. For only a third wish's payment, you truly dig deep into your pockets."

The girl frowned and fidgeted with her mother's jewelry. "A third wish?"

"You also seem very determined to aggravate me today. I've enjoyed the time we've had, quite a lot, in fact, but I'm not immune to anger. Giving me your life was the ultimate price for something as little as a wish, girl. I see you're trying to barter with something else, though. Wish I could say I was interested, I really do, but you cannot rescind an agreement. Maybe with some sprite child, but not with me."

The girl only stared, teeth biting down on the inside of her cheek until it hurt, until her mouth filled with the taste of pennies and salt. She figured asking the faun what she was talking about would make her angrier, so she kept silent. The faun reached under her furs and retrieved what looked like two thin birchwood flutes, tied at one end with a length of tanned leather.

"I'm tired, girl. The year drags hard on we who still live in the wild. Best you get back home."

"But...I wanted to..."

The faun's eyes glimmered like water on quartz. A vein of amber coursed down her forehead and dripped down her face, tracing her lips and chin. "There are worse things in the woods than wolves or bears, girl. Now go away." She turned, putting the twinned flute up to her lips, and as she played a threnody, or a dirge, that wove melancholy through the linden grove, the girl gladly left.

It didn't take long for Edith to guess what had happened. She had hoped it wasn't true, but all the possibilities pointed to it. There was no other explanation.

When she got home, Dena was milking the cows in the barn. She walked up behind her and slapped her face as hard as she could, knocking her sister off her chair and into the hay. The cow twitched and scurried away, knocking over the pail and sending milk into the hard dirt.

"What did you do!?"

Her sister stared up at her, terror gleaming in her eyes. Terror and perhaps triumph. Red was spreading on her cheek, her hair a tangled mess.

"She gave you a wish, *my wish*. What did you do with it?"

Her sister stood up, slowly, brushing hay off her dress. She hid her face, holding her cheek. "It's not yours, Edith, and it's not mine. I don't want the kinds of things you want, or the things you already have. I gave your wish to mother."

"What?"

Hurt and vicious, righteous fury in Dena's eyes, like a forest fire. "You heard me. I wanted you to stop this, just stop going out there and talking to that thing. It's not right. And I just wanted you to come back to our family."

The accusation hung in the air, charring everything, and for a moment, all Edith could feel was a dimly growing rage. She wanted to punch her sister in her teary face, thrash her, strangle her. "Everything that I did has been for my family!" she screamed. "I wanted my family to have better things, to be happy and prosperous!"

"We would have had all of that without that friend of yours! You don't think any of this has been without consequences? Did you think I

208

didn't have my suspicions when the Calhoun baby went missing? This isn't some childish fantasy, or a dream you can forget about! This is happening!"

"What the *hell* is going on in here?"

The doorway darkened, and their mother stood there, baby Johann on her hip. She looked up at the sky, grey as wet linen, looking for an answer. "I've just about had it with you two. We can't waste time. It's almost winter, and there's still so much we have to do, and no time to fucking waste it bickering like children. You're both adults now! Now get moving! Edie, get back in the house and see what you can do with that venison. Dena, pick up that bucket."

The two sisters muttered thin apologies to their mother and moved. Edith grabbed at her coat as she headed for the house, seething.

Behind her back, her mother said "*Det var droppen*…Really, Edith, sometimes you make me wish I'd never left Sweden."

A gust of wind blew over Edith's face, whipping her hair around her face. There was a thump, and baby Johann's screams reverberated off the barn. She spun on her heels. Her mother was gone.

She rushed over and picked up her baby brother and held him, stroking his head and trying to get him to hush.

The farm was silent. In the barn, there was only the cow, a pail that had been knocked over, reset on its bottom, but her sister was gone, as well. Payment paid in full.

And the wind blew like the dolorous piping of a birchwood *aulos*.


Joe Bellamy came to see her after Edith's fainting spell. He had little to say outside of the thin commiserations for her daughter's divorce, but prescribed some pills and a couple days without work. Sally made little effort trying to hide her disappointment, but promised she would stay with her as long as she wanted. Edith let the comment alone, knowing that her daughter will change her mind in time.

Whatever her daughter did, she was doing it for her family. That much Edith knew.

In the kitchen, Sally was mixing lemonade in a glass pitcher at the counter. Some of the blueberries that they'd picked yesterday spun at the top, spilling purple juice into the cyclone. When Edith walked in, Sally glanced up and gave a small smile. "How are you doing, mom?" she asked. "I was scared you'd broken something when you fell. Joe said he didn't see any broken bones or sprains, but you shouldn't take any chances."

Edith smiled and touched her daughter's shoulder, reminding herself she had a family of her own now, reminding herself it was still 1979. She grabbed her favorite mug, the blue one with a baby polar bear on it. "I'm okay, honey. Takes more than a fall to knock down a tough old bird like me. Are you and Mike okay?"

Sally clenched her jaw and tipped the pitcher over Edith's mug. "He's gone. He left a little while before Joe showed up. Asshole. He couldn't bother staying long enough to see if my own mother is okay. He said something about the store going into default so he just…I don't know what to do, mom."

Edith sighed, tapped her daughter's back. "You'll be okay. You're strong enough, Sally. Like a linden tree."

Sally just shook her head and breathed heavily. Edith stood with her a moment, sipped her lemonade, told Sally it didn't need so much sugar because the berries were already sweetening it. After Sally felt better, she walked out into the daylight.

On the porch, it was nice and gentle as satin. It was noon, late September, and the sky like a ceiling made of hydrangeas or pansies. Mabon, according to her new calendar, and the winds were unseasonably warm this year, not that that was anything to complain about. She fell into her rocking chair, watching a woolly bear caterpillar strut along the banister. The rusty band of its hair was wide, its black tips like simple cuticles. It would be a mild winter.

Around the house, the orchestra of siblings fighting or playing shattered the calm. Billy came running around the corner, clutching a bundle of fabric to her chest. Roger was behind her, pelting her with handfuls of leaves and sticks. "Stupid Billie, doesn't have any friends!" he yelled.

"No, get away from me!" Billie was smiling, but it was the kind of smile that treaded distress, wondering how far her brother might take his antics.

"You simmer down, kids," Edith said. "*Tagga ned.*"

"Gramma, save me!" Billie screamed, darting around the porch and up behind Edith's chair. Roger, seeing his prey had cheated and entered neutral territory, waved his hand and stalked off, kicking the heads off of sunflowers.

Edith grinned and reached behind the chair, tapping her granddaughter's sleeve. "What's that you've got there, Billy?"

"Just something," Billie said coyly, like giving a secret while trying to keep it a secret. She stepped around the chair, hiding her toy. "My friend gave it to me."

"Really? May I take a look?"

Her granddaughter, smiling, proffered the old doll up to her. Edith ran her fingers through the little twigs woven into the pale blonde hair and the hem of the white and blue dress soiled by dirt and lichen, but it was the simple red curve of the smile that made Edith's heart shrink in its confines. The smile that had carried her across the sea to Minnesota. The smile of a friend she gave away for a dream she regretted.

# Tarina Keväästä

There was no indication in the morning and noon hours of that cat-soft late February day in 1983 that the rest of the week was going to be as horrible as it was. When folks in western and central Minnesota woke up from a cool, newly-minted spring night, they only noticed the wide China blue surface of the sky, a gentle but insistent breeze murmuring through the aspens and conifers, and the way the sunlight bore fiery gold across the tall grasses, rivers, and woodlands like a platoon of royal bannermen. Snowmelt was filling up ditches and burying sidewalks, turning fields and plains into soggy marshland; both farmers and urbanites were cleaning up what the snow left, replenishing their livelihoods; patches of lupins and bluebells were already popping up along roadsides, telling everyone who saw them that they wouldn't have to worry about the nasty old ice again for another eight or nine months.

An hour until noon, and Michelle Cophen began her second week at the National Weather Service station in St. Paul by drowning the butterflies in her stomach with hard black coffee, knowing full well that it was the last thing she needed. It could only excite her nerves, not stifle them.

So far, everything had been going just fine. Nothing wonderful, nothing terrible, which was exactly what she had been hoping for once she'd received her degree. For her, contentment could only ever be achieved when things were in that wonderful spot between absolutely terrific and wholly awful.

But sweat was beading on her brow and her hands were shaking. You're being childish, she accosted herself, stupid and childish. Sighing in the station room, she tried to focus on the computer monitors and readouts; she already knew how to comprehend the messes of numbers and symbols, so she fed the data into her own computer terminal. This information would later be released for national syndication.

This was only Michelle's second job – she liked working at the Broken Paddle Hotel a lot less than this, practically danced out the door on her last day – so there were naturally lessons she hadn't yet learned to consider. First and foremost, that you can still accurately perform your job's tasks and still bungle everything up.

Michelle's coworker had neglected to inform her that, out of boredom, he'd been checking the data for the Limited Fine-Mesh Model from the past two months, and had forgotten to correct it before clocking out. So, Michelle was working with a mixture of *current* and *outdated* info when she began feeding it into her computer.

But the blame couldn't only be traced to Miss Cophen; the radar system itself had failed to scan the cold air cell that was rapidly developing over Manitoba, accelerating like a cruise missile as it slipped into a low-pressure zone. At noon, it was only thirty miles across, not even close to the system's sight. It traveled like a lumberjack's arcing chop straight downward, cleaving through the U.S.-Canada border, relentless and hungry, gorging on the flat lands and strengthening on conquest. Its wake brought awe and confusion as it buried the springtide, the kind of awe and confusion that was traced in underlying terror.

In a matter of minutes, many roads and highways – such as I-94 – had become a pale ribbon of anxious, frustrated people.


Tom Brody flicked the last couple drops of Pabst Blue Ribbon out of the can with his tongue and tossed it into the backseat. It was either dumb luck or his own breed of Brody stubbornness that made sure he had a twelve-pack in the passenger seat of his Chevy, and good thing, too. He sat back and squinted through the passenger window at an old green Lincoln in the other lane; all he could do since the only other thing he could see was the big truck ahead of him, or at least its rear lights. Two red eyes peering back at him from all that white.

Betty Boop was staring at him from the corner of the dashboard. All she had on was a grass skirt, lei necklace and a ukulele to cover herself. Paint was missing from her right eye so it looked like she had a cataract. He gave her a smart tap and her hips waggled.

"Don't think that's regulation attire for this, Betty. Can't dock you points for trying, though."

Damn freak of nature, he decided, damn stroke of ill fortune. Tom had woken up that day in his boat, somehow stirred out of the cottony hell of his cousin's moonshine by the breeze or the sunlight. He'd been in there all night, covered up in so many layers of wool clothing. He'd been doing his best to meet his allotment of pike and perch and damning the DNR and what they say his allotment ought to be. He supposed that by two in the afternoon he'd be on his way to the Blue Bear Bar & Grill to sell his catch; by four-thirty he'd still be haggling with Rudy's little shit of a son over payment. He didn't expect a case of gold, but that's what it seemed to take to pay the utilities these days.

Beer was getting expensive, too. Not like it used to be. There used to be a whole string of little honkeytonks around here in the sixties that would sell a whole mug of lager for eighty cents. All of them gone now, swept away by the '74 recession and Ford's half-assed attempts to clear up the inflation. These days, he'd had to tranquilize that monkey on his back by going to Charlie's House in town to get a six-pack for nine bucks.

Tom sighed and reached over for another beer. He didn't pop the tab, just sat with it in his lap, tapping his fingers against the cool aluminum. The heater was on, but the beer was still warmer than the air.

It just came out of nowhere. While Tom had finished business in town, it was pulling up to six in the afternoon, and there were only a few cirrus clouds looking like stray bits of cotton torn out of a pillow. By the time he'd reached the freeway, the sky had filled up, swelled, and fat drops of rain began dotting the windshield. As the evening cooled, that rain turned to a slushy snow mixture, falling in sheets so thick that using the headlights would be futile. Soon enough, the trees along the freeway became obscured and he'd had to use the truck ahead of him as a landmark, a safety marker.

Some safety marker, he ruminated as he tapped a Reba McEntire song on his beer. It's easy to delude yourself into thinking you're safe when you were stuck on the freeway along with dozens of other drivers too eager to get home. Too easy to think you still had a chance before the shit really hit the fan.

An apt axiom says that it's better to get home late than to not get home at all. Tom grunted and glanced into the rearview mirror. Salt and pepper hair, heavy stubble, the different odd jobs he'd had throughout his life hardening his skin and eyes. He looked like an old muskrat, a bit worried the he might not make it home to his burrow tonight.

Betty gave him a sidelong glance while she continued to sachet, and he pretended it was more than just paint in her plastic eyes.


She could have picked any other day. Any other day of the full week he'd managed to get off from his foreman would have been just fine. But someone's luck – his, hers, or someone else's on this godforsaken freeway – didn't stretch as far as that, and he dared another couple of inches closer to the Silverado's back bumper.

But Jill was determined that today was the day she wanted to go see her mother at St. Mary's Hospital in Minneapolis. They were relieved to hear from the doctor that it had been nothing serious, but some miniature voice in Isaac's head told him that that made the current situation all the more aggravating.

"Is it still spring, dad?"

"According to the calendar, it still is, but I don't think Mother Nature got the message."

Jill was fiddling with the radio, trying to find a station that was offering more than the same weather reports. "Would you turn on the heater?" she said.

"It *is* on, Jill."

"No, it's not. It's freezing in here. I can see there's no condensation on the glass."

"Yeah, the slush is turning into ice. It's going to take a while for the heater to kick in."

"Then don't you think you should have started it earlier?"

Isaac sighed, made sure she heard him, knew it was the kind of sound that grated on her. "Yes, frankly, I do. Now would you just pick a damn station already?"

She gave him the briefest of glares, her green eyes bright with rage beneath her brunette hair. Those eyes used to make him feel bad whenever they got into it, but they'd been married long enough that that look didn't do anything for him anymore. When Isaac realized that, a small smile flickered on his lips, before the situation doused it.

It was bad. Worse than most blizzards he'd witnessed down in the Twin Cities. He supposed he had a good bit of luck, in the sense that he had a job that was close to home, and he didn't get out much anyway so most snowstorms just howled over their heads, except for when the pipes decided to freeze up. It was an altogether different beast, he realized, being away from the safety of your home, the roads that were wet before now frozen over, and they were totally blind. Being able to see only five or so feet in front of him with low beams, that distance cut in half with the headlights on. Uncertainty pockmarked every decision he didn't think he'd had to make tonight.

Jill finally settled on a radio station and sat back, bitter scowl on her face that always reminded him of a mouse. It was never a secret in either of their families that when they recited their nuptials that she was marrying down; it was almost like some bastardized fairytale, and he supposed that's what had been fun about it, in the beginning. She was the silver child to a family of dentists and he was the underachieving offspring of the foreman of the county sanitation department. Real Dickens-meets-Bronte kind of shit.

Truthfully, the scope of it didn't hit him until Jill started showing. He wasn't merely married, he was honest-to-goodness 'til-death-do-we-part *married*, with a kid on the way. It didn't strike him what he had, how fragile it was, and how every single thing could be a danger until he saw her sitting in the hospital bed with their son swaddled in a minty green cloth.

Jill said, "See if you can pass them up here, Isaac."

He looked at her, but she was resolutely staring at the window. "Are you nuts? We'd be lucky to get this wreck of mine going even if they could get out of the way."

"There's a clear path! Can't you just –"

"No, I can't just! It's too dangerous, Jill!"

"Oh, godammit, Isaac." She huffed, glaring.

Behind him, their son's little voice said "Would you two stop fighting?"

Jill put on her costume smile, angled her head and said "Daddy and me aren't fighting, honey. We're just having a discussion about things."

Isaac smiled at his son in the rearview mirror. "That's right. Mommy and daddy like having *discussions* because it makes a bad day seem even worse."

Jill could have done in the whole bear population of the Midwest with the expression she gave him, but Isaac didn't see it. Somewhere in the evening, the bleating of a car horn sounded, and they both looked through the windshield, deer-eyed. A series of sharp honks, an engine gunned to its limit, and then the shriek of metal grating against metal before a thunderous boom.

"What was *that*?" Jodie said in the back. He'd slipped out of his seatbelt and sat up on his knees, hands and nose pressed against the window, trying to peer through the icy glaze outside. Jill turned to look at Isaac, looking back at her, both quiet and secretly content to stay put.

"Think your mom can wait a bit, Jill?"

"Yeah, I think so," she said, and she wiped away a veil of sweat he hadn't noticed before.

From the back seat, Jodie wanted to rub his nose or rub his hands together so fast until they were warm again. He really wanted to, but he felt that if he took his eyes off of whatever he was looking at beyond the window, it might go away. It was a blur – no, that wasn't the right word for it, but he didn't know what else to call it. The snow was falling, but at a spot just in front of him, the snow was falling *around* something, and where it was supposed to fall the fat flakes were moving in different directions.

In the other lane, Sean Steeds was trying to scratch an itch by doing the worst thing he possibly could do; ignore it completely. While the boy was straining in his seat to see the wreckage, Sean adjusted his half-frame spectacles and feigned ignorance to what the bad nervy feeling in his guts was supposed to mean.

A little longer, he told himself. Once you're in Maple Country, you can take that baggie out and enjoy that soft banana taste in your mouth, fuzzy euphoria filling your head that makes you think of pussy and tequila…but not before, never before. Don't fuck this up, too.

"Did you see that, dad?"

Sean brushed away a curtain of dark blonde hair that fell across his spectacles. "Yeah."

His son waited before continuing the conversation; that's what he hated most about the boy, truth be told. He was so much like his mother, so soft and hesitant. Probably would have grown up to be just like her, if

Sean hadn't intervened. Once they were in Canada, there wasn't nothing she could do about it, either.

"What do you think happened?"

Venting frustration through his nostrils, he said, "I don't know. Dumbass probably thought he could play Mr. Hero and got himself more than he bargained for. This snow screws up your sense of place – he must have thought he was closer to the center line than he really was, so he must have been inching to the right. He jolted into that semi there, which made him start to fishtail on the ice, and he went right into the ditch. Wham!"

His son coughed into the sleeve of his yellow shirt and said "Are they okay?"

"How'n hell should I know? Look, just sit there and don't move. You're makin' me nervous."

The boy frowned and sat back in his seat. At least he did what he was told. Sean could tell by the burn on his cheeks and the runny nose that the boy was getting a cold. Not much he could do about that, not until they crossed the border, at least.

His eyes kept darting to the glove compartment – he felt he could just about see the little bag inside, full of powdery gold and tied off at the end with a rubber band. Even his sweat started to smell like bananas, though he couldn't be sure of that.

It had been going so well; that's what hurt him the most, that everything was going so *perfect* before this storm blew in just as he was blowing out. There's nothing more appealing than the intermediary periods between getting the job and getting it done – he ruminated on that little lie, wishing his predecessor, a big Irishman who called himself "Bear," could have seen him a week ago, a bleached blonde on each arm outside the nightclub, double that in the gold medal suite at the Daisy Hotel up in Montreal, and no church would ever want that choirboy back if they found out what those women did to him, did for him. No cheap-ass bottom-of-the-barrel beer that night, just top of the line wine and tequila, and it all looked the same coming back up anyway.

He would have laughed in Bear's face, would have explained as pretentiously as he could how he had taken Bear's mediocre hundred-dollar hustle, given it a good kick in the ass, and built it up into an international enterprise that raked in more in a night than what they'd made in three years. If Bear wasn't lying at the bottom of a lake in Chattanooga with his feet tied to a truck engine, Sean Steeds would have made it all seem as big as it was. A glorious week spent sampling the local wares in wonderful Montreal before he had to head back down into the states. Down to Chicago to accept another shipment of coke which another group brought in from Bolivia. The feds would be watching the airports by now, so they'd had to learn to get clever.

And that was when the cake started to rot. He must have left something behind, a plane ticket or receipt that had slipped past his notice, something that his wife had found in her skulking. He had to give her credit for connecting the dots so fast, though it made him no less chagrined during their confrontation.

She thought she could hide away his son from him. Nothin' doin'. He reminded her how idiotic a decision she'd made, and again when she tried to talk back to him, and then he'd taken his son away from her. A dubious action, now that he'd had the time to reconsider the past twenty-four hours over and over again while stranded here with a hundred Midwestern idiots.

A sharp knock at his window jolted him, and he just about pissed his pants. A big man in an officer's uniform stood there looking in on him, big badge emblazoned on a pine tree, close enough to see the fine black stubble on his jawline. Sean took a deep breath – burnt sugar – and rolled the window down. The night rushed in.

"Yeah?" he asked.

"You folks alright over here? You probably noticed what happened just around the corner."

Sean followed the man's gesture toward the ditch, the upturned headlights. "Yeah, officer, we did. Real bad luck."

The officer had hickory skin and a nervous smile, real bright teeth like snow caps. "Ain't that the truth, for all of us out here. Just thought I'd do some checking up on everybody, make sure everything's alright."

Sean had to clear his throat before saying "Well, thanks, buddy. We really appreciate it. Don't we, kid?"

Before the cop was even able to lean in and glance at his son, his head snapped around to look at the lane behind Sean's yellow Coup. All the joviality that had been there was gone. As he darted away to be swallowed up by Sean's taillights, Sean heard a sound tear through the night. At first, he thought it was the metallic shriek of another car ramming up against another, but then it dropped in pitch, and he recognized it as a scream.

Everything happened in quick succession – there was the unmistakable *pop-pop-pop* of small arms fire, hurried shouting and screams, a tumultuous chaos that was quickly opening up. Sean whipped his head around, trying and failing to see anything but the rippled layer of ice on the windshield.

He couldn't take it anymore. The pang in his stomach echoed through the webwork of veins and arteries, made his skin burn. There was no way to know how they found him, or even who they were, but sure as shit they found him out. He leaned over and wrenched open the glove compartment, fingers shaking when he took out the little baggie and the shiny .38 next to it. Safety policy, and he was glad to have it.

The boy's eyes went wide. "Daddy, what's going on?"

The driver's side window was facing the ditch, and beyond it was a congregation of poplar and balsam leading into the night. "Alright, champ…when I say go, we're gonna get out of the car and rocket straight for those trees, okay? You're gonna stay right by my side, okay?"

The boy's mouth was a dark circle. "Huh? I don't wanna go out there…"

Sean already had the door open before he shouted "Now!" His shoes were pounding snow so hard it sounded like he was running on potato chips, and the wind immediately embraced him.

Not far away, a scruffy-looking man held up a hand and hollered. "Hey, buddy, what's going on?"

Sean scanned him with his pistol, and the man flinched away, ducking behind the nearest vehicle. Had to be one of them, Sean thought, some agent in civilian clothes. It was how they operated.

There was a snowdrift of some two feet at the ditch, and he made a good leap of it – good, but miscalculated; the angle was steeper than he expected and he slid on his back, the slush wetting the back of his jeans and Chambray shirt, collecting in his shoes.

The gunshots weren't any closer, but there certainly were enough of them to make the fine hair on the back of his neck stand at attention. He turned back only once to see if his son was keeping up, and when he did, he saw all the lights from the trapped vehicles caught by the falling snow, creating a brightly hellish horizon. Like a muggy evening in Los Angeles. He didn't see the boy; probably still fumbling around the hood of the car.

Screw it. The boy would keep up if he really wanted to. Sean slipped unnoticed into the trees.


Sergeant Neil Walker didn't know what he was seeing. The woman was leaning out of the window of her truck, too far to make it seem like she was merely leaning. She looked like she was levitating, most of her torso hovering so far across the open window she was casting a blue shadow over the snow, mouth working in total silence, the next car's taillights catching in her eyes. Blood was pooling in the snow beneath her, steam rising and dancing like reveling ghosts.

Neil Walker, sergeant of the Douglas County police department for eleven years, had not been exempt from seeing some terrible things. Assaults, domestic battery, tragic accidents. A drunk driver had rammed into a bull moose at fifty miles an hour – the moose's body was lying in a shattered mess in the road, while the decapitated head was still attached to the windshield, its antlers impaling the driver. One very dry spring, he was called to the Native school on the edge of the county after reports of kids being reckless with fires. He found no kids, but he did see a number of small spheres floating there, just floating less than a foot or so above the ground. Ten seconds later, one of the lights flared to a brilliant light – Neil remembered thinking of ghosts and stars – and his partner at the time, Wyatt Sebastian, stumbled a few feet before falling into the tall grass, dead.

Months later, he learned about ball lightning, perused what little research there was about the phenomena. It didn't stop the dreams.

Those things he could compartmentalize, stick off to the side and observe from a distance, after the craziness had died down. He could look to books or papers, if not to completely excise it from his mind, at least rationalize it.

There was no way he could rationalize this. He pulled his sidearm from its holster, tried to remember the last eleven years and all it taught him but he was coming up blank – the woman was hanging in the air, and from the sounds carried on the wind, was being eaten alive.

Sergeant Walker leveled his pistol at a point above the woman, squinted, trying to see the thing that was gripping her. There was something wrong with the way the snow was falling – it was refracted, as if there was a mass of glass there.

There was a lot of blood, too much for the woman's survival to be remotely possible. But Neil didn't want to think about that. He brought up his gun—

Something smashed into him from the side, driving him down into the slush. The suddenness of the attack tore away his breath, but his gun still hung onto his hand by the grace of his thumb.

Hard ice crunched against his face and sloshed into his collar – he tried to get up but the thing that gave him a quarterback slam felt as though it was still on top of him, driving him deeper into the slushy road.

He couldn't see it, but he could certainly feel it, something dry and cold pawing at him. A bitter wind whispered in his ears. He beat at the unseen thing with his fists and he knew he was striking something solid, something that was there, but it looked like his fists were just stopping in midair.

*It* grabbed his free hand and wrenched it to the side – it felt like his hand had plunged into an icebox. And then the pain, bright and volcanic, shooting all the way up to this elbow. Like splintered glass grinding, chewing on his hand, and Neil felt his own blood spatter his face.

He managed to get control of his handgun, wedged between him and his unseen attacker. He angled the barrel up and pulled the trigger, feeling the force jolt his wrist and slam against his stomach.

Chips of ice pelted him like shrapnel. Spiderline cracks like calved ice appeared in the air above him, and the thing paused gnawing on his hand long enough for Neil to get off another shot. The weight left him, vanished. There was only a gust of wind that blew snow in his face.

He managed to stand up – every part of him felt coiled, shaking, like summer thunder about to strike. His hand looked like a piece of mangled steak, the flesh of his fingers peeled off so that the pallid peaks of bone were showing through in some spots. He stuffed his hand into his armpit and tried to push the pain out of his mind. He turned back to the woman. She was now lying face-first in the bloody snow, a drift already forming over her.

Glass shattered somewhere. What was happening?

Everything started out just fine, how a fine spring day was supposed to. Neil woke up in bed and the painter he'd met over in Asenath surprised him by kissing him on the mouth, coffee and cherries, and Neil twined his hands in the man's long black hair. Sunlight was streaming in from the window, closed because spring at Neil's house meant droves of mosquitos to deter any hope of cool air, forging them together until Neil had to get to work.

Paul had received a call from a family down south, asking to purchase a couple of his pieces, and he was going to drive down there this afternoon. Neil thought about that, wondered if Paul was somewhere in this mess. If the freeway was paralyzed, then what about the other routes that saw less travel, or were more remote? Dread filled up the spaces where the physical agony of his ruined hand couldn't go.

Backup. Reinforcements. Neil turned back to look for his cruiser, somewhere in the distance past the tractor trailer that flipped over and created the pileup that paralyzed traffic. Somewhere that was covered in icy slush.

No, bad idea. Neil wasn't going to risk bringing in more vehicles to get stuck out here, calling in armed men who had no idea what was going on. Not his call. And what was he going to say to explain it?

A whole family seemed to be screaming not far away, a child's desperate terror. Neil began running.


When the skinny blond man (obviously an out-of-towner, what with that shirt and snappy haircut and all) levelled that squirrel-puncher at him, Tom Brody felt like he was in two places at once; back home just outside of Asenath, years ago while his parents were still alive, and standing right here in the middle of a frozen-over I-94, a step away from wetting himself. He went back to his car, concerned that the order which civilization and modern social mores had brought had begun to dissolve.

After those first shots, he'd figured it'd been some frustrated asshole letting loose on the side of the road. Could be a communist vanguard, although, in spite of all the made-for-TV movies attesting to the point, he doubted that the soviets would start the revolution on a Minnesota freeway in the middle of spring.

Regardless, the blond man had sealed the deal, far as Tom was concerned; the moment he got back into his Ford, he reached below the seats in the back and pulled out his 30-30. He'd kept it there since he'd had to put down a deer he'd hit three days ago, and he was thankful for his laziness.

Fine time to start listening to little voices, Betty said with her mismatched eyes. He rocked the car when he exited, and she gave a little shimmy that made him feel a little better. Somewhere, not too far away, a window shattered.

Tom stumbled onto one knee, his gut reminding him of times that were decades and a hundred pounds ago. He fumbled out a couple rounds, jamming them into the breech. He had to wipe away all the melted snow from his face every five seconds and swore each time, but Tom grew up in the fraternity of Brody hunters, weaned on autumns and winters in the Brody hunting cabin over in Waseca. Snow was just snow.

There had to be someone around here trying to set order to all of this. Tom peered into the cold night and saw what Sean Steeds had seen, the bright corona of all those vehicles stretched out along the freeway, so many people stranded and wanting. Some were crying for help, angrily shouting, screaming.

One so close that Tom gasped. It was shrill and piercing, the kind of thing he expected sailors would hear in a great gale. He moved toward it.

If pressed, Tom would say he'd led a sheltered life – he was drafted into Nam, but much of his time was spent onboard a patrol vessel, going up and down the coast looking for Vietcong forces or for downed fighter pilots, with hardly any gunfire support. In the seventies, he was transferred to the East German border, close enough to have a staring contest with the Russian forces there. Once they found out *nobody* wanted to be there, Tom and his friends traded with some of them; mostly chewing gum, cigarettes, and porno. Living in the sticks brought its own special snarling faces around the corner, some smelling of booze and aftershave, some grinning while wearing snappy suits. But it was a sheltered life.

Tom saw a little yellow Chevy with one of the rear doors open, its wipers working like mad. Behind the windshield was a portrait of a family in mortal horror, father and mother throwing punches at something that wasn't there. A little boy was hanging onto the back of a seat, half of his body floating in the air.

The sounds the boy was making brought Tom back to some muggy day in 1970 when one of his fellow sailors had his arm caught in a piston, and how they couldn't halt the mechanism a full six minutes later. Agony congealed, liquefied, spread apart. That young man was howling the whole time, until they'd given him enough morphine to stop his heart. The boy was making the exact same sounds.

Tom felt his body relax, edges smoothed down, took aim, and fired.

In a fraction of a moment, he thought he'd hit the boy, the way he dropped out of the air and thumped against the car. But the bullet struck something solid. He saw something in the air crack apart and reveal an outline of something hunched, something big and threatening.

Tom chambered another round and fired at where the crack was most definitive. Ice splintered and jangled along the frozen snow, and Tom saw the shape reel away, weaving between the vehicles until it was lost to the night. The wind chittered.

The father got around the side of the car and met his wife as she knelt by their son, already wiping away the blood on his leg. The boy's pants seemed pretty shredded and his legs were torn up, but he wasn't bleeding as bad as he could be, far as Tom could see. The father stared at him as he got closer, his eyes sighting the rifle in his hands.

Tom held the gun close to his chest and pointed it up to the sky. Not thinking of anything else to say, he straightened up and said "You folks need any help?"

There were others.

The traffic backup comprised a stretch of some five and a half miles along I-94, and in each vehicle, life with its own promise and direction. Evening brought workers who were returning from their jobs down in St. Cloud or up in Fergus Falls or Moorhead; couples or friends heading to their special places; loners who either have somewhere or nowhere to go and who just like the smell of the land and the air at night.

Approximately two hundred people were there when the storm struck, and about fifty more showed up by the time the snow really got in. When the initial attacks began, some were equipped to defend themselves, and their confusion – compounded by their concept of good intentions – led to many people getting shot by accident. Some grouped together, holing up in their vehicles to wait out the night.

Most didn't; most just wanted to get the hell out of there by any means available. Get home. Get to safety.

What was left of them was buried under the falling snow, secrets to be found some other day.

Sean Steeds bounced painfully off another conifer. Snow leapt off of its branches to cover him and make his clothes even wetter. He was convinced that the FBI wouldn't hunt him down through the forest at night (The FBI had to be the ones who engineered the chaos back there, all of it a wild ruse just to get to him. How clever. Who would ever notice if someone would vanish without a trace under the government's

231

stern hand under the guise of some shootout?) The chill was biting into him now, the kind of teeth-numbing cold that was deeper than the snow or the ice.

When he got to the trunk of a particularly thin silver birch, Sean stopped to catch his breath. He hadn't had to run like this since high school Track & Field. The sounds of gunfire and honking car horns were coming from all directions, hovering all around him in a cloud; the trees were playing with the noises and throwing them back in jumbled pieces.

His son wasn't around, either. Shame. Sean actually liked the kid, but there was no way he could go searching for him. The feds would take him in, poison his thinking. Lost cause.

Now would be a perfect time to get that bag out and calm down, he thought. He leaned up against the smooth bark, felt its coolness on his skin, alleviating the hot spasms under his flesh. He dug out the baggie and fumbled off the rubber band. He sniffled, wiped his nose and then his face when melted snow got in his eyes.

Something under the snow – a displaced root, a hunk of ice – bumped against his shin when he tried to get more comfortable. He caught his balance but the baggie spilled open, and he watched in benumbed shock as the powder disappeared into the snow.

"No..." He gasped, and the breeze felt like it blew right down his throat. "No, no, no..." He bent into the drift, put his whole body under the snow while he scratched and scrabbled at the two hundred dollars of uncut. He grabbed handfuls and put his face into it, hoping that some of it would bring him that calm floaty feeling he needed. There was no floaty feeling, just cold, just ice particles offending his sinuses, sending him into a fit of sneezing.

"Fuck, man." His nose dribbling, outwardly crying now, Sean Steeds smacked the tree with his fist, punched it until his hand bled and the dull *thocking* noise faded away. He sat down, leaning against the trunk of the tree and becoming aware of the disgusting sensation of the fabric in his sodden soles tearing away underneath his toes. The night was so clear; he could make out a couple stars behind the scaffolding of branches, leaves and needles making mournful whispers.

The night was whispering too loudly, too closely, for Sean to settle down. His nerves were so jangled, he realized, that he was starting to see the snow falling at funny angles.


"Sorry about that, fella," Neil said, practically shouted over the wind. He stood in a pool of light, trying to keep one eye on the small party that had found him and another on any changes in the way the snow was falling.

Tom Brody wiped his face and smiled – Neil thought he looked a bit like an otter when he did, the way his moustache unfurled and his cheeks hid his eyes. "Don't mention it, buddy. Would'a done the same in your position."

"Really?"

"Hell no, but I feel better knowing there's two of us out here can shoot."

When Tom and the family in his tow appeared around the corner, they just about surprised Neil out of his skin. Tom had his rifle shouldered and ready to fire; Neil instinctively pulled up his service pistol and fired off a round that, thankfully, went wide. The bullet threw up a cloud of snow at a nearby snowdrift, and Neil felt an extra flavor of stupid. In spite of the faux pas, they recognized his badge and decided to follow him.

They asked him where they had to go. No other option came to him other than his own cruiser; it wasn't any more concealed or armored than any other vehicle here, but there was the radio, and the tools in the trunk. Medical supplies in the glove compartment.

He had to get these folks out of here. That was the important thing, everything afterward was superfluous. He didn't want to think about what was happening.

"You got a notion where we're going, officer?"

"My cruiser," Neil said. "My cruiser isn't too far from here. Got some supplies that we'll need, get some heat, too. Wait it out."

"My son needs bandages," the woman said, busy enough wiping snow off her son's face and her own. Neil felt she was handling this pretty well. "His legs are still bleeding."

"There's bandages in the squad car, I promise."

Neil didn't know if there were bandages in there, but surely a bit of hope outweighed the worry. There was an owlish screech in the distance, and he paused while the hairs on his arms gave a little jump. Sounded human to him, but then, so did the wind tonight. He heard furtive whisperings at his back, but that could have been the night as well. He put half a dozen cars in his sights before he was convinced they were good to go.

The man with the gun, he thought he heard him say Tom, stepped up to his side, sweeping the muzzle of his rifle between the vehicles. "What's going on here, officer?"

"I have no clue, sir. I really don't. Wait, what makes you think I'd know?"

Tom sniffed and drew his lips into a small grin. "Oh, come on, man. Isn't there some old Indian legend or folk story that has these things in 'em? There's gotta be, ain't there? What're they called...manitous or something?"

Neil scoffed and rolled his eyes. Man didn't know what he was talking about. Truthfully, though, Neil didn't really know. He never knew his grandparents, and if his father knew anything about their cultural beliefs, he kept it to himself.

Where was the cruiser? Already, half a foot of snow covered the road, growing by the second, threatening to block out the lights and remove anything they could use as a landmark. There was an ambulance in the other lane, its lights flashing in vain attention, but there was no other vehicle to tell apart from all the lighted mounds of snow. Neil was in awe of this storm, how hardly anything at all preceded its arrival, and when it arrived it shut down everything. And the things that were attacking everyone – did they come with the storm, or have they always been here, hiding until the conditions were right?

Neil rounded the corner past an old van and his foot went through something red. He looked down and moaned – there was no other reaction he could have made to properly elicit how he felt when he saw it.

It had been a child, without identity with the head missing, a layer of snow accumulating over the small body. At first glance, Neil thought its right arm was curled under the body, but he realized that was missing as well. There was blood on the yellow Coup above him.

He started to tell them all to wait up a moment when the mother rounded the corner and screamed. The father said "Oh, Christ" and the boy said something Neil couldn't hear.

"Jodie, don't you look at it," the father said, covering all of his son's face with his palm. The look on the boy's face before it was obscured told Neil that the briefest glimpses can convey everything that needs to be told, and a father's defensive hand doesn't mean much in a situation like this.

"Let's keep going," Neil said, motioning with his pistol, but the others weren't moving. They were congregating around the mess.

"Goddamn," the father said. His hand was still clamped on his son's face.

The mother had slipped behind the Coup to vomit. She came back wiping her mouth and gasping for air. "Isaac, what's going on? We have to get Jodie to a hospital."

"Ma'am, we need to get—"

She rounded on him, eyes so big that he could see them glinting in the snowlight, reflections of reflections and filled with rage. "Why aren't you doing anything to *help*? How come there aren't any other cops out here trying to save anyone?"

Neil held up his hands. "Listen! We can stay here and bark at each other until those things come and get us, or we can get out of this storm and into some shelter!"

The man with the rifle sniffed at that. "Yeah? Don't think there's much shelter in all of this shit, buddy. Those things seem like they can tear right through a car like a sardine can."

"This isn't a discussion, sir. I know where we're going, and we're going to follow me. Now let's move it."

"Look, just relax, officer," the father said. "We're all just—"

Neil had enough time to see a shine of apprehension in the father's – Isaac's – eyes before he was thrown to the side, the boy hurled out of his

236

grasp. The mother let out a choked squeal and Tom gave a shout before misfiring into the air. Isaac was screaming and Neil watched as he writhed into the snow like he was on fire; something was tearing into his stomach and chest, painting the snow red.

Neil aimed and fired, and Tom fired off a round from his rifle. The bullets chipped off hunks of ice, making bright jagged wells. Isaac's blood was painting a rough outline of what Neil supposed was the thing's face, all sharp angles, reflecting and refracting its own menace.

They filled the air with gunfire. Ice rained over the snowdrifts but the thing wouldn't go down. Blood was spraying in a broad dark jet, oxygen-rich and in spite of what he knew about arterial spray, he didn't want to believe that the man was beyond any help. There was still a goddamn chance.

A sharper scream stole his attention. The woman was kneeling down over her son, shielding him, the back of her shirt coming away in lacy wet strips. Neil didn't know how many bullets he had left but he fired until the thing got up and skittered away, a low howling wind trailing it. A large dent suddenly appeared in a truck's side, scraped as if by steel wool.

Just then, Tom Brody gave a wheezy shout, and Neil watched another of the things carve a chunk out of the man's waist before he fired the rifle and hurled the thing backward.

His hand was stinging like a bitch. You'd think the cold would have provided succor from the pain, but it only amplified it. There was no hope getting to the cruiser. They needed something much closer, needed it now. In the tumult, he spied a big red-and-white vehicle lying on its side off the road like a dead beetle.

"Get in that ambulance!" Neil shouted. "Get down there and get in the fucking ambulance. Now!" His pistol felt lighter than it did a moment ago, and he knew he didn't have much left in the clip. A couple, if even that.

Luckily, they listened. Jill appeared to deliberate with herself about who she should try to carry, her son or her husband, when Isaac stood up and urged her forward, the whole of his blue jeans stained black in the dimming light; Tom Brody was doing a full day's work trying to heft himself toward the ditch, keeping his insides where they ought to be with one arm.

What a shitstorm, Neil thought. He wiped his face and kept his eyes on the air around the group. Jill gave him a desperate look as she passed, her eyes so stark against the blood on her face, like dew on a forest red cap, and an unreasoning pang of guilt hit him, guilt and shame.

Blood was streaked along the side of the ambulance, leading into the woods. We're not going to make it through this, he thought to himself. Almost said it aloud, but he didn't think speaking it would be any help to anyone. Better to keep that tucked away.

Tom gave him a small grin as he strode past. "Now I know how the deer feel every autumn." He gave a garrulous, wincing chuckle, but Neil didn't laugh. After they'd all made it down, Neil took a step into the ditch. The snow rose up well above his shins, and the bottom four inches felt like he'd stepped into a milkshake.

The group was lingering at the ambulance's rear doors, kneeling or shifting glances between them and the shadows around the woods. "How do we get it open?" the boy whispered, and Neil's heart sank; snow blocked the lower door from opening up, but the top one was bare. The doors might still be locked from the inside. Neil went over and kicked apart the ice, hoping that the first responders had been just careless enough, or the crash might have jostled it apart. He leaned down, straining the last shred of hope he had that it would work, and unjammed the upper door.

The interior was lit in pale yellow light, thrown back by scattered instruments and emergency equipment. A gurney was lying at an awkward angle near the entrance until Neil reached in and dislodged it with a loud clatter.

He pulled out, looking up at everyone. Isaac's wounds made him the top priority, but the truth was that everybody was bleeding. He motioned for them to crouch down.

"Go on, Isaac," Jill said, pushing her husband forward. He groaned and clutched at his stomach, but he made it down to his knees beside Neil. He looked at his son and gave a small smile.

He said "You're going to be alright, aren't you, Jodie? You're going to be strong for your parents, right?"

The boy was crying, but he quietly nodded. Neil saw he wanted to hug his dad, but Isaac was already shuffling around to get through the door headfirst. "You might have to give that door another kick, officer," he said with a little champagne-colored grin, "I don't know if I can make it in by my—"

For a moment, Neil thought whatever Isaac was going to say had just slipped out of its socket, the words there but the thought derailed. Then, Isaac's leg jolted up and his body lurched backward. His chin knocked against the bottom door and his body hit the snow hard. The thing that had him began dragging him back, the frozen snow crunching beneath and, Neil realized, inside of him.

"Fuck!" Tom shouted. He fired round after round into the night. Some struck their mark, but Isaac's body faltered and veered sideways, crunching and flailing, until it vanished into the trees. A red stain like an ugly finger drawing left a path. Jill began to scream and dashed for her husband; Neil attempted to grab her but her shirt slipped out of his grasp, and then she was just a receding form between the trees.

"Son of a bitch! Get in the ambulance!" Neil shouted. A feeling of loss seemed to pull him down, weight on his bones.

Tom was firing his rifle without hesitation or aim, just pulling the trigger on any shadow he didn't like. Jodie was screaming now, the trees bouncing back the sound and amplifying it a hundred times over. Neil grabbed the boy and tried to shunt him toward the door, but Jodie was putting up too much of a fight, desperate to get to his parents. They had left him here in the cold and the darkness, and he wanted out. Before the boy could get far, Tom reached out and caught him by the elbow, kicking up a string of curses.

The snow around them changed, whirled about in a small gust and then was thrown apart, as if something ran through it. Like wolves, Neil thought; they hunt in packs, make ambushing attacks and then scatter when the prey lashes out.

He grabbed for his pistol with his ruined hand and spent two bullets – all that was left in the clip. One bullet missed, the other pinged off of solid air.

Before he could do anything else, he watched as Tom's head jerked backward at an impossible angle. His eyes were transfixed, bewitched, as if by the starless sky. Neil barely heard the crack, but he watched as the boy was torn from Mr. Brody's grasp, the man's body crumpling to the

240

ground. Red stains appeared on his shirt, painted the ground, and the boy was hauled screaming back up the ditch.

There was something louder than the mournful wind, growing into a fevered pitch and desperate frequency, and Neil realized that it was his own breath. His lungs felt like they were going to break into a run straight out of his mouth. Somewhere up the road, in the orange freeway corona, the boy's screams transfigured into something beyond screaming, something altogether animalistic.

A few yards away, the snow was moving in strange patterns.

Neil knew there was nothing left, nobody to rescue. Failure. He lifted the upper door and scrabbled inside, finding the latch and locking it. On his heels, something incredibly dense slammed into the door, made a ripe bubo out of the steel.

For a long time, nothing else happened. Eventually, all the screaming and echoing gunfire ceased. He hoped that it didn't take too long for them to go. He threw up, tried to get into a corner but his breakfast spilled across the wall, now the floor, in a long diagonal line.

One of the things began snuffling and scratching at the door. Neil retreated into the far corner by the lights, his gun empty, but it gave him some meager comfort. He thought about faces, a handful of names hastily remembered, a handful of lives snuffed out and thrown to the wind. He thought about the painter he loved, the one who made him feel embarrassed and hopeful, hoped he wasn't on the road tonight.

Neil settled into the corner clutching his ruined hand, and waited.

The storm began to break apart two hours after midnight. It was a slow, hesitant process, like some meteorological commiseration was interceding its rage, but it was clear by then that the storm was on its way out. All the woodlands and geographic ridges in the state acted like speed bumps, giving the clouds enough friction for them to slow, halt, and eventually, dissipate. Below, the snow stopped falling, the wind quieted to a perturbed hum, and hundreds of residents caught in the wake of the storm were left to wonder in bewildered awe.

Emergency crews across the whole western half of the state would be working deep into November on downed power lines, clearing out windfalls, and repairing the damage to infrastructure. Septic statistics would be drawn up to illustrate the loss of human and animal life and relayed on the television, but couldn't properly indicate the details that could make those numbers important. They couldn't show that, once the snow had cleared away and the macabre spoils of the storm discovered, bodies were frozen so solidly they would give off a sound that was almost metallic when touched.

In the congested stretch on I-94, the abandoned vehicles would conjure the sensation of a ghost town, a mechanical graveyard. Some bodies would be discovered with marks and wounds attributed to coyotes or other scavengers. Some bodies would not be found at all.

There was a small pocket of survivors, huddled away from the windows, in shock or mortal terror. They could offer no answer when interviewed, no suggestion of why nearly everyone had up and vanished. For years, decades, they would be silent about the storm, cursing it when pressed. When news reporters, college students, or historians came sniffing for information, everyone – Neil among them – would wall themselves in their minds, shutting out anyone that dared to suggest the storm had even happened.

Life resumed – families were raised, generations perpetuated. A help group was formed by some of the survivors of the storm in 1995, but would be disbanded a couple years later.

The fading years are never kind enough. During the first snows, whether they fell on November, October, or – say it ain't so – September, this handful of survivors would go to the window and look up at the sky, then down to the fat little ice crystals that congregated on the ground. They would stare with concern, heedless of family members or nurses trying to call them back; they would stare and look for funny patterns in the falling snow, things that shouldn't be. Neil Walker, soon enough retired from the force and living alone, would wonder what happened that night and why.

Sometimes, no answers could be made. Sometimes, the yearly snows were just merciful enough to provide none.

# Keepsakes (1910)

Statues. That was the word that came into Maarja's mind when she looked up at the men and women gathered around her small home. All staring eyes as blank as the full September sky, all the vehemence and mistrust that had been growing now gone, tension relieved, now that her husband lay dead on the ground.

She knelt by her husband, rain puddles soaking through her skirts and wetting her knees. The air was still yet cold that smoke was wafting up from the bullet wound in Tuomas's skull. She wanted to pretend it was her husband's soul that was circling and passing around her, as if his last dying desire was to caress her face one last time, but she knew better.

"We told your husband to get out, woman," the man with the rifle said. She recognized him only as another man who worked with Onni at the lumberyard. "We told you we don't want you damn Finlanders around here. You wouldn't listen."

He looked behind him at the crescent of the gathered townsfolk, wiping away a layer of what forms when sweat meets dirt and grime and sap from his forehead. "They wouldn't listen, right?"

The statues nodded their stiff necks and some gave voice to their approval, muffled by the wind that whistled through the north edge of town. In everything, heat and color were starved as autumn made itself known. Baby Eino was screaming somewhere inside the cabin. Maarja's mother was staring from the porch, old owl of a woman bundled in her frocks and white hair, diamond willow broom gripped in both hands like a ward.

The man with the rifle wasn't holding the gun directly at her, but it was a damn sight close. "Maybe now you gonna listen to us. Just get on out of here."

"Let me bury him," Maarja said through the horror in her throat, her accent thickening. "Please, let me just..."

The gunshot echoed louder than thunder ever could. Some of the statues gasped and there were some reprimands, but the man with the gun seemed as stalwart as the trees. His eyes, bright blue like lake water, were wide and fascinated by what was happening, like he was watching someone else's dream unfolding. "We said get, so you get. This is the last time we're gonna tell you, you hear me? We don't want to see you around here again."

Exhausted, with her bad ankle sending a spark of the memory of how bad it used to be, Maarja stood, keeping her dark brown eyes trained on the man with the gun. She let him be the first to look away before she trudged back to her cottage. The statues, having sensed that whatever important thing had already ended, began to disperse, confident with the knowledge that they had homes to walk back to.

"Don't try sneaking back in, either, Missus Halonen," the man with the rifle said. "We'll be right here to make sure you get gone and stay gone. Won't we?" There was still some of the rabble behind him, filthy rats to a man, and most of them muttered a few words of agreement.

Statues. Maarja saw her mother hop off the steps, broom still gripped in one hand, baby Eino now cradled in the other, mewling. They met near the well some yards away from the house – she thought about the flower seeds she'd sent away for so she could plant them in the spring, her tulips and begonias, and mama simply needed to have her St. John's Wort and Lilly-of-the-Valley. All lost now, all pointless, just warm dreams cooling in the dirt.

The men broke through the front door, and the symphony of things being smashed, shattered, ripped, and gouged opened up the evening. It was the sound of the universe splitting apart.

Even when she could smell the flames licking at the timbers and could feel the heat of the flames, she just kept her eyes on her husband. Even when they tossed him into the inferno as well, she kept her eyes on him.

Soon enough, her mother took her away, speaking in small, strict sentences. Where would they go? Maarja's mother told her they'd make a go of it in the woods – better to live there now. How would they survive? They would survive, was all her mother would say, so Maarja followed behind as her mother called in the goats and the chickens.

The animals always did what Mama Helka asked them to.


Days were measured in torn skin and tears, in flesh ripped from scabrous trees and being filled by the memory of a moment, a single moment that peeled everything else away to make room for only itself. If nothing else, the work helped her avoid her inner thoughts, but not by much.

It became apparent to Maarja that the hovel they were building was, more than anything else, a memorial to hopes that would never come true. Low and squat with a vaguely triangular shape, thatched with mud and loam, it looked like a primitive hut, feral, but they were building with only survival in mind. Winter was already howling through the trees, announcing itself with breathy gusts of chill wind and dead leaves, and they had no time to debate.

Those first few nights, when the smoldering wreck of the house was still hot enough, she and her mother would huddle near the charred ruins. Then the wind took that heat away. During those nights, rubbing at her swollen ankle, Maarja would still pray and hope for tomorrow.

Baby Eino died on the third week. He had stopped crying and simply slid into sleep, but he wouldn't wake up. His skin was white and cool as birch bark, and no matter how much she asked, pleaded, demanded, he wouldn't wake up.

The ground was harder than stale bread, but she managed to dig a grave; it was only a couple feet deep, just enough of what the ground would give her. She wrapped him up in a potato sack and placed him in the hole, muttering small prayers that she knew wouldn't break through the thick, pewter ceiling of clouds. After covering over the grave, surmounting it with a meager cairn, she fastened a small cross from two sticks and plunged it into the earth. Two days later, she woke to find the hole had been dug up, the dirt littered with large paw prints.

"They did this, *aiti*," Maarja whispered to her mother as she knelt on the cold hard dirt. "All those respectable, honorable people in town. They did this." Her voice was choked with all that she wanted to say, barbed curses and vicious lamentations that struggled and settled in her throat like bitter silt.

Her mother sat down beside her, wincing as her knees popped like pinecones in a fire. "I know, I know, darling. It hurts inside, doesn't it?"

Maarja grabbed a handful of dirt, put it in the hole because she couldn't think of anywhere else to put it. The knowledge that it wasn't her soil, her property, was an ache. "I can't even describe it, *aiti*. It feels like I drowned on that ship long ago, and I'm only now waking up under the ocean. As if the wind is tearing away more and more pieces of me."

Her mother nodded, a shared memory of despair in those hard brown eyes. More than anything, it was that look of despair that Maarja had always associated with her elders; communal pain. The silence took their breaths and sighed away to nothingness.

"You can bring them back, Maarja."

Maarja thought she misheard. She thought her mother had tried to intimate some concept that was too complex to be put into words. Her head seemed little more than a sack filled with cotton, and every word going into it was garbled. "What?"

"You heard me, girl. You want the pain to stop? You want them responsible to feel as deep in the darkness as you do now? You want them to hurt, my darling?"

No thought, no conjecture. "I do," Maarja said, completing a pact as divine as the one she shared with her husband.

"I can show you," the old woman whispered. "I can show you how." And she proceeded to tell Maarja a story.

Helka often told her daughters stories, tales that could be pretty as lilac bushes or grim as blood in the moonlight. In her youth, Maarja sometimes hypothesized that they were memoirs rather than fiction, seeing her mother as profoundly glamorous. After her sister Anna finally succumbed to the worm of starvation in Finland, her mother had stopped telling stories. Not one had passed her lips in nearly ten years.

And while she heard her mother tell the story of the thing she called the many-bag, she felt as though she were sinking even deeper into some awful dream. What her mother was telling her was horrible, blasphemous; something not meant to be in a rational world, where she knew night followed day, where spring followed winter.

She wanted to say all of this, but it came out as a choked sob in her throat. Her mother gave her a sad look, mistaking her disgust for sentimentality. A story about a lonely man who went out looking for Vainamoenen's *Sampo*, but couldn't find it for all the world, so he decided to make his own...

"You can do it, Maarja," her mother hissed. "You can teach those monsters a lesson they need to learn. Teach them what it means to hurt."

The world was a muddle, a mess of images that swam around in Maarja's head. Her husband lying dead on the ground; the faces of the men and women (no, statues) that took them in, made them feel welcomed, and then spat in their faces, drove them out as though they were animals, subhuman. They listened to those idiots in the capital who told them how to think, listened to the lies and forced simulacrum of scientific conjecture.

She thought about that bronze French woman standing on Ellis Island with her torch and book, mute and blind.

She thought about burying her son in the cold ground – her son taken away, a gash opening wider inside of her.

From that gash, a deluge of anger and sadness poured forth, seeping out of every pore on her skin, drowning. "How do I make it?" she asked.

"It will require all of you, dear, every ounce of your want and pain. It will need a lot of work, a lot of time to grow."

She wiped her eyes and flung the tears onto the dirt. "But will it work?"

Her mother gave her a look that she couldn't place. But Maarja recognized the glint in Helka's eyes, always there when she was thinking about the long ago summers and winters from her past, and that made frost grow on her back.

"Oh, yes, it will work."


Birch bark and twine wrapped up in chords of pine boughs and small windfalls, stones knotted in them, and this was to be the bag itself. Her mother helped her drag Tuomas's body to a clearing behind their hut, heavier now that all traces of life had left him. Maarja grabbed whatever she could find from her child's pilfered grave, the few meager scraps of swaddling, and her tears.

She remembered how her husband had created a bouquet of flowers for her by wrapping a piece of birch bark into a cone; she utilized the same principle as she held the container under her cheek and allowed the despair to fill all of her. It seemed so endless, a plain wider and deeper than the sea she crossed to get to this.

There were moments, of course, when she felt she shouldn't be doing this, or that this was just a silly curse that her mother conjured out of fantasy, or that she was merely seeking something to do, something to occupy herself with so she couldn't be left alone with her own thoughts. Those moments were easily dispelled as soon as they appeared, blown away with all the frustrated screams that were filling her.

The day was waning when the bag was finished, lying on the ground behind the hut. Maarja stood against a boulder near the front of the hut, tired and stinking of sweat and sap. The cows and goats spoke together with small solemn voices. At the end, Maarja turned her head up to the mauve sky and sighed. The air was so clear, so cold.

Trees. Everywhere, trees. She'd read so much poetry about trees that spoke and danced and did other sufficiently equivalent human actions that the words no longer held any meaning for her. She had been staring at the trees all around her for so long, tamarack and pine and birch, forming a webwork of claws across the sky, forming odd shapes when they wanted to. She wondered about the forests, and about the people who lived with them. She wondered if trees could move, they'd goddamn *run*.

The wooden panel they used as a door creaked open and shut, and she heard the familiar shuffle of her mother. Without turning away from the sky, she asked "Is the bag yet ready?"

Silence, long enough for her to become concerned. She was about to say something else when her mother said, "Yes, just about ready. There's just a couple more things need to be done."

Maarja huffed. "I don't know how much longer I can wait, *aiti*. I feel like I'm in two places at the same time – as if I was a giant bird and could tear apart everything beneath me with my claws…but also hiding underground, cowering in the dirt with the moles and the field mice. I feel stretched too far to even see how things are anymore. I don't suppose any of this makes sense to you. I just hope this spell of yours will work."

Her mother give a derisive sniff. "Not my spell, girl. You don't *own* what can't be controlled. I thought I taught you that."

Maarja glowered. "What will it take to finish it?"

"Not much left." Whispers of her mother's coats brushing against the forest floor.

Maarja waited, the sky grew darker. Then she heard a hard thump behind the house, a clatter of sticks and stones. A cow lowed. Maarja felt the sounds seep into her skin, cling to her like regret and become worry. "Mother?"

Only the trees answered her, creaking in the cold. Maarja stepped around the house and saw her mother, face down on the many-bag, staining it red.

"Mother!" She ran over and knelt beside her, turned her over, grunting out her frustration.

Blood. Blood was everywhere. Red patterns were stained onto her mother's face, in her clothes, all over the dead leaves about them. It was still spurting from the slit on one of her thin wrists, arcing onto Maarja's clothes, warming her. Her husband's *puukko* knife was lying on the ground not far away, the thinnest red on its short blade.

"*No!* No, no, no, no!" A scream was hurled into her mother's face, vain defiance, rejection, a command for her mother to stop. Maarja grabbed her wrist and pressed down hard to staunch the flow, but it was slickening under her palm, sticky. Her mother's head was lolling on her neck, like a daisy. She pulled the old woman closer and rubbed at her cheeks, looking into eyes that saw past her.

"What did you do, *aiti!?* What did you think you were doing?"

A smile, sad and small, on dry lips. Her mother was crying, but Maarja couldn't tell what kind of tears they were. "Listen to me, girl. Everything's a door...you hear me? Every little thing is a door to

253

something else. You just…just open your door, and everything…it will follow right along."

That smile held strong, but when the last hunk of life shivered out of her mother, that smile tilted downward into a grimace, and Maarja was left alone.


Despair, horror, and desperation are sisters, and each is a door to the other. Each is a door to things quintessentially awful, geologic steps toward monstrous conceptions. Maarja flitted about from one to the next.

For the next two days, she didn't eat anything. The meat stored in the tiny larder had gone bad anyway, and even if it was in prime condition, she didn't think she could put anything down. The chickens had all been taken away by scavengers, and except for a couple cows, the other animals had all scattered, wandered off through the woods. Hunger was just something that was there, and then gone, and she was happy to see it off.

The bag was her only concern. She made sure all the parts were together, and, like before, she scratched out another hole in the ground, one big enough to set it in. With the slivers of whatever remained of her strength she pushed all of it, the whole leaking mess, into the pit. Then she spent an hour covering it up. Even when she patted down her mother's stiff hand back into the soil, she hardly felt as if she were in her own body, but somewhere high above herself, watching from afar.

The moon peered through the claws of the trees as she stumbled back into the hut. She didn't know how long she slept, but the dreams she had lasted for more than enough lifetimes.

When Maarja was a little girl, she loved to get out of the house and walk through the woods. The Finnish woodlands were a wondrous and mysterious place, where you were liable to become lost at any moment, and find yourself back where you started just as quickly. The best time was in the spring right after the snows melted and gave up all the treasures that had been buried.

One of her earliest finds was a box – her mother would later tell her it was a woman's hat box, but in those initial moments it was as good as a pirate's treasure chest, and she made sure it achieved its function. It was crinkled and the lid did not fit right, and no doubt before it had been lost and forgotten, its paper had been white or pink instead of a stained yellow, all but making the dyed lilies hidden from view, but she cherished it.

Often, the box would become misshapen for all the rarities she would put inside – river-smoothed stones, old coins, some of her dolls, piecemeal arrangements of her mother's makeup routine and, later, when girlhood left her and she found her mind settling on other topics, it became her beauty care box; she'd put in knickknacks from the boy she'd been sweet on. Not Tuomas then, but a young Swede named Lars.

Lars died with the rest of his family, both parents and all six siblings, when their farm suffered from the geist of the famine that flew across all of Europe. Just like Maarja's family – just like thousands of families.

That hat box must still be in her old room, hidden underneath the two loose floorboards closest to the window. In one of her dreams, that hat box was waiting for her exactly where she had placed it before her father came to tell her they'd be leaving for America. Lucidity transmuted the old house into a shack of old timbers devoured by fungal rot, of foul-smelling age and pregnant shadows. Moonlight, or perhaps sunlight filtered through a thick fog, illumined the room for her, revealing each sad detail. She had pulled up those old boards and found the box. Its pretty paper much paler than she recalled it, those lilies so bright and artistically rendered to such perfection that they seemed to waver before her eyes. She swore she could even smell the flowers through the sharp stink of decay.

The lid hung ajar when she pulled it up out of the floor, setting it beside her. Only a sliver of shadow peered out at her. Maarja set the box on the floor and stared at it – only looked at it for a while, overcome by a surge of warmth and joy.

Then the box began to shake. A teakettle wail issued from the opening, rising into a horrid scream that made the rafters jitter and dance. Something inside was pushing against its interior, its walls bending so that eggshell cracks split along the paper.

"Stop it!" she ordered, commanded this corruption of a memory she kept tucked away. A nightmare intrusion, that's all it was, and in this dream, she had enough control of her mental faculties to know she could stop it at any time. She lashed out and put her hands on the lid, pressing down with all her weight to keep the thing shut tight.

"I said stop it!"

The box lid split apart and Maarja screamed as her hands plunged into something impossibly, unendingly cold—

Despair, horror, and desperation are sisters, and they welcome everyone.


Maarja's hands were numb when she managed to pull herself out of her stupor. It might have been sleep, what she'd experienced, or maybe some kind of madness inflicted by her empty stomach. She thought about the goat and the cow, imagined herself tearing into soft warm flesh, guzzling meat and blood and fat until the pain would stop. Yes, she thought about that so hard she could just about smell it.

The *puuko* knife lay next to her. Did she have enough strength to use it?

The day was lost in grey again, making it impossible to tell what the time was – what could have been dawn might as well have been dusk. It smelled of fall – sweet earth and decay, the past summer and spring stuck in a state of putrefaction, transmutation. A thin fog hung low over the ground, hardly noticeable at all, just diaphanous sheets of moisture that whirled around her legs as she glided away from the house. Everything seemed like a dream.

No goat here. She saw some red stains around the hovel, and some odd tracks. Wolves must have taken it. Maarja winced; better the goat than her.

A faint breeze caressed her face. Nearby was the thick bough of an elm tree where she'd tied up the cow, or at the very least *remembered* tying up the cow. The cow looked at her with its big eyes, full and bright with emotion and frailty. The cow had been starving as well; not enough food for anyone to go around, and there were bite marks on its rear legs. It made Maarja think of a worm dangled in a river, one that the fish would only play with and never wholly take.

She stroked its head and muzzle. The cow snuffled into her grip, expecting food that wasn't there. She even let it sniff the knife. That it wasn't afraid was its own fault.

She brought her hand around, a step from running the edge across the cow's throat – warmth, blood, fire and meat, the pain would go away – when a sound made her pause. At first, she thought it was some vestige of her dream, or another steam train rolling through the back of the county. It was far away, beyond the trees, and she had to think for a second before realizing it was coming from the town.

It was a scream. She'd made the sound herself so many times already.

She left the cow where it was as she walked toward the sound – it made a low grunt as if to thank her. Maarja inhaled the air. The sharp sting of burning wood cut through the smell of the forest.

Where the woods thinned, there was a clearing. There used to be a house there, now a burned-out heap. A family might have lived there once, Maarja thought, a husband and wife and an old woman who helped care for a young son, with a modest but growing farm. Now char and ashes.

Beyond that, she could see the outskirts of the town.

It was on fire.

Maarja walked no further than the border of the trees. The townsfolk had been clear that they wanted her in the woods. She watched as the sky was wreathed in black smoke, and she listened to all the voices – much more than just the one now, men as well as women – adding themselves to a choir of horror, lamentation. Maarja watched and listened until she grew bored. She walked back to the cow; her stomach guided the knife to where it should go.

By the time night fell, she'd managed to gather up enough birch bark and windfalls to make a fire, a big one. She sat down in the dirt, watching the brisket strung up from the willow rack, saliva flooding her mouth. Her legs were twitching, daring her to spend what energy she had to leap up and rip at the flesh, to hell with the cooked hair and the melting fat.

Her mother would have barked at her for allowing the fat to go uncollected. She would have thrust a fat coffee tin into her stomach and tell her to mind her work. Would have given ample reasons explaining why Maarja was wasting good time daydreaming.

The fire spat. A gob of fat fell into the fire and shrieked.

That was long enough. She tore at the flesh with her knife, slicing off thick pink pieces and jamming them into her mouth. It felt like she was devouring heat, energy, life, her body suffusing with everything. She ate until her stomach repulsed what she was delivering it, and then she ate more.

A dry rustling sound came from the trees behind her, a snuffling noise behind it. Some animal that smelled the meat, deciding to wander closer. She held onto the knife; sharing was not an option she could accept. She stood taller and turned to look. Immediately, whatever cry tried to leave her was choked away.

At first, the thing was little more than an impression, a tracing of firelight set against the forested dusk behind it. But then her eyesight adjusted. It was tall, much taller than her, a bundle of rags and sticks covering a vaguely humanoid shape. As it moved closer, she noticed it didn't appear to move by putting one leg in front of the other, but by sidling back and forth, ophidian in its movement. It was a misshapen thing, painfully so, and it made a mewling noise as it drew into the light.

Her body twisted toward the hut, toward safety, and she held the knife out in front of her. The thing stopped and stared at her, its body moving back and forth in the wind like a tree.

"Go away!" She shouted in both English and Finnish. The thing shifted backward a little bit, cringing. She thought she heard sticks bending under its rags, and its breathing sounded like wind passing through a field of dry wheat.

It moved closer, but she didn't flee, couldn't move. It walked up to the meat and reached out – there was a hand covered in scabrous bloody skin, maggots coming out of the forearm, clawed worms, or maybe extra fingers – and tore off a piece of the carcass. The steaming flesh disappeared under its hood, and wet sucking sounds emanated from its confines.

When it finished, it stepped toward her – her hands had been lowering but now she brought the knife up again. It was her meal, and it was her damn land, and she wasn't going to allow herself to be killed so easily. Not anymore, not after what she'd already been through.

The thing rasped forward, dropped down at her feet. It shuffled side to side, almost in supplication, like an anxious little boy in church. A stench rose up from its rags, like cheese or milk gone bad and left in the hot sun. It almost sounded like it was weeping.

It raised its head, and the firelight caught up under it and she saw a face that was too familiar, with its bushel of black hair and pale blue eyes so bright they refracted the fire into a million gemstones. "Tuomas?" She stared at him – Don't be stupid, Tuomas died when a bullet went into the back of his skull like a rock through a window so he can't be here now – and a little smile curled up the corner of its mouth.

The figure noisily shuffled closer until it was embracing her legs. She knelt down and threw her arms around what she presumed were its shoulders. It gave a shuddering sob and sank into her. She tried her very best not to wretch when the stink of rot and earth rose up to meet her.

He was cold. That made sense, given the circumstances, so she tried to stand and pull him toward the fire. Some of the rags fell away, and she saw what was making it so misshapen, and then her horror went unrestrained. Another face looked up at her from behind her husband's shoulder, her mother's piercing gaze staring from the nape of Tuomas' neck. Her mouth worked, but no sound came out; the keening was coming from somewhere else, where the rags were still covering him, and she didn't want to see what was making it.

Her husband made a sound in his throat, a kind of mute gurgling, and she leaned in to ask what he was trying to say. Something began prodding at her – she looked down at her breast and saw where the rooster's leg was connected to Tuomas' body, its talons twitching as it groped her. A feather fell in the firelight.

She groaned and backed away, leaving the thing that the many-bag had given her on the ground. She backed away, expecting it to start bounding after her, but it stayed right where it was. It was kneeling in the dirt and making pitiful sounds, goat-like, child-like. Sounds of her husband and mother and infant son. Maarja slammed the door shut, and even then, she stared at its charred surface, *puuko* knife at the ready, daring it to open.

As she rested on her straw-and-cloth bed, she wondered if she'd ever sleep again. Eventually, it was the meat in her stomach that finally helped her.


Rationality is a road with a beginning and an end, and even when you reach that destination, you never realize the extent of the energy spent to get there. As Maarja's father was once fond of saying, "You can go a hundred miles and not feel a thing." It was one of his favorite little aphorisms, and he had spouted it even when he died on the ship somewhere between Norway and North America.

Maarja was somewhere in those hundred miles and already wheezing, hacking up blood and struggling for air. It had been so long since she'd smiled, or at the very least since she'd had a day that didn't cause her heart to hitch up in her throat, or her head to ache with worry. If it were all to stop when she woke up, she doubted she'd even be a step close to happy, but it would be easier. God knew her life hadn't been easy, but surely dying in her sleep, garbed in her memories, wouldn't be so bad.

In that murky area between waking and sleep, she thought about how, if she was allowed to wake up, she could do it herself. Bleeding out would take too long, and it would leave a mess. She didn't want to think what her mother or father would say, or her husband, if they knew what she was thinking. But they were dead, all dead, and she was left to die alone in the Minnesota cold.

No, not cold. Not today. The sun must have been on her, peering like a kindly voyeur through the beams and bracken walls; she felt warm. Not the kind of fire that consumes with a fever. A pleasant warmth was spreading all along her.

An arm as strong as oak wood reached up and rubbed against her sternum, coarse hair tickling at the fleshy bottom of her breast. She grinned and opened her eyes, and it was around that moment, when she could hear the wheezy snoring behind her head and smelled the stink of an old forgotten crypt, that she realized she'd made a colossal mistake.

Tilting her head around, she saw that the door was open, the stick she used as a deadbolt lying ineffectual and splintered on the ground. Her eyes went down to the arm around her, skin pale and scabrous like the victim of a hard winter. Blue-green lichen was caught in that hair, like unwanted stowaways on a lifeboat. The nubs and protuberances and other things that tried to resemble fingers waggled when touched by her breath.

Maarja had only thrown up twice in her life, both times when she was pregnant with Eino. But right now, an intense wave of nausea rose up and tickled the back of her throat. Clapping a hand to her mouth, thinking of the smell of spring rains, she tried to put her stomach back on its leash.

The thing settled deeper into the straw, gave a heavy sigh that smelled like swamp fungus. She jumped up and twisted around, feeling as though it had left something on her, something creeping through her skin. The maggot surveying its dinner before making purchase. The thing had divested its coat of rags and sticks and she was granted the curse of seeing all of it. Every part that was more or less human, more or less animal, every stick and stone jutting from its skin like unfeeling fractured bone.

It began to make a pining, cat-in-heat sound that started soft and unsettling, but quickly grew to a volume that made the hut shiver. She covered her ears as she ran to the door. It shifted off the straw, all of its appendages moving in tandem, its lithe body following its digits; she felt she would faint from the sight alone. Three pairs of ruined pale blue eyes watched as she fled.

The first gusts of winter were whistling through the skeletal trees, ripping away the last vestiges of sleep. Fear made everything so clear to her, every detail held in exquisite accuracy; the smoldering remnants of the fire, the ominous smell of the woods, a pair of blue jays winging away from the ruckus, the wood hatchet stuck in a tree stump. It was on this that Maarja's eyes focused, and she grunted low in her throat as she wrenched it free of the stump.

It gave a low snuffle just before the door was flung open, thrown from its hinges, and the thing growled like a wounded bear. It was glaring at her, and she saw the hurt in its faces, betrayal and rage mingled into doughy grimaces.

It rushed at her on its atrophied torso, hands hooked into rakish claws, mouths hanging open and dribbling a dark-green substance that illustrated jawbones. Maarja ran around the nearest tree, an old elm that was ripping itself apart by its own weight.

The thing was right behind her, practically digging on her heels, and as she had hoped, it saw the bare opening between the boughs as a better access to grab at her. When she saw the thick, mossy arm reach for her, she hauled back and swung down as hard as she could.

Without a file to be found, the iron head was terribly blunted, little better than a narrow hammer, but it still held to its own lethal efficiency. Meat tore, bone crunched, mouths worked in agony. Maarja swung again, and everything seemed louder.

Voices screamed so loud she thought her ears were being pulled apart. The sound was like a shovel piercing her heart, drove tears to her eyes that made everything grey and blurry. But stopping meant death. She pulled back for another swing—

She didn't see the other arm circle around with hideous alacrity and cuff the side of her head. Its talons ripped loose a flap of skin on her forehead, and the grey world turned red. The pain was ferocious, and she felt it all the way through a dizzy spell.

Maarja thumped to the ground, equilibrium wounded and her head flaring white-hot. She imagined it was steaming, steaming like a bullet wound. It grabbed at her from behind, one arm stiff and cold, the other broken and limp. It held her up firmly, almost gently, and it twisted her around to look into its eyes, all of them.

Tears. Tears were streaking its faces in glassy rivers, running from eyes wide with agony. In those all-too-familiar, familial faces, she didn't see any anger. No hatred or malice, just pain and guilt. Frustration. And she hardly felt herself pull her arm back, hatchet somehow still in her hand, and put the blade into the creature's skull.

An expression of confusion stemming through the fear before its entire body went down, pole-axed and twitching, and brought her down with it. Her arm struck the tree, releasing a new bright knife of pain all the way up to her shoulder. It landed on top of her, wriggling and mewling in that awful not-quite-a-language, a river of brackish effluence coursing over her. The thing Tuomas had become stared down at her, bleary and sullen, his broken mouth trying to form words.

There was a small grouping of rocks beside the tree where she had fallen; she was lucky enough to have fallen away from them. She reached for one, just one, one that she hoped was hard and sharp enough. The thing slavered and whined at her face, and in her scrabbling, she tore loose a fingernail.

The world smelled of rot and remorse.

Finally, her hand found purchase on one of the stones – she gave a small prayer of thanks to any god that was listening and swung. The rock connected with a dull *thock!* sound, what you expect to hear when taking a boot to the trunk of a tree. The thing grunted from three mouths and rolled off of her.

Her hand went up and down like a mad piston, hearing that *thock!* sound grow softer and softer. When the rock split apart in her hand, she pulled out the hatchet. Gouts of brackish blood surged up and onto her.

Old Helka was saying something to her, owlish eyes bright in the grey dawn. She didn't hear a word.

Her son was forming words from the flap of skin that was his mouth. His eyes were filled only with horror.

She swung until the noises stopped, and even then, she didn't want to see those faces. When it was over, she stepped away from the bloody mess, feeling like she was floating in herself, outside of herself. She was seeing everything as a bird might, looking at everything with a tired, forlorn eye.

The day was cold, colder. She wove through the trees until she came to the hedge, the threshold between untamed forest and tameless civilization. She stumbled through it, feet wholly numb, just as the first snowflakes began to touch down like fey heralds. She hardly noticed anything; images of her family, scraps of memory, cut up and randomly sewn together like a mourning shroud, wove themselves into her vision. At first, the images were formed from her imagination, but then they took on a ghostly quality that covered and merged into her vision. Her mother stood at the broken well; her son was playing by the charred wreck of the house; her husband stood on the little hill in the front yard, pipe in his mouth and looking proud.

She had hatred in her heart when she made the many-bag, filled to the brim, in fact – but truthfully, she knew that the keg from which flowed that hatred had been nothing but love. And she thought about how a monster can be made of love and hate as she walked past the cadaver of her home, past the necropolis of the town, kept right on walking, as the snow continued to fall from a pregnant ashen sky.

# About the Author

Matt Anderson is an author of horror and fantasy fiction. He was born, raised, and currently lives in Minnesota, where he learned to take inspiration from nature, history, folklore, and nightmares.

Twitter: @Mattyinthewoods
Instagram: @Mattyinthewoods

www.ingramcontent.com/pod-product-compliance
Lightning Source LLC
Chambersburg PA
CBHW070813180626
46818CB00001B/237